EARTHWEEDS

SONS OF NEPTUNE: BOOK 1

by Rod Little

Earthweeds
ISBN-13: 978-1547268566

For other books by Rod Little:

www.rodlittleauthor.com

PART I

"Nothing is so painful to the human mind as a great and sudden change."

— Mary Shelley, Frankenstein

CHAPTER 1

A curved ribbon of dirt split the forest and formed a thin, uneven path to the lake. At the end of this path lay a portly man from the city. His body rested slightly askew in a seated position at the base of a maple tree, his back pressed against the trunk. One lifeless eye stared blankly at the peaceful lake; the other eye was gone. The right hand grasped a rolled-up piece of paper that now trembled in the breeze. The other hand still held the gun.

Two brothers, a high school student and a college student on summer break, stood over the dead body for several minutes, studying it. After camping in the woods for over a month, this disturbing scene was the most interesting thing to happen all summer.

"I guess this ends our vacation," said Shane, the older brother. "Soon the woods will be crawling with cops. All the game will be scared off." He didn't really care; the trip had been lousy from the start.

"*Geez*, man, the guy is dead," Sam spoke in a half-whisper, the way everyone instinctively lowers his voice in front of the dead. "Think of someone besides yourself and your vacation."

"I didn't mean it that way."

Shane's younger brother, Sam, crouched down and took the piece of paper from the man's hand, trying not to touch the skin of the dead fingers. He unrolled it and read aloud: "If anyone finds this, I saved another bullet in my pocket for you."

"That's weird," Shane said, resting his hands on his hips, but keeping his distance.

Sam squinted up at his brother against the morning sun. "Why would he save a bullet for us?"

"I guess he's saying whoever finds him will want to kill himself, too."

"Why?"

"I don't know," said Shane. "Why don't you ask him?"

"Weird," Sam mumbled. He stood up and pushed his bangs out of his eyes.

The dead man wore a business suit and tie. His shirt was immaculately pressed and clean, as was his tie – except for a splatter of blood across its knot. This was no hunter. This man came from the city to end his life outside in the open air, here at the lakefront.

"Do you suppose this lake meant something to him? He came up here to look at it before he... you know, cashed out?" Sam asked, but it was more of a statement than a question. He took another step back away from the body. The paper clung to his hand.

"Maybe we should put his body in the jeep; take him back. Animals might drag the body away. They might eat it." Shane finally stepped forward and rifled through the man's clothes for a wallet and ID, but all he found were two dimes and a quarter.

"I don't think so. We shouldn't touch it. This might be a crime scene. Maybe the cops should look at it as it is."

"You watch too much TV."

"Maybe. But don't move the body. Okay?"

Shane was happy to comply. He certainly wasn't looking forward to carrying a dead body anywhere.

They passed the man's Prius on the way back to their campsite and peered through the windows. The seats were empty and clean. A new box of bullets sat on the dashboard, minus two. Sam still held the man's crumpled note.

I saved another bullet in my pocket for you.

Sam neatly folded the note and slipped it into the pocket of his shirt. Then he reconsidered and slipped it under the windshield wiper of the man's car.

Let the police find it, he thought.

The boys pulled up the tent and packed their gear. Surrounded by the deep green of the forest, Sam stopped to look around one last time. The trees, rich and abundant with life, filled the air with clean oxygen while their leaves chatted back and forth in the wind. He took a deep breath of fresh air, maybe the last pure air for awhile.

Sam Summer was a tall boy, an inch over six feet, but slim. Being the tallest boy in class, or in any room, made him uncomfortable in a way that only abnormal kids can understand, whether they are fat, short, handicapped... or tall. He avoided attention at all cost, and craved solitude. Rarely caught wearing anything beyond his jeans and white sneakers, and usually a rock t-shirt with a blue flannel over it, he blended as best he could. His thick blond hair was always a bit too long for his mom's liking. She said he looked too much like one of the *Hardy Boys*, whoever that was. Often going out of his way to make himself smaller, either by sitting or hunching his shoulders, he received more than one scolding from their mom when she was alive. She wanted him to stand tall and stand out; he just wanted to fade into the wallpaper.

Shane Summer was two years older, sturdier, but not as tall. At five-eleven, he had a strong, athletic build, and Sam envied him for that. While Sam's hair was always long, Shane's was forever cropped short. Shane wore hunter's boots and jeans, and always a flannel shirt. His color palette was wider, but the material stayed the same – and his sleeves were eternally rolled up a few inches to the elbow. When he found something he liked, he stuck with it.

Both boys had perpetually tan skin from spending most of their time outdoors. Their mother often complained they should use sunscreen, as she worried about sunburn, cancer or premature aging. She nagged out of love, and they had only fond memories of her. And the problems of sunburn would seem absurdly minor in a few days.

The world had actually begun to change three days before the boys stumbled onto the dead body. Before the next sunrise, Shane would shoot both bullets and arrows to save the life of himself and others. Sam would do much more. They didn't know it yet, but these would be the last restful moments of their lives. It's funny: since we never know such events are in motion, we never take the time to enjoy the calm before the storm. Sam was no different, and failed to appreciate their last few minutes of tranquility deep in the woods.

Soon they would drive back to Shane's college campus and find it empty. The mystery would take them down a dark road. For now, that road was miles away.

The boys' two-month camping trip was supposed to be a last attempt at clinging to their youth. This marked the end of a school break for Shane, soon to start his third year at the University of Pittsburgh, and the start of Sam's freshman year at the same school. The recent high school graduate was eager to be rid of his elementary years, but was nervous about going to a new school. Things hadn't always gone so well at high school, partly because he wasn't the same as other kids.

Sam wasn't just tall. Sam was different.

For several days they had seen no deer – or any other animals, for that matter. The hunting had been thin this year, and the woods a bit too quiet. The boys always hunted by longbow, so as not to scare the game. If anything had spooked the animals, it was something or someone else. Nothing felt right today; they had sensed it was time to get back home, even before the dead body. Finding the suicide victim merely clinched their decision to head back a week early.

They hopped in the jeep and drove out of the woods on a bumpy path made up of dirt and rocks. The ride was rough and uncomfortable, but the path eventually became a real, paved road. It would take a few hours to get back to the city.

"Can I drive?" Sam asked.

"Yeah. That would be: No." his brother said smugly. "I drive my sweetheart. She only responds to me." Shane thought of his jeep as his best friend. In a creepy way, maybe even his girlfriend.

Sam gave in and leaned back in the seat. He watched the trees flick by, one after another, like a filmstrip, as the wind flipped his hair back and forth in his eyes. He played with a spark of electricity between his thumb and forefinger, then rolled it into a small sphere, like a marble, over the back of his hand and in between his fingers.

"Be careful with that," Shane said. He always said that. Much more mature, he kept an eye on his brother, partly because he had promised their mom; mostly out of his own concern.

"Yup."

"I mean it, someday you're gonna forget people are watching."

"Yup."

"That would be bad. You got that, right?"

"Yee-up."

"I'm gonna kick your ass someday."

"Yup. I look forward to it."

Shane growled, took a deep breath, and cranked up the car's MP3 player. Rush sang "Closer to the Heart" as they broke out of the woods and cruised onto the main road. The lake and green forest disappeared behind them, too quickly gone from the rear-view mirror.

They passed a ranger station along the way, but it was empty.

Typical, thought Shane. Budget cuts had most of the park services and other needs on a shoestring.

Ahead lay an open road. The boys exceeded the speed limit, and their jeep ate up pavement like a hungry hippo. Sam closed his eyes and went to sleep, trying not to think about the gruesome scene back at the lake: the dead man and his neatly pressed blood-splattered tie.

A pain in his ear roused Sam back to life.

"Hey, wake up!" Shane said, flicking his brother's ear.

"What?" Sam shook the sleep from his head and brushed the dirty blond hair from his eyes. "How long was I out?"

"A couple hours. We're almost on the turnpike. We'll be there soon. But hey... look."

Sam looked around at the empty road.

"Yeah? Not much traffic."

"Exactly. No other cars. The only car we passed in the

last two hours was a breakdown left on the side of the road."

Up ahead the Pennsylvania turnpike was deserted, except for half a dozen stalled cars parked in various skewed positions on the shoulder.

"Is that the turnpike? Geez."

"Yeah. Where the hell is everybody?"

"Steelers game? I guess we'll see people soon enough. Cheers if they win, riots and fire if they lose."

"Funny. Hey, try to call the cops about the dead body. You should have a signal now."

Sam dialed 9-1-1. The phone rang, but no one answered. "I'll try again in town."

They spun onto the ramp and entered the turnpike. At less than 30 mph, their jeep eased past the first parked car. The boys didn't see anyone inside – the car was empty, and the driver's door was propped open.

Shane sped up faster to put more road behind them. The sooner they got into the city, the sooner they could shower, relax, and report the suicide victim.

"You think it's a curfew?" Sam offered. "I mean, like a virus, that SARS thing, or something like it?"

"Yeah, maybe, but why would everyone need to stay off the road? Earthquake warning? Tornado watch? What would keep people from coming out?"

"Terrorist attack? Remember how empty the streets were on September 11?"

"Not really. Anyway, it wasn't this empty."

"Beats me. Let's get back home." By home, he meant

their grandparents' house, before going back to the dorm.

Their parents had died two years earlier in a car accident. While on vacation in Colorado, touring the mountains by car, their brakes went out. They slid off the side of a steep road and into the canyon below. The car exploded on impact – no survivors.

After that, the boys moved in with their grandparents in Schaler Township before heading off to college. Grandpa's house was only 25 miles from school, but this year they had opted for dorm life instead of living at home. As college students, they needed more freedom. And Sam needed a private room – sometimes he generated an electric cloud when he slept. Not even their grandparents new about that.

Sam wasn't normal. He had an unusual ability that, to his knowledge, no one else shared – the ability to generate electricity at will. He could contain it in a ball in his hand, or throw it like lightning in any direction. His power could start a car, heat any object, or even light a room, if he was so inclined. And if he was careful to control it. It was a useful tool at times, but not always easy to manage in his young hands. He was far from a master of the spark, and much more inclined to suppress it than use it.

With a little tweaking, it could also be a weapon. That's what usually got him into trouble. He rarely hurt anyone, but an electric ball hurled at someone's chest wasn't about to go unnoticed. And secrecy about his ability was key to his happiness. He didn't want to be known as *the freak* again, not at the new school.

His older brother knew, but no one else did. Even his parents hadn't know about his ability, and certainly not Grandma or Grandpa. Shane alone knew about Sam's gift, and he carried the weight of that secret like a backpack of snow in summer.

That was part of the reason for the annual camping trips. They both felt relaxed and comfortable in the woods and in the mountains. The pressures of life, school and classmates were far away. The birds didn't care if Sam started a campfire with his electric fingertips. There was no one out there to judge him.

Shane had always made great efforts to help Sam keep his spark a secret. The two brothers would be roommates this year on campus. Normally freshmen stayed in a separate dorm, but when your parents have died recently, universities are willing to bend the rules. It was bad publicity to create any extra hardship on grieving students. The faculty consented to almost everything the boys wanted, and they wanted to stay together.

Shane turned up the road toward Grandpa's house, and still saw no one alive, or at least awake, in the suburbs. Several driveways had cars parked in them, but no sign of people. Another abandoned car was parked in the street, blocking their way home. Shane steered the jeep around it and rode up onto a neighbor's lawn. They crushed a small shrub getting back on the road and then turned up their grandparents' driveway.

"Try not to kill any cats or dogs," Sam scolded.

"Hey, I'm trying to get us home. And by the way, you see any freaking cats or dogs? Or hear any?"

"I guess not."

The emptiness was more than the absence of people; they had not seen any pets or wild animals either. Except birds. They heard scores of birds chirping and squawking, and saw a few flutter around the trees in the yard next door. Nothing else stirred.

One page of a newspaper swirled across the lawn, and Sam bent down to catch it. He lifted and straightened the front page – half expecting to see a headline: **Evacuation of Pittsburgh**. But there was no such headline, just a report of a senator being bribed by a Russian diplomat. Same old news, and no hints about any catastrophe. Sam folded the page and stuffed it in the newspaper holder under the mailbox.

They peered through the garage window; Grandpa's car was parked there – same as always. They reach the front door to the house and found it unlocked. That wasn't so odd, because sometimes Grandma just forgot. The boys crept single-file into the living room and listened for any signs of life. Several creaks lived in the floorboards. With each step, they sounded especially loud today.

Shane called out. "Hey. Grandpa. Anyone home? It's Sam and Shane. Grandma?"

Sam grabbed his brother's elbow. "If Grandma's a zombie, you gotta stake her. I'm not doing it!"

"Stop joking around."

"I'm just saying..."

"Cut it out! Look, you check upstairs. I'll look down here."

"I'm not doing the basement either!"

"Sam, go!" Shane ordered. "Look for any clues about where they are. Anything at all."

Like the floors, the stairs creaked under the boy's feet. Until now, he'd never realized how old those stairs were. His sneakers felt heavy. Every creak betrayed his rise to the top, so there was no chance of surprising anyone. Or anything.

The two upstairs bedrooms were perfectly kept, but vacant. The bathroom still had a few toiletries strewn around as if in the middle of being used. An open bottle of after-shave lay by the sink, and he instinctively screwed the lid back on. He thought of *Psycho* as he pulled back the shower curtain. It revealed an assortment of soaps, and a water bug that now dropped from the shower head and scurried along the edge of the wall.

Back downstairs, Shane hadn't found anything of interest. A box of cereal had spilled on the table, and Shane started to clean it up. A cockroach crawled out from the box. Sam reached down and zapped it with a tiny shock from his finger. It fried and curled up dead.

"Did I scare you?" Sam asked.

"No. I could hear you on the stairs from a mile away."

"No one's upstairs."

"Yeah. This is freaky. Not like a video of dogs playing the piano. That's a different kind of *freaky*. More like: the body is buried in the backyard *freaky*."

Sam pointed to the basement stairs. "Go down yet?"

"I was waiting for you."

The basement stairs sounded even worse than the steps leading upstairs. Under the weight of the two trespassers, each stair groaned as if about to give way. They stopped one step from the bottom and looked around. Weak light shone in from two small window wells; it cast delicate rays filled with dust particles all the way to the concrete floor.

Their attention was drawn to a strange mass packed into the far corner. It looked like a giant butterfly cocoon, roughly the size of a dog. Shane aimed his flashlight in its direction. The motionless cocoon shimmered between black, dark green and blue, depending on how the light hit it: shiny, silky, and creepy.

Sam stepped forward and nudged it with his foot, but there was no reaction.

"Weird, man. Looks like the neighbor's dog."

"Yeah, but I don't wanna meet the spider mom who's saving it for later. Let's get outta here. I want to go check out campus."

"Weird," Sam repeated.

Sam's intrepid spirit was waning; he just wanted to solve this mystery and get back to normal. He backed away, turned and climbed two steps at a time.

"I want to shower before we go."

While Sam showered upstairs, Shane used the downstairs bathroom. He screamed the moment he stepped under the water. It was ice cold. There was no electricity or hot water left.

Sam dressed and came back downstairs to find Shane eating cereal and putting on a new shirt. He was talking to himself, complaining about the cold water.

"Oh sorry about that," Sam said. "I heated mine up, you know..."

"Yeah. You couldn't do that for me?"

"Actually... I don't know how to do that for someone else. Unless... I'm in there– "

"No no. Never mind. I shower solo."

"Good to know."

Sam picked up the phone receiver. Grandma still had an old-fashioned wall-mounted phone, the beige ceramic kind usually only found in the suburbs of the seventies. He heard a dial tone and dialed 9-1-1. It rang; still no one answered.

"Nothing? Cops on holiday too?" His brother talked while scooping handfuls of cereal into his mouth.

"Or too busy. Uh, is that the cockroach cereal?"

"I'm hungry." Shane groaned and grabbed another handful. "Let's go!"

"Hey, look... a cat," Sam motioned out the window. A gray cat stared back at them through the neighbor's kitchen window. It was the first live mammal they had seen since leaving the woods "You see. We're not entirely alone."

"You think the Willards are home?"

They crossed the lawn and knocked on the neighbor's front door. When no one answered, Shane tried the door handle. It rattled in the frame, but was locked. He pounded harder and called out Mr. Willard by name. Nothing but wind and birds replied.

"Should we at least see if the cat's okay?" Sam asked.

"You mean break in? No way. Let's go. We need to find someone who can help us."

CHAPTER 2

THE drive to the University of Pittsburgh campus rolled out the same as the trip from the mountains. They had the streets to themselves with no one else to share the route. No people, no animals, no moving cars. A few more derelict vehicles littered the streets, some partly blocking access ways. They drove through an empty downtown block. Nothing but ghosts now stood at the bus stops. Pigeons scattered as the jeep drove up Fifth Avenue.

"Isn't this a one-way street?" Sam asked. "In the other direction?"

Shane ignored him and kept driving. The traffic lights were all dark, no longer fed by any power.

A chill raced up Sam's spine. It was one of those moments when you realize your life has now changed. The moment the doctor comes in with your test results, and you can see the disappointment in his eyes. The moment you hear your parents have died. The point in time when you discover body parts in your neighbor's back yard. These are the moments that turn our lives in a new direction. For better or worse, the train is derailing.

The suburbs had been deserted, and now the city appeared to have been forsaken, too. Only the pigeons and crows remained, scavenging for the last bits of food left behind by humans. Sam guessed that cockroaches and rats must also be around somewhere.

"Well, the pigeons survived the apocalypse," Shane noted with a degree of satisfaction. "Good for them."

"You think it's the apocalypse?"

"Not to be too dramatic, Sammy, but... it's not looking good. If everyone evacuated because of a flu, we're right in the hot zone. It means we've got it. But it's probably something else."

"So what is it? Invasion?"

"Well, I doubt it's the Russians. Despite the hype, they couldn't wipe out a city. They couldn't find sand in a desert with two shovels and a map." That was their dad talking. Shane agreed with Dad on everything, back when Dad was alive.

"It happened while we were camping. Something happened here, Shane. All while we were up there in the mountains."

"There's not much sign of gunfire. Or blood. So they didn't fight anyone. At least not here."

"That man at the lake, he saw something here... something that made him kill himself." Sam paused and lowered his voice, looking out over the empty streets. "What did you see ol' man?"

An empty shopping cart rolled across the street, pushed by the wind. It rested a moment, then rolled back, as if some phantom shopper was trying to decide where to go. It was likely not the only ghost haunting the street today. They waited for it to roll out of the way, on the ebb of its constant journey back and forth, and then quickly drove around it.

They passed a store window that had been shattered, and a mannequin lay headless and lopsided, half in the store, half out. Broken glass littered the sidewalk. A crow picked at something inside the display box. It might have been a body part, or maybe just a dead mouse; Sam hoped for the latter.

Shane stopped the jeep and rifled through their gear. He pulled out his longbow and a quiver of lead-tipped arrows, then leaned them against the front gearshift next to his leg.

Sam looked surprised. "Really?"

"Just in case. And yours?"

"No. I'm good."

They parked abruptly in front of the Litchfield Towers dorm, halfway across two parking spots, and made their way into the lobby. Shane carried his bow, but Sam (always the optimist, and – some would say – foolishly upbeat) remained unarmed. The front glass door was ajar and badly cracked with a piece missing. When they pulled it all the way open, the rest of the glass fell from its frame. The crash of splintered glass echoed through an otherwise hushed campus. Pieces cascaded across the floor and bounced all the way to the other side of the lobby.

They stopped to see if anyone, or anything, would respond to the ruckus. They waited for the last clatter to land, but when no reaction came, they continued inside.

Shane's dorm offered no surprises. Like the rest of the city, it was vacant, lonely and hollow. The only difference was blood and glass in the lobby leading up to the elevators, which no longer worked. The blood, at least, offered a sign of life. The boys worked their way up the long winding stairs to their dorm room on the fifth floor. Only a few floors would be occupied during the summer session, but fall classes were to start in two weeks, so the building should be teeming with students carrying boxes, moving in.

"Hey, anybody!" Shane shouted in the stairwell. He rapped on the banister, but no one replied.

In Shane's room, he started gathering some of his things into a backpack. He stuffed an extra shirt, socks, and underwear into the bag.

"Get some things together, just the necessities."

"Where are we going?" Sam asked.

"To find people. To find answers. We kind of need to find out what's happening, don't you think? What if our friends are just a few miles away?"

"Like they evacuated?"

"Maybe to Chicago. Maybe all the way south to New Orleans. I don't know, Sammy. But we need to find out."

"What should I take?"

"Whatever you can't live without. I get the bad feeling

23

we're not coming back."

Another chill ran down Sammy's spine. This was the second moment of realization. Their lives had splintered again; the derailed train wasn't getting back on the tracks.

In that instant, a gunshot broke the silence. It echoed from somewhere outside on the street. A second shot cracked the campus wide open. The boys ran to the window and peered out from an uncomfortable angle. They were careful not to show their faces, to avoid being a target for a sniper.

A shadow flew overhead and blocked the sun for a second, then passed out of view. They couldn't see what it was – a plane maybe, but without the roar of engines. Someone fired a gun again, but they still couldn't see who or where.

Shane stuck his head out the window and looked up, but the glare of the sun blinded him. It was impossible to tell exactly what had caused the shadow, but he did see something in the sky. A dark blue object disappeared into the one single cloud.

He turned back to his brother. "Spaceships from Mars, Sammy."

"Stop kidding. What was it?"

"I have no idea. But there aren't many clouds up there, so it's gotta show itself again soon. You can't fly in a cloud forever."

This time they both stuck their heads out and looked up. More clouds were moving in, and a storm loomed not far away. Shane scanned the ground to see if the gunman might show himself. Or herself.

A quick glare of metal shone from the lobby of the University Inn, less than two blocks over. *That's where the gunman must be*. The boys backed away from view, waited and watched. Unsure what to do next, they froze in place, the victims of hesitation. It had an iron grip on them.

The gun fired again. They chanced a peak through the open window just in time to see a black creature running up the street toward the Inn. It looked like some kind of monitor lizard, about three feet in length. Although closely resembling a Komodo dragon, it had the speed and agility of a large dog, with longer legs than a normal lizard. The creature maneuvered fast. Its shiny black skin shimmered with a rainbow of colors in the sun, and its long white teeth stood out when it opened its jaws: the fangs of a killer. The creature ran toward the sound of the gunshot.

A teenage boy stepped out of the Inn, a pistol in his right hand. He had just killed a similar creature, its body now lying motionless in front of the hotel. The boy knelt and began examining the dead animal's hideous form, when he noticed the second creature screaming toward him, fast and agile. It made a horrible hissing sound. Shane readied his bow, unsure if he could help at this distance, but willing to try. Fortunately, there was no need. The boy raised his gun with both hands and fired a single shot at the animal's head. It dropped to the ground just a few feet from him.

The boy stood up and looked around. He muttered something inaudible at this distance and rubbed his head; then went back inside the hotel. The street fell quiet again. It was the unsettling silence of an empty tunnel after a truck has barreled through. The entire scene carried an unreal, hypnotic effect.

Sam was first to break them from their stupor.

"We have to go talk to him. He knows something about … all this."

Shane agreed. "He knows more than we do, that much is a safe bet."

"He looks like just a student, though."

"Yeah. Get your bow."

They returned to the jeep where Sam strapped on his bow, and Shane loaded a pistol they'd always kept in the glove compartment. At this point it was unclear who they might be fighting: the boy or more new creatures. They took precautions and loaded everything that passed for a weapon in their possession.

The jeep drifted toward the University Inn at a slow 10 mph. The hotel wasn't far, but it seemed to take forever to get there. It was vital not to surprise the gunman, but equally important not to stir up any new animals lurking in the streets. They didn't want to get eaten or shot before getting answers. Sam's eyes darted back and forth, checking for any signs of more creatures, while Shane kept his focus on the hotel door.

They parked in front of the Inn and got out of the jeep, their hands held up, and no weapons drawn.

"Hello," Shane said clearly, but not too loud. "We need your help. We... We're not armed."

"Well..." Sam pointed to their bows, and the gun.

"I mean, we won't shoot. We need help."

The gunman threw open the hotel door. "Stop making so much damn noise. Get in here. Now!"

His rifle was raised to his shoulder and pointed at their heads. He didn't waver, and followed their every move with its barrel. They took slow steps into the building, arms raised, and he closed the door behind them. Once inside, he started to question them.

"Where did you come from?"

"I'm Sam. This is my brother Shane. We're students–"

"I didn't ask who you are. Where have you been?"

"In the mountains. Hunting. We just got back."

The boy studied them a full minute, not moving. He wore an army camouflage jacket and matching fatigues, and had incredibly long brown hair – nearly to his chest. He resembled a sixties Vietnam War draft dodger. Finally, he relaxed the gun against his side, so it pointed to the ceiling. He pointed a finger at Shane.

"I know you. I saw you at school."

"Really? Sorry, I don't remember..." Shane lowered his arms.

"I'm Jason Briggs. We had Econ 101 together. But I almost never went." He sat down at a table and began reloading his gun. His fingers worked fast; this was not his first time.

"Oh yeah. I remember you now." Shane remembered

the kid was usually late, absent, or high. "So, where the hell is everyone else?"

Jason finished loading the gun and pulled his long straight hair back behind his shoulder. "No clue."

"So where have *you* been?"

"I was drunk," Jason said in a matter-of-fact tone. "After Cheryl Russet's party, I was wasted. I barely made it back to my room. I woke up the next day and didn't even open the shades. I ate cold pizza and went back to sleep. A couple days might have slipped by. And then... I went outside and found everyone gone."

"And those lizards?" Sam asked. "Someone flush an alligator down the sewer or something? And it had babies... or what?"

"They're new. They started popping up today, from outta nowhere. I killed one out back while getting food from the place next door – this afternoon. And then those two just now. Ain't got no idea what they are, or where they come from."

"You think that... they ate everyone?" Sam asked.

Jason shrugged. "Could be. I mean, something got rid of everyone, and I ain't seen no sign of a body, blood, or guts anywhere. So if these things are what's eating people, then... they clean their plates. They don't leave anything behind."

There was a pause. The brothers took a moment to drink that in. *They don't leave anything behind.*

"Awesome." Shane said sarcastically. When he said that, it usually meant: *we're screwed.*

"But they seem easy to kill," Jason offered as consolation. "One bullet to the head will do it."

"But they're fast," Shane pointed out. As an experienced hunter, he knew fast game. These things would be hard to hit from a distance. Still, if only a few roamed the city, defending themselves wouldn't be very hard, especially with three people now on their team, watching each others' backs.

"We should stick together," he said. "More eyes, more weapons."

Jason nodded. "Fine with me. I've been talking to myself for a week. About to go crazy."

"You've been here a week?" Sam asked, his eyes widening in amazement. "It's been empty like this for that long? So all this went down more than a week ago?"

"I think so. Seven or eight days, at least." Jason stared into space, suddenly preoccupied with counting the days backward.

Something occurred to Sam. "Back at our house, there was a cocoon of some kind in the basement. Maybe these lizards... or whatever, maybe they created it. Maybe they cocooned all the people."

"I didn't check any basement," Jason said. "It's creepy enough up here. I've been staying on higher floors for safety and to keep an eye on the street."

"Does this place have a basement?"

Sam looked around for a door. The hotel lobby was sparsely furnished with cheap chairs and a couch covered in plastic. A metal card table stood in the middle of the room; that's where Jason now finished reloading and checking his rifle. A poster hung on the wall for a concert by a Pink Floyd cover band, called Pink Bricks, with a subheading: "Pink Side of the Moon, a charity event for world hunger."

"Yeah, they have a storage cellar," Jason said. "Stairs are in the back. Why?"

"We should check it out." Shane drew his revolver.

Jason shrugged and hoisted his rifle to his shoulder.

The three boys tiptoed down the first few stairs with their weapons drawn and ready. The steps were dusty, and the air smelled dirty; this cellar hadn't been aired out in months. Shane took up the point with a pistol in one hand, a flashlight in the other, and a good mixture of curiosity and fear in his head. The flashlight's narrow beam pushed against the darkness, which reluctantly parted only a few feet ahead. They moved lower, listening, peering into the gloom. The boys descended to the bottom step, all the way down to the musty cellar's concrete floor. What they saw surprised them.

And what they realized horrified them.

CHAPTER 3

A low muffled bang broke above their heads. The boys recognized the sound of the front doors slamming shut. They waited and listened as a chair scooted across the floor. Another noise, muted footsteps; they strained to hear who or what might be in the lobby. They hadn't thought to lock the front door! If one of those creatures had managed to get inside...

Softly they crept back up the dirty staircase. Sam was happy to leave the musty smell behind, but feeling foolish now – at least one of them should have stayed upstairs to guard the door.

Have to think smarter, or soon we'll be dead... or worse.

At the top they could see shadows move across the wall, but nothing more. Then a voice muttered words in an irate tone, and a second voice answered. It sounded like a girl. The voices were too low to make out specific words, but at least they were human.

"People," whispered Sam.

Caught between the horrors of the basement and the unknown voices in the lobby, the boys stood motionless for a full minute. Shane was first to move, taking up the front again, and stepped over the top stair and into the lobby, gun raised at eye level. Sam noticed sweat trickling down his neck.

At the lobby table sat a boy and a girl, university students. They were intently poring over a map. When they saw Shane, they jumped up, startled, and spilled a chair. The girl pulled out a large knife, and the boy grabbed a shotgun, which he immediately brought to his waist and leveled at Shane.

"Take it easy," Shane said, lowering his own gun.

The other two boys appeared behind him. He motioned for them to lower their weapons, too.

"Look, we're in trouble, same as you," Shane said. "We're not a threat to you. We just didn't know if one of those things had gotten in."

The boy lowered his shotgun. He had short black hair and wore a skin tight t-shirt with a cartoon that said: *I'm not drunk, I just act that way.* "I'm Ken. This is Tina."

The girl had long blond hair. She was beautiful. That's all Sam noticed. That and she had a great knife – a ten-inch hunting knife and a leather sheath on her belt. She wore a blue flannel shirt that roughly matched Sam's, a pair of pink sneakers and tight bluejeans. He felt a tiny spark at his fingertips, and fought to suppress it.

"We heard the shots," she said.

"Yeah. My girlfriend and I came over as soon as we heard. Been trying to find more people."

Tina flinched at the word 'girlfriend' like it wasn't

entirely mutual, but she said nothing. She sheathed her knife, brushing aside a small feather dreamcatcher that also hung from her belt.

"You seen any more of those lizards?" Jason asked.

"Yeah, we've been running into them for a couple days now," Ken explained, sparing a glance out the window. "We killed four already, over on the South Side. We came back to check the dorms, and that's when we heard your shots. What about you?"

"We've only seen two, so far," Shane said.

"Three," Jason corrected.

"But the basement is full of cocooned people. Must be forty or fifty of them. All lined up, like some kind of animal is saving them for a rainy day."

"It's messed up," Jason said. "Total freak show."

Shane looked back toward the stairs. He closed the basement door and secured the lock.

"I don't think three of those things could have done all that," Jason added. "Must be more of them around here."

"What do you mean: done all that?" Ken asked.

"I mean, three lizard mothers couldn't have cocooned fifty people. I don't think so, anyway. Must be more of 'em out there somewhere."

Ken shared a curious frown with Tina, and then stared back at the others. A bemused look crossed his face, like he knew something they didn't.

"The creatures don't cocoon people," he stated grandly like Sherlock Holmes revealing the murderer. He looked back at his girlfriend.

"So, what does?" Shane asked.

"Those cocoons *are* the creatures," Ken said. "They hatch from the silk wraps and become those unholy hell hounds, or hell dragons, whatever you want to call them. And they're hungry at birth! Hungry and mean."

That took a moment to sink in.

"You mean the people down there, our classmates, are gonna hatch into... *those?*" Shane pointed outside. "Our friends and relatives are gonna become lizard things?"

Ken and Tina both nodded.

"We've seen it," she said. She raised her hand to her hair, and Sam noticed she wore about ten leather bracelets of various colors. "We saw a few hatch."

"Holy hell," Sam murmured. Again he felt his hands warm up, but this time for a different reason. He palmed a marble of electricity, then quelled it. This was his coping mechanism.

"So who is cocooning them?" Shane asked. "Who, or what, *is* doing all this? What could put a million people into cocoons, in basements, and cause them to hatch as a totally different... thing?"

"Some serious genetics bull going on here," Jason said. "It's the damn government!"

"We don't know who, what or why," Ken chided flatly, clearly thinking Jason's conspiracy theories were ridiculous. "We just saw them hatch. No idea what's causing this."

"The government, it's a covert lab experiment gone

wrong," Jason ranted. "Or maybe it's the Russians!"

"Why didn't we get... you know, mutated?" Sam asked. "Why are we still human?"

"Because we weren't around, or awake, to get stung," Jason spouted. He was on a roll.

"Maybe some of us are immune?" Sam said. "Like a virus."

"And what stung them?" Shane asked. "If that's the running theory. Some giant insect from Mars?"

"We saw something big in the sky," said Sam.

"We didn't see anything like that," Ken stated.

Jason shook his head. "Ain't seen nothin' up there."

"I watched a dozen classmates go into the cellar of my dorm and fall asleep," Ken told them. "I watched them just go, like in a delusional state. They crawled into a ball and slept. Then the cocoons formed. After about a week, they hatch as... whatever these are. But I had no urge to join them. I wasn't affected by whatever made them do it."

"And I was away," Tina said. "I was locked in the..." She interrupted herself. "I was in a hospital for evaluation. And after all this, Ken came and got me out. The staff had been gone for days. I was just locked in a room."

"You were locked up? In a hospital?" Sam asked. He imagined a straight-jacket and padded walls. This was probably no ordinary hospital. He sent a look to Shane, who sent it back: *loonies, be cool.*

"So we're immune," Shane said to relieve the awkward

moment. "Or we were away at the right time, when the green cloud was sprayed, or whatever. Good news. But we won't be alive for long if all those people hatch."

"We should find other people," Ken said. "I mean the whole world can't be like this. It's just this area, right?"

"Sure," Sam said, trying to sound positive. "But where? Any ideas where to start looking?"

Ken pointed to the map. "Maybe a bigger city. Chicago. Or New York. Better chance of finding people." He paused, then added: "Human people, that is."

Shane shook his head. "No. That's the opposite of what we should do. We need to get out of the city, go to the country."

"He's right," Sam agreed. "Pittsburgh is bad enough, a few thousand raptors ready to hatch. Maybe a couple hundred thousand. But imagine Chicago with three million lizard creatures. New York with six million lizards. All trying to eat us."

"We need to get away from people. Far from any city."

"But we won't get answers in the countryside," Tina argued.

"For right now, answers take a back seat to survival."

"Regardless of where, we gotta move now," Ken said. "More of them are gonna hatch soon. By tomorrow, I'd guess. They have a six to eight day gestation period. This is all just by my observation. No science to it. But, it seems a week is all they need to transform."

"So tomorrow the streets might be filled with lizards,"

Sam murmured, staring outside.

"And in here too." Jason motioned toward the basement, reminding them of the cellar full of potential problems. "Maybe in every building that has a cellar."

"Back near the mountains, we passed the Peak Castle Lodge," Sam recalled. "It's a hotel, but it's also a damn fortress. And it's on high ground. Easier to defend."

Shane nodded. "And far from most people. Except for the resort guests. But that can't be too many this time of year. It's not ski season. Might only be a few."

"I think it's closed for summer," Jason said. "My cousin worked there over Christmas last year. There might not be anyone there at all right now."

"By the way," Ken snorted. "Those creatures outside are just dogs. Cocooned dogs, after the change. The changed people are much bigger."

Shane looked outside at the dead creatures. "Awesome."

Ken and Tina exchanged a whisper then agreed to come along.

They gathered supplies: food, water, weapons and extra gear, such as binoculars, walkie talkies and batteries. They even raided the sporting goods store for knee pads and bulletproof vests. While they had no idea how effective these might be against rabid dragons, they wanted the extra protection. Sam's idea – he always favored a good defense.

At the sporting goods store, they scanned the shelves

for anything else that might be of use. Sam was overpowered by the smell of Tina's perfume, which aroused him. It was a relief when she moved outside to help Ken load the jeep parked at the next corner. Sam went back to searching the shelves and packing supplies. His stayed focused on the task at hand: finding useful provisions.

Suddenly, Tina punctuated the air with a scream.

Sam and Shane ran outside to find a lizard ambling toward Tina and Ken. This one was bigger than the others, more than five feet long. It snarled and leaped forward. Tina stumbled and fell. Ken ran ahead and fumbled with his gun. The lizard went right past Tina and aimed straight for Ken. It was frenetic, taking long strides and baring its teeth. Just as it reached Ken, Shane let an arrow fly. It sank into the creature's neck, and the creature collapsed. Jason stepped out of the store and shot two rounds into its skull.

Tina picked herself up and joined her boyfriend. Despite a few scrapes, they were unhurt.

"It went right past her," Shane said. "Does it only eat men?"

"It's her perfume," Sam suggested. "They can't smell her. They can hear and smell us, but I think their eyesight is poor."

"Let's get back inside."

Back in the shop, they bandaged the scrape on Tina's knee. The incident had succeeded in making them aware of a great big hole in their supplies: first aid. They now added some bandages, antiseptic and first aid kits to their backpacks. Sam wanted some aspirin, but the first aid kits were all Ted's Sporting Goods had in stock.

"We should hit the drug store. There won't be any in the countryside."

A thud shook the room. Something hit the back door hard – the door to the storage room. The door shook again. Something was hitting it from the other side with a serious measure of brute force. Dirt shook from the hinges; it wouldn't hold for long.

"I'd guess something hatched in there," Shane said. "We should go. Now!"

"Come on." Sam slung his backpack over his shoulder.

A loud crash from the front stopped them cold.

They turned in time to see two lizards throwing their bodies against the front doors. The weight of their fury shook the double glass doors, and one pane cracked. Both creatures made another volley, hurling their weight against the door frame. Behind them, a dozen more lizards could be seen running at full speed to join them, their powerful tails thrashing side to side. A few looked more than six feet long – massive creatures. Their fangs might have been seven inches by Sam's guess.

The glass doors cracked again.

"Upstairs!" Shane yelled.

They slung their backpacks, grabbed their gear, and headed up the narrow staircase to the second floor. Ken closed and locked the door behind them. They passed up further to the third floor, and then to the roof access hatch. It was stuck. Shane thrust his shoulder against it. It opened a few inches and stopped.

Below them they heard the front doors give way. Glass could be heard shattering.

"Something's blocking it. Help me!"

Sam and Jason threw their weight against the door. The three boys were able to get it open wide enough for Shane to crawl through. He spilled out onto the roof, landed on his hands, and then scrambled back to his feet. The roof was clear, nothing up here but the debris blocking the access hatch. He kicked some of it aside.

"Come on!" He urged frantically, and helped the others get through. Sam, Tina next, then Ken and Jason crawled through and pushed the door shut. They arranged the debris to block the door once again.

The roof was flat, empty. Shane ran to the edge and looked down. Below them lay a terrifying sight: the entire street was filled with lizard creatures of all sizes from two to six feet long. All of them looked angry and hungry. Their black scales gleamed under the late afternoon sun, almost blue at times, and their eyes glistened red. Now hundreds, maybe even a thousand, swarmed the streets. They burst forth from other buildings, from every dark corner and basement.

The great hatching had begun.

CHAPTER 4

A few of the lizards snapped at each other savagely, fighting for a chance to get into this one building that held the five students: the meal. The sound of gunfire had drawn the creatures here. And the smell of fresh meat.

"Holy crap!" Ken rubbed his hands on his neck. "We are screwed!"

Tina backed away from the edge, squatted down and held her arms to her chest. Vertigo paralyzed her.

Jason leaned over the side and fired a shot from his newly acquired hunting rifle. He aimed through the scope and fired again into the street below, into the mass of chaos.

"Stop it!" Sam said, "You're just attracting more of them."

Jason ignored him and fired again at the swarm.

Shane grabbed Jason's shoulder and pulled him back hard.

"Look, we don't have enough ammo to kill them all. And you're just riling them up! We can't shoot our way out of here."

"He's right." Sam said with forced composure. He held out a hand to stop Jason, who looked like he might throw a punch at Shane. "Relax. We need to think."

The creatures were loud in the street below. Some black, some brown, some changing color, they struggled to clamber over each other and gain access to the building. It didn't appear they could climb up walls. A few tried, but failed. That, at least, was a blessing.

Ken sat down next to Tina and put his arm around her while Jason laid down on the roof, rested and caught his breath. Looking down at their fate below wasn't helping. The late afternoon waned and began to weave into evening. The night loomed ahead, less than an hour away, and with it: darkness.

Without speaking, Shane shot Sam a look that asked if he was okay. He was always able to understand his little brother, and always able to look out for him. Tonight would stretch the limits of that ability.

Sam whispered, "There's no way out down there. Unless they get bored and go away."

"Which isn't impossible." Shane reminded him. "Dogs get bored and stop barking. Animals usually move on, look for food. If they can't get it here, they might move on."

"Or they smell us and don't give up."

"Our options are limited, Sam. We have nowhere to go."

"Rescue helicopter?"

"You really think someone's coming to rescue us?

Sammy, I think that ship has sailed into the rocks. No one's coming."

"Yeah." Sam bit his lip. "Yeah."

Hours passed. The night closed in, until the envelope of darkness was complete. That made it all feel worse, scarier. In the dark, the hissing and growling from the street below sounded demonic. The moon offered only the smallest bit of light – just enough to make the eyes of the creatures glow red. Sam looked over the edge, and imagined falling. He shuddered.

"Don't look, man," Jason warned.

Good advice. Sam scooted back and looked up at the moon.

Then fresh sounds came from the floor beneath them. Several of the creatures had made it to the top floor and were destroying it. Something metal fell over with a clatter, then something made of glass shattered.

Shane stood up. "We need a plan. We need to get out of the city. We can't fight our way out."

"There's none of 'em near that jeep," Ken said. "Not yet, anyway. But it's a block down. How do we get to it?"

"That's our jeep." Shane pointed to the next roof. "We can jump roof to roof. They're only two feet apart. And then shimmy down the fire escape at the corner. The jeep isn't far from there."

Jason shook his head. "Look. Even if we do make it, and even if the princess here makes it too, how do you expect to drive out of here without leading those things behind us?"

"They might follow us all the way to the Peak Lodge," Ken agreed, "...if that's where we're going."

Tina stood up again. "I'm no princess. I can make it to the Jeep. Can *you*?"

A thud shook the roof access door. Their guests inside had found the roof, could smell the human meat. Another thud, followed by snarling and hissing. Dirt particles shook from the door frame.

"We don't have a choice," said Sam. He backed up, then ran forward with his arms swinging. He jumped to the roof of the next building and landed on his hands and knees, picked himself up and looked back. He made it look too easy. "Come on!"

The roof door cracked open. The debris partly blocked it, but a claw came through. It raked at the air. Then a creature popped its head out and growled – the low pitch growl of a crocodile. A smaller creature climbed on top of it, and pushed its way through. It ambled toward them, and Jason put it down with one shot.

Tina and Shane jumped next. Then Ken. Jason kicked the dead creature and joined them last. He jumped just as the bigger lizard shattered the door into a pile of shards. Three more beasts lumbered onto the roof.

Sam didn't stop. He leaped to the next roof, and then the next. He knew if he kept going, the others would follow him. Shane would follow to protect his little brother, and the others would follow Shane. The elder brother had the innate quality of a leader, and people naturally took to him.

Landing on the last roof, Sam scuffed his elbow. It hurt, and a jolt of electricity shot from his arm to the roof shingles – a reflex action. Part of the roof singed black, but none of the others had seen it happen. They were busy jumping for their lives.

He watched them jump and roll, roof to roof. Behind them, the lizards were stranded. One tried to jump after its prey, but fell to the street below, badly wounded. Four other creatures pounced on it and tore into its flesh. Apparently, they ate their own wounded.

Ken landed on the last roof, out of breath and the last to arrive. The fire escape stretched before them; it spiraled to a garbage bin just twenty feet from the jeep.

"Well, at least they can't jump," Shane said, gasping for air. "Or fly!"

Jason raised his rifle and aimed for the roof far behind them, but Sam stopped him. Winded, he put a hand on Jason's shoulder and shook his head. He pointed to the fire escape.

"Save the ammo. And don't make any noise."

"Those things on the street don't know we're over here," said Shane. "Let's keep it that way. Stay quiet. Move slowly down the fire escape, and be careful. I'll cover you with a bow, and come down last."

The metal fire escape was old and rusted. Bolted to the side of the building, it wound down to a point just two feet from the bottom, which was hidden by a garbage bin.

Sam thought of something.

"Tina, do you have any more perfume?"

"Yeah, why?"

"We need to mask our scent. Give us some. Spray it on all of us."

She had half a bottle of it left, and sprayed it generously on all the boys. They choked on its pungent sweet aroma. It was too much – like a 70s disco – but at least now they didn't smell like human meat.

They negotiated the fire escape as fast as possible without slipping, one rung at a time. Sam went first, followed by Tina and Ken. Then Jason slid down, skipping a few rungs, while Shane kept his bow poised and ready. They kept an eye on the mob of creatures just a block away, continuing to pile into the sporting goods store.

Sam landed on the ground. It made more noise than he'd liked, so he waited a moment before standing. When nothing moved around him, he helped Tina land, cupping his hands around her slim waist. She fell back into him, and he supported her. Sam blushed with guilt, but no one noticed. Ken and Jason reached the ground, and Shane crept down to join them. The five of them crouched behind the dumpster.

The jeep lay in plain view. The plan was to tiptoe along the wall to get to it, climb inside and start it up. The sound of the engine would surely attract unwanted attention; so after start-up, they would need to speed out of town as fast as possible. Sam wondered: *how fast can those lizards run?*

They crouched down and made their way to the open vehicle. Ken helped Tina into the back. Sam and Shane took their seats in the front, and Jason stood outside. He opened his backpack and fished out something red and long. It was a pair of bottle rockets: fireworks.

"We'll need a distraction after you turn the ignition."

"Good thinking," Shane whispered. "Point them in that direction."

Jason aimed a rocket over the creatures' heads, in a flight path that would take it in the opposite direction from the jeep. He had a lighter in one hand, the rocket in the other, and stood ready.

Shane turned the ignition. The jeep started, but the noise was low compared to the melee of creatures growling and scuffling with each other down the street. Jason hopped in the back, but stayed ready.

Shane gently applied the gas. The jeep backed up, then rolled ahead toward Fifth Avenue. They would head for the Parkway, exit to the interstate, then off to the mountains.

As the jeep sped up, the noise attracted a band of lizards who broke off from the pack. They scurried after the jeep at a frighting pace. Jason fired the rocket. It sailed upward and whooshed into the distance, past the throng of creatures, and exploded at the other end of the street. The noise engaged the reptile swarm, including most of those chasing them – all except three. Three of the lizards stopped and considered the pack running after the explosion. Then these three unique animals turned back to the jeep. They jolted again, like prehistoric crocodiles with the speed of a gazelle.

The jeep turned a corner on two wheels and sped up Fifth Avenue toward the exit to the turnpike.

The three lizards scurried after them, and it was clear they would overtake the jeep in a matter of seconds. Sam drew an arrow and tried to steady his bow. He released the string and let the arrow fly free, but it missed, deflecting off the pavement. He wasn't as sharp at this as Shane, and the vehicle was bouncing too much.

Jason raised his gun, but knew he couldn't fire. They couldn't risk the noise.

Sam drew another arrow and pulled it back taut in the bow. It made a sharp whisk sound as it flew, and sunk directly into the skull of the lead creature. The beast fell dead, and its mates stumbled over its body. This bought them a few precious seconds, but the beasts recovered quickly, remarkably, and pursued the jeep with even more vigor.

Shane drove faster, regretting his decision to drive. He needed to be the one shooting arrows. Sam drew another arrow and fired, but it just grazed a lizard's leg. This didn't slow it down at all, a useless effort.

There was no more time for arrows. Both creatures were at the jeep. Tina screamed, and Jason yelled for Shane to "stop driving like a grandma! Move it!"

A lizard jumped up. Its front claw found traction on the jeep's bumper, where it raised its body onto the jeep, its jaws wide open. In seconds it would sink its teeth into Ken. This outcome seemed inevitable.

Then Sam reacted without thinking. He raised his hand and shot a wide arc of electricity forward and outward, fueled by the adrenaline coursing through his body. He opened his fist and the arc widened, intensified. For a split second, the air sizzled with iridescent blue fire. It scattered the darkness like a camera flashbulb for an explosive blink an eye, then went out.

Both lizards flew back a hundred feet, stunned by the electric charge. They did not get up.

The jeep sped on, and put distance between them and the university campus. Everyone looked at Sam, surprised and scared, but also relieved. They watched the stunned creatures get smaller and smaller, left behind, as the jeep entered the highway and departed the infested city. The group also watched Sam.

But no one said a word.

CHAPTER 5

WHEN Sam was ten years old, he experienced his first real problem with his spark at school – the kind of problem that stays with a child forever. Billy Morski had enjoyed teasing Sam and all his smaller classmates throughout several years of grade school. By now, it was old habit, but the kid had been growing more sadistic every year. On this particular day, Billy had managed to shove little Timothy Taylor in his locker and shut the door. Tim was one of Sam's good friends, and Sam knew that the small frail boy was claustrophobic. Tim cried a bit and pleaded for Billy to let him out. After ten minutes, the locker became silent.

Sam was a bony kid, afraid of the overgrown bully, but he couldn't stand to watch this. He stepped up.

"That's enough," he said. "Let him out. He can't breathe so good in there."

"You do it," Billy said. "If you like him so much, why don't you marry him?" A few kids snickered.

"I don't know your locker combination, Billy. You need to open it. Please, he might not be okay in there."

"Yeah, come on," someone said in the crowd of kids

in the hall. "It's not funny anymore."

"Come on," Sam echoed. "Let him out."

"I'm busy," Billy gloated. "Class starts soon."

Sam knocked on the locker door. "Tim? You okay?"

There was no reply.

Mr. Jackson came along about that time, and asked what was going on. Billy claimed it was an accident, and that he was trying to get the door open. He fumbled with the lock and giggled to himself. Finally, it made the familiar *chikt* sound and swung open. Tim's small body fell out onto the floor. He looked dead.

"Get the nurse! Now!" Mr. Jackson shouted, and some kids ran screaming down the hall. As it turned out, Tim was fine. He had passed out from a panic attack. His parents took him to the hospital, but he recovered, at least physically.

When Mr. Jackson asked why the kid was in the locker, Billy lied. "He bet me he could fit in the locker, and when he got in, the door shut by accident. Honest, Mr. J. It was just an accident."

"Is that true?" Mr. Jackson asked a group of five kids, including Sam, still in the hallway.

The other kids were silent, but a few nodded. They were all afraid of Billy, afraid of a painful reprisal at the hands of the sadistic bully. But Sam spoke up:

"It's a lie, Mr. Jackson. Morski put him in there, and made him stay. Then he closed the door."

Billy glared at Sam as he was hauled off to the principal's office. Billy wasn't the smartest guy on the block, he was just the meanest. He didn't think his lies through – or his actions, for that matter.

After school, Billy waited at the top of Sam's street. It was a new subdivision with as yet only a few houses built, and few witnesses to a beating. On this day, Billy set out to beat the crap out of Sam. He wailed on him like "the devil beating the sins out of hell" as his mom used to say. He bloodied Sam's nose, blackened his eye, and broke one of his ribs. About the time it looked like Billy might kill the smaller boy, Sam's older brother showed up.

Shane had a temper, too, and he was highly protective of his brother. Shane was bigger and knew how to fight. He pushed Billy off Sam, and then punched him in the gut. It was when he turned to help Sam up, that Billy took a gun from his book bag. He pointed it straight at Shane's head, and fired.

That was the first time Sam used his "spark" in public. He sent a small dart of electricity at Billy's head. It was enough to knock Billy off balance and send the bullet off target, far over Shane's head and into the trunk of a tree. Shane knocked the gun out of Billy's hand, and punched him in the face until he stopped fighting back. Billy just lay there, moaning.

From that day on, Billy's life took a tailspin. The gun was eventually discovered in his locker, and he was kicked out of school. Later, he spent a year in a juvenile prison facility. Other than spreading rumors about Sam's freaky abilities, he kept his distance from Sam and his brother. At least until years later, when opportunity for revenge came. Sam remembered that day forever.

The five of them rode silently out of town: Sam and Shane, Jason, Tina and Ken. They had less life experience between them than a single adult, but they were full of survival instinct and the will to try. Sam and his brother had hunting skills, at least, and that was going to prove helpful in the coming days.

Their plan was to reach the Peak Castle Lodge by noon the next day. It was still 120 miles away, even with the night putting miles of road behind them. If the roads remained free of abandoned cars and other obstacles, it might be possible to arrive in late morning.

Thick clouds covered the moon. Thunder rolled in the distance, and small drops of rain started to fall. The jeep was uncovered, which meant this night was about to get uncomfortable really fast. Heavy rain would dampen an already bad day. Sam suggested they try to find shelter before the storm broke, but in the middle of nowhere their choices were slim. The woods beside the road would offer a small amount of cover, but not much, so they continued driving northward.

The rain intensified, and lightning cracked the sky. They were drenched within minutes. The wind stirred up, and this was beginning to look like a full-blown storm, worse than they had expected. Any shelter would do.

Not far ahead they spotted a broken down car, a '98

sedan with its hood open. They drove onto the grass, pulled up next to it, and the five of them piled inside the car. It might not run, but it had a roof. Sam and Shane got in front, and the others jumped into the back seat. When the doors were closed, they instinctively locked them.

Rain spattered the roof. It made a helluva racket, but it didn't leak in. Their clothes and gear were soaking wet, but at least now they had cover. They took comfort in this small bit of luck the world had thrown them.

But still no one talked about Sam's bizarre electrical stunt.

Tina found a towel in the back seat and started to dry her hair with it.

"That's probably not clean," Ken warned her. But she didn't care.

They all relaxed and took a breath. That's hard to do when you're wet, scared and miserable. Jason broke out some snack cakes and passed them around. At least they could eat. It wouldn't lessen their fear, or discomfort from damp underwear, but their stomachs thanked them. Nutritious or not, the spongy yellow cakes tasted great in that moment.

Shane was first to say what was on their minds. "This day is one for the books. If 'the books' are volumes of the damned, that is. What do you suppose is happening?"

"Government conspiracy," Jason told them flatly. It was obvious he believed this. "Some virus got out. I bet you it was meant as some kind of germ warfare weapon.

And it got out."

"Our government?" Ken asked. "Or some other? Or terrorists?"

"Take your pick. Or all three."

Sam disagreed. "That's ridiculous. Maybe the Earth just gave up on us. We treated it so badly, maybe it's forcing a new evolution. Earth is changing up."

"You think all this happened naturally?" Jason raised his voice and was becoming animated, waving his hands about. "People turning into monsters? Nature doesn't usually change course in eight days, you know. Can't trust any government, it's gotta be commies!"

"Aliens," Shane said. He paused, then added: "From Mars."

Sam rolled his eyes. "Come on, we need real answers"

"I'm with your brother." Jason patted Shane's shoulder. "You might be right. But not Mars. Further out."

"*Planet of the Vampires*. Remember that movie. Very cool flick." Shane loved fifties sci-fi movies.

"Was that the one that got the chick and the skin-tight leather outfits?" Jason asked.

"Yeah. It is. But *Demon Girl from Mars* also wore something like that – ."

"Can we talk about something else?" Tina interrupted.

"Something else?" Jason asked. "Sweetheart, this is the topic of the day. We're at the end of the world. What else do you want to talk about? Your SAT scores? I got news for you, they don't friggin matter no more. This...

all this crap about monsters and Martians, this is what matters now."

They sat without speaking for ten minutes and ate yellow cake.

"I keep wanting to check my phone messages," Tina said. "I still miss that. I hope the phones and wi-fi get back up soon."

Sam didn't think that was likely, but he gave her a supportive smile.

"Well... we don't know it's Martians... yet." Shane said, to defuse the tension. "It might just be Republicans." He was rewarded with a snicker from Sam and Jason.

"We'll find out what this means... at some point," Sam said. "Everything has its day. Every mystery has a solution. Isn't that what Sherlock Holmes said?"

"The mystery is only your eye," Jason said. "Is that right?"

No one knew, but they were surprised Jason, of all people, had read Sherlock Holmes – or read anything at all.

"Do you read a lot?" Tina asked.

"I do," said Jason quite simply. "I do."

Books and their covers, don't judge, Sam thought.

And that brought them to silence again. Listening to the rain had a peculiar calming effect.

The rain lasted the better part of an hour, then trickled to a drizzle. When it had completely stopped, they got back in the jeep and headed north once more.

The seats were still wet, which made the ride uncomfortable, but at least they were moving again. Tired and damp, they listened to the noise of the jeep's engine, and said nothing.

Before dawn, something caught their eye on the road ahead. They observed a large shape blocking the road about a mile further north. It was a barricade made of stalled cars and trucks. The first rays of morning sunlight glinted off the car mirrors, but it was difficult to see more. A few of the vehicles were badly damaged, with dented sides and cracked windshields. The road appeared to be totally impassible, and the barricade looked man-made.

They stopped the jeep about a half mile from it.

"This looks on purpose," Shane said in a hushed tone. He didn't want to break the eerie quiet that had settled in this morning. "That's no accident."

Sam agreed. "It's a roadblock. Someone wants to stop cars from passing here. Or stop something else."

Shane looked through the binoculars. Jason peered through the scope of his rifle. A single man sat on the pile of cars. He had a shotgun in one hand, and a beer in the other.

"Well this looks inviting," Shane whispered. "Two of us go talk to him. The rest of you, stay here."

"You sure?" Jason asked. "He doesn't look friendly."

"I'll go with you," Sam offered.

"No. I'm taking Tina," Shane said. "She is the least threatening. We'll look like a harmless couple of kids.

And no weapons. We won't carry any, so you guys need to keep yours trained on us."

"No, I don't want Tina going," Ken objected.

"It's okay. I'll go. He's right, I'm not threatening."

"I'll go with her," Sam insisted. "Shane, you need to stay here with bow drawn. If anything goes down, I need you to rescue us."

That did seem to make sense. The group agreed to send Sam and Tina out to meet the stranger. After all, Sam had clearly demonstrated his ability to protect them in a jam, and Shane was by-far the better bowman.

With the modest protection of Tina's knife and Sam's hands, they stepped forward onto the road. The others watched anxiously from a pile of rocks near the jeep. Shane kept the binoculars glued to this eyes, and Jason followed them through the hunting scope, one finger ready on the trigger.

The old man was sitting on the hood of a car near the top of the barricade. He put down his beer and shotgun, and lit a cigarette. He seemed at peace with the world. As Sam and Tina got closer, they saw he wore a Pennsylvania State Police uniform.

It was cool in the early morning. Every step could be heard, their sneakers crunching on the dirt road. That was fine, they wanted him to see and hear them coming. Sam lifted his arms to show he had no weapons. They stopped about forty feet away.

"Hello Sir."

"Hello," Tina said in a soft voice.

The old man dragged on his cigarette. He did not reach for his gun. "Hello back."

"Um, I'm Sam. And this is Tina. We're with friends. From Pittsburgh."

"Oh yeah?" The man put out his cigarette and climbed down from his perch atop a brand-new silver pickup truck. A short jump to a Corolla's bumper, then he landed on the road. He seemed more agile than Sam would have guessed for the man's age; he still held the beer in his left hand without spilling a drop. "Come closer. Let me have a look at you."

They walked right up to the man. A few gray hairs remained on the sides of his head, but otherwise he was bald. He had a kind look about him, but Sam didn't doubt this guy could wrestle a bear, if needed. The corners of his eyes were wrinkled from age – eyes with decades of experience. Sam wondered what those eyes had seen this past week.

"My name is Stuart Reese. But I guess you can call me Stu."

Sam shook his hand. He knew that this scene was being closely watched by Shane and the guys. He wondered if Stu had someone watching them, too.

"So, how's the Burgh this time of year?" Stu asked.

"Sucks," Sam said honestly. "Really sucks."

Stu laughed and coughed. "You got the critters there, too?"

Sam nodded "And then some. We barely got out alive."

"Well, here's to you!" Stu raised his beer and drank. "So your friends gonna join us?"

"Yeah. We just... want to be careful."

"I hear that." Stu said. "Smart to bring the pretty girl up with you. Help charm your way into a newcomer's heart. And I do admit, it is working."

"What are you doing out here, Sir?"

"Stu." he corrected the girl. "I'm waiting for you."

"Me? Us?"

"Well, not you in particular. I'm waiting for anybody. I didn't block the road, mind you. These cars were here like this when I arrived. I'm just sitting here waiting to see who comes along. Safest place to watch from. And if anything inhuman comes crawling along, I can pick 'em off one by one." He pointed to his shotgun resting atop the pickup.

Tina held Sam's arm for safety and stood close to him in the morning darkness. He certainly didn't object to it. She kept glancing back at the others and the jeep back down the road.

"Go ahead," Stu waved his arm. "Invite your friends over. I won't bite."

Sam sized up Stu in a flash, and felt no threat. He turned on the walkie talkie and told the others to join them. There was a pause before they replied "Right," and the jeep started up. Shane stopped the jeep about twelve feet from the pile of cars, at the mouth of a dirt path.

Sam introduced the others to Stu, who nodded and wordlessly waved a hand that looked rough with calluses.

It was a single gesture wave, almost like a salute. The meeting had a surreal aspect to it, out in the middle of nowhere, and again Sam wondered if they were being watched.

"You can take that jeep of yours around by that path there," Stu said. "It'll be rocky, but it's short. You come out on the other side."

"We're trying to find shelter," Sam told Stu. "At the Peak Lodge. See if we can get our bearings. Just until help comes."

Stu nodded. "High ground. Surrounded by a wall. Makes sense. It'll probably have a storeroom stocked with canned goods. And probably no people this time of year."

"You can come with us," Sam offered.

The others were surprised and shot him varied looks of uncertainty. Jason shook his head silently, as if to vote *No* on this issue. Shane pulled Sam aside, asked if he was sure.

"Not sure, but we may need help. More guns, more people. And he knows more about this area than we do."

It was a moot point, though, as Stu politely declined.

"It's okay, Stu. You can join us. Safety in numbers."

Stu lit another cigarette, dragged on it, and leaned back for a moment. "I don't know about safety. These days it's in short supply, seems."

"But if we stick together," Tina said. She shrugged. "It might help."

"That it might." Stu mumbled, looking down the road

at nothing. "But somebody stacked these cars here. And I want to know who. And why."

"What does it matter?" Sam asked.

"It might. It might not. But you kids go ahead. I'm gonna stay put for a bit."

"You plan to sleep here?"

"I'm camped not far from here. I'll be all right. By the way, no offense, but you guys reek. You get into some perfume war, or just coming back from Studio 64, or whatever it's called?"

"It masks the scent," Sam explained.

Stu grinned. "Smart. I'll keep that in mind."

"Well. Good luck to you, Stu."

Sam shook Stu's hand again, and the five of them piled back into the jeep. Tina waved at the man, as they disappeared into the woods. The path was rocky and rough, as promised, but the four-wheel drive got them through to the other side. They regained the main road, and sped ahead. Soon the pile of cars, and Stu Reese, were out of sight.

CHAPTER 6

OTHER than a few more derelict cars peppering the landscape, not much caught their attention on the way to the Peak Castle Lodge. One car had been burned to the frame, the others simply abandoned. The day unfolded warm and bright, and revealed the resort hotel a few miles ahead. Perched on a hilltop, it was easy to spot, but would be a valuable strategic vantage point for anyone inside. The hotel was large and impressive, like a castle from Europe, a defense of eighteenth century kings. It would make a good fortress, but a fantasy castle was its artificial theme, not its true calling. Tourism was its true purpose, which meant they could expect to find some items of comfort inside.

The wind picked up, and the clouds moved on, letting a little sun in. Two flags whipped violently from atop two of the watchtowers. One was the American flag, the other a fictitious flag with a crest: the Peak logo. Both were tattered and worn from many nights of wind and rain. No caretaker remained to bring them in or to tend to the hotel. The area appeared deserted, save for the birds and butterflies fluttering here and there; even those now disappeared, scared off by the newcomers.

They drove up the hill to the front gate. The gray stone wall rose more than twelve feet and surrounded the entire lodge. The gate presented no opening from the outside. Someone would have to climb over the wall.

With the skill and ease of a monkey, Sam climbed a knotted maple tree growing closest to the wall, and looked down from a branch into the courtyard. Other than a swarm of bees, it appeared uninhabited. Sam gauged the distance.

"I think I can jump onto the wall."

Shane put a hand to his forehead and shielded his eyes from the sun, now showing its face through an ever-thinning cloud cover. He watched his brother scale the branch. "Be careful, Sammy."

Jason walked around the side of the wall, checking the area for signs of anything alive. His gun never left his hands. The others stayed at the jeep and watched.

Sam moved to the end of the tallest branch, which started to bend and creak. He pushed off with both his arms and legs and landed chest-down on top of the wall. He started to slip down, clawed back over the rampart, arms straining, but did manage to find purchase and climb to safety. He stood up and smiled down at the others.

"I'm Batman," he boasted.

Shane frowned. "Yeah, you're the Batman. Let us in."

"I'll jump down and open the gate. You drive the jeep

inside."

"If the gate's electric, it won't open. Look for a manual release," Shane told him.

Sam searched for the best way to climb down into the courtyard. He found a point above a shed, then jumped onto the shed's roof. With eight more feet to go, he began to shimmy down the side when a familiar sound stopped him.

A five-foot lizard crawled out from the thick garden bushes. At first it looked lazy and sleepy, but the sight of a new meal brought it to attention. It raced toward the shed, growling and beating its tail against the ground. When it threw its tail against the rickety wood structure, Sam nearly lost his balance. The creature grunted and jumped, snapping the air just inches from Sam's feet. Sam scrambled backward, but had no weapons on him, nothing to help fend it off.

"I need something, a gun!"

Shane tossed him a pistol, but it flew too high. Sam reached out to catch it and missed. The gun fell to the ground, and the lizard licked it with its forked tongue, then turned back to Sam.

"Another one. I missed!"

Shane was already up on a tree branch, now cracking from his weight. He hopped onto the wall before the branch snapped. He aimed and fired two rounds into the lizard as it made its second attempt to jump the shed. It fell dead.

The blast of the gunshots echoed for several seconds

through the resort ground and the valley beyond. Sam's ears began to ring.

The brothers jumped to the ground. Nothing else moved in the courtyard, so they turned to the front gate. Hitting the button on the control panel didn't produce any result; the gate did not open.

Outside, the others inspected the wall and waited. Ken got behind the wheel, ready to drive inside, but bigger problems were about to descend on them.

They heard the sound of bushes being crunched under feet somewhere behind them. They turned to see five large lizards crashing from the forest into the field, and then up the road. The creatures moved incredibly fast, their bodies twisting and their tails thumping the ground. They destroyed the reeds and brush on their way to the opening that lead them to their prey.

Jason yelled over the wall. "Guys, you better hurry! We got company..."

He raised his rifle and aimed through the scope. He pulled the trigger once, twice. One of the lizards fell. Ken aimed his pistol and took down the next one. He aimed between the eyes and killed another, but it took him three shots. Two more creatures still tore at them.

Less than two feet away, within bite's range of his leg, Ken shot one of beasts in the face. It spun around and smashed into its mate. The last lizard rolled over and lost its balance. When it regained traction, it circled the jeep and hissed.

The gate groaned and opened, like a mighty giant

spreading its jaws for a wide yawn. Sam and Shane appeared with guns drawn.

"It's behind the jeep," Ken shouted.

Shane circled around to the other side, but the lizard jumped on the jeep's hood. Jason took it down with one shot. Its body slumped down on the hood, leaving a dent.

It took three of them to push its body to the ground where they left it, then drove the jeep into the resort. Sam and Jason shut the gates, then manually lock them. There was a manual lever, not electric, and it took two people each time to open and close the massive stone doors. After being slammed shut and locked, they hoped the lodge belonged to them.

A quick tour proved the grounds to be empty, except for a fluffy white cat. It roamed the top floors and was happy to find the crew. They brought it downstairs and fed it part of a prepackaged yellow twinkle cake. The other floors, even the kitchen and basement, were empty. The lodge harbored no more surprises. As they had suspected, no one was up here at this time of year.

Sam climbed the watchtower from the staircase inside the hotel. Five stories high, it provided a good vantage point to survey the land. He didn't see any more creatures or people for miles in all directions. The open fields surrounding the lodge would show anything that might come out of the woods, at least during the day. That was small comfort, knowing how fast the creatures could run. However, it seemed unlikely that the lizards would be able to climb the wall. Across the courtyard loomed a sister tower, but not as tall – only three stories high.

Thunder rumbled, even though few clouds now dabbed the sky. In the distance, Sam thought he heard the single faint shot of a gun firing. He wondered if it was Stu. No more shots followed, only thunder again. Exhausted, he lumbered back downstairs and joined the others in the hotel lobby.

"We need to take turns in the tower. On watch."

"Right," Shane said, "in shifts."

"Did you find any supplies?"

"Enough for now, a few cans of food, and a stream runs out back. We'll have water, at least"

"Can we get rid of... *that?*" Tina asked, pointing out the window to the lizard's body next to the shed.

It took all four boys to drag its scaly carcass outside and drop it next to the other dead creatures. Flies were already feasting on their remains.

Back inside the safety of the Peak Castle Lodge, they set up camp in the lobby. It was elegantly decorated with high ceilings, glass chandeliers, and big windows. A plush red couch and several armchairs filled out the main reception area. To one side sat a cafe with one large oak table and several small tables for guests. Another building housed a fancy reception hall and restaurant, so this small venue was just for coffee and tea. A long reception counter jutted from the opposite side of the room, and had more than enough space for several clerks to stand behind it. In a resort of this size, the staff would be large.

A narrow staircase accessed both of the watchtowers from the lobby wings. Each of the boys would take four-hour shifts keeping watch in the taller east tower. With binoculars they could see for fifteen miles, except for the areas hidden by dense trees. There was no way of knowing what lurked in the dark cover of the two forests on either side of the road.

By afternoon, the incongruous thunder had stopped, and the sun came out in full force. Sam briefly wondered if it had not been thunder at all, but cannon fire instead. He climbed the stairs and took the first watch while everyone else explored the remainder of the resort. They looked for food, supplies, firewood, and containers to fill with water. Jason checked the club house and buildings in back.

High in the tower, Sam stood alone and enjoyed the solitude, keeping one eye on the grounds below. He removed his shirt, jeans, and socks, and hung them in the afternoon sun to dry out. After making sure no one was coming up the stairs, he removed his underwear and hung them out on the window sill. The tower windows stayed propped open; the breeze caressed his body and soothed his mind. It felt good to be dry again.

He rubbed the palm of his hand, still sore from the electric charge he'd generated last night. His clothes were drying fast; and the sun felt good. It felt good to be sheltered again. This whole place felt right, and it should be able to protect them from the rain and cold, and with any luck... from monsters.

While standing watch, a calm washed over him. He was dry, protected, and five floors high. Heights made him feel safe. He pressed the binoculars to his eyes and looked out. Some movement disturbed the trees. *Probably squirrels or birds*, he thought.

After an hour, Tina climbed the steps to the tower. He had just enough time to grab his sun-dried boxer briefs and pull them on.

She whistled. "Wow. Nice body, science boy."

He blushed and covered himself with his hands. "I uh... swim a lot." He was aware of how snug his briefs fit.

She herself had changed into dry clothes from the hotel staff quarters. She wore a tight t-shirt that revealed her belly button, and showcased her ample chest area. She handed him an apple and more snack cakes.

"Thanks. I'm starving."

"The guys are working on getting hot water for the showers." She threw a plush towel over his shoulder. "This is a hotel, after all."

"Thanks, but I'm dry now." He took the towel anyway, and wrapped it around his waist.

She put his right palm in her soft hands and rubbed it gently, as if polishing glass. Her curiosity was obvious and understandable.

"How did you do that?" she asked. "Back there. Static electricity?"

"Something like that."

"Have you always been able to do that?"

"Yeah. Pretty much, since I was a kid."

She released his hand and felt the muscles in his arm. "You have any more super powers?" She wasn't flirting, it was just her way; this was how she acted around all boys.

He blushed again, and started to feel uncomfortable. He shook his head. "No. Not really."

"Well. I'm glad you saved us back there."

He turned to look outside, and changed the subject. "So Ken and the other are getting the showers going?"

"I hope so. I'd love to get that hot tub running again, too." She snatched the binoculars and looked out on the still road. "We seem to be totally alone here."

Sam took advantage of her distraction and brought his clothes back in from the sill. He quickly pulled his jeans on. Still warm from the sun, they pleasantly hugged his body. He put on his flannel shirt, but didn't button it yet. The wind kicked at his hair.

Abruptly she handed the binoculars back, turned and headed for the stairs. "See ya later." She waved and hopped back down the steps, out of sight.

Sam thought she was a bit odd, but liked her. He'd try not to like her too much. The group didn't need any more complications this week. Survival looked like it was going to be a full-time job.

Jason took over the next watch, and Sam descended

the stairs to see what progress had been made down in the hotel lobby. The others had stacked all the canned goods and safe food into neat piles on the tables in the cafe. They pushed a few smaller tables together and stacked the food for rationing until more canned goods could be found. Ken and Jason managed to fill several bottles and jars with stream water from the back. Luck favored them; they hadn't run into any dragons on the way to or back from the stream.

"Everything okay up there?" Shane asked his younger brother.

"Yeah. Nothing moving."

"We've got enough food to last a few days here. We'll need to make a supply run tomorrow. No idea where. What's the closest store to this place?"

Sam picked up a can. "Peaches? Really?"

"Hey, beggars can't be whiners," Shane scolded and pointed to some cases behind the bar. "We've got bottles of wine and beer, some top-shelf whiskey, a few soft drinks, but... only for emergencies – if we ever can't get to the water."

Tina and Ken returned from the garden that spread next to the hotel. They had a basket of apples, a few greens and a couple carrots, which they plopped down on the table. Apple trees were abundant around the grounds, so they would probably never completely starve.

"These are all we could pick for now," Ken reported. "There are other trees in the back, pears I think, but the fruit is too high. And the garden has some vegetables, I guess ripe enough to eat, or close enough to ripe ...considering."

Shane poured Sam a glass of stream water. Parched, he gulped it down gratefully. He tried to avoid looking at Tina. He always felt guilty for things he'd never done; even guilt for his thoughts. Shane picked up on this and steered them back to the maps laid out on another table.

"So," he said, "where do you suppose the nearest store might be? Fayetteville is seventeen miles east. But St. Marks is easier to get to."

"That's almost forty miles," said Ken.

"But it's a straight road. Easier, faster."

"If it's not blocked," Sam grumbled.

"Hey, which one is smaller?" Ken asked. "Smaller towns are better. Fewer people. I mean, fewer lizards. Fewer cocoons."

"About the same. Both are small towns. Population maybe a thousand people in each. Before all this, anyway."

"They won't have much."

"A drugstore and grocery store, at least. That's all we need."

Shane clapped his hands together. "We'll go tomorrow morning, early. Okay?"

"We need a new car," said Sam. "The jeep isn't protected."

"But it's got four-wheel drive. We'll need that here. It'll be muddy after the rain."

"Okay for now, but let's keep our eyes open for a better vehicle. A van or a truck maybe."

Shane wasn't giving up his precious jeep just yet, but he agreed to "keep his eyes open" for now.

They gathered together and ate a nice dinner of apples, carrots and canned peaches. They even splurged on one soda and one beer, split among them. The cat ate with them, content to have company again.

Several of the showers still operated with running water, even though they couldn't get the water heater working yet. Cold showers were better than no showers and were a welcomed extravagance; it felt nice to be clean again.

They wrapped themselves in plush robes from the hotel suites, and chose their rooms. Physically and emotionally drained, used up by the day, everyone welcomed the release of sleep. A bed for everyone tonight, so there would be no guard shift. It was decided that sleep was more important, to be fresh for the supply run the next day, so the guard tower sat empty from midnight to five.

That was a mistake.

CHAPTER 7

THE Peak was a four-star resort with plush, king-size beds and over a hundred suites, complete with red carpeting and large panoramic windows. Except for Ken and Tina, each of them took a separate room. However, for safety they decided to stay close together on the second floor, the rooms closest to the stairs, instead of scattering around the nine-story hotel. This also put them at the front, closest to the watchtower.

A new thunderstorm swept in and pounded the outside world. The wind picked up speed; their flags might not survive the night. Rain battered the windowpanes. Their frames vibrated.

Sam nestled in his bed and listened to the storm. It felt good to be snuggled in, ensconced amid lots of amenities: two big pillows, and a pile of sheets and blankets on his body. Like a bird in a nest, he curled up and tucked in for the night.

He remembered Saturday mornings in the winter when he was about six or seven. Their house was always cold in winter, and he didn't want to get out of bed.

Wearing his footies, he'd shuffle to the TV in the living room. He'd wrap blankets around his body and watch "Saturday morning cartoons."

Sam also remembered when he was barely eight. He used to practice warming his dad's coffee with his fingertips. The first few times had been failures; he'd boiled the liquid and nearly shattered the cup. He had to pretend to have dropped it, but Mom wasn't angry. She was never angry. He missed her.

Many years of practice had taught him extreme control over his sparking ability. He had acquired a finesse to his art — because that's what he considered it: an art. By the age of fourteen, he was able to warm a cup of coffee with one finger just by shooting a tiny jolt of static shock into it. His art of sparking had become as natural as walking or riding a bike.

Now, in this new version of the world, he knew his sparking power would be needed. Was there any point to continue hiding it? Not anymore, he guessed. No more classmates remained to tease him for being different. *I guess the end of the world has its perks,* he thought wryly.

Shane also settled in for the night, but he slept on top of the covers. He didn't share the same nesting instinct his brother possessed. Instead, Shane liked to stay ready to charge and fight. This lodge was a tactical advantage to him, not a cozy home. He lay on the mattress and stared at the ceiling, his bow at the side of his bed. Twice he got up and looked out the window. The view from the second floor wasn't great, but he was able to watch the storm wail down on the Earth. Ironically, the storm made him feel safer, since it seemed unlikely anything could move through this tempest. Most people, friend or foe, would have to stay put tonight. And the creatures, too.

Ken and Tina cuddled together and slept like logs.

Jason paced for an hour and also watched the storm from his window. But eventually sleep took him, as well.

Sometime in the middle of the night, a howl broke through the rain. It was a terrifying screech, like a wounded animal. The storm continued without caring. The cry was distant, but Shane distinctly heard it. The cat joined him for awhile, curled up on the bed. It had heard it, too.

They woke up much later than planned: a bit past 8:00 in the morning. The storm was over and only sparse traces of it remained. Everything outside was wet, but drying fast under the kiss of the yellow sun's warm rays.

Shane sat in the watchtower, as the others got up and ate their breakfast of dry cereal – no milk, and more apples. When the others had finally assembled in the cafe, he went back down to the lobby.

"Come on," he said, "I want to show you something."

They followed him to the front gate. Two of them opened the heavy doors again, and they followed him out onto the wet grass outside the gates.

"Look." He pointed to a dark spot in the grass.

The dead creatures were gone. Only blood-stained

grass remained, and the impressions their heavy bodies had made. A line of damaged grass revealed they had been dragged away.

"Someone, or something took our friends here."

"Why?" Ken asked.

"The meat," Jason said with some authority. "To eat them. Food has gotta be getting scarce out there. That was a lot of beef they got hold of here. Maybe we should have kept 'em."

"I'm not eating lizards," Tina said. "I'm not."

"You might," Jason laughed. "People do strange things when they're hungry."

Shane bent down to look at the tracks. He couldn't tell what had dragged the bodies away. "People or creatures. Not sure."

"You think people are here?" Sam lowered his tone to a whisper. "That means they might be watching us right now."

They surveyed the road, field and woods. The flowers swayed back and forth, tugged by the wind, but nothing else moved. It was a peaceful tapestry filled with color, but it didn't feel that way. It felt like they were on a beautiful deserted island surrounded by sharks.

"Okay, from now on, we have someone in the tower at all times," Shane said. "It would have been helpful to know who dragged those things away."

"Yeah," said Jason. "Let's head out. Supply run, remember?"

Everyone agreed, but Sam lingered a moment and

stared into the woods. He felt someone, or something, was watching them.

They geared up for the day's supply run. Tina and Ken stayed behind to guard the castle and to open and close the gate. Jason and the brothers took the jeep out on the road for Fayetteville, the closest town.

The jeep jostled and bumped over the wide dirt path before finding the paved road. Ken watched them disappear, and wondered why a hotel this fancy didn't have a paved road to the gate. Rustic appearance, or country atmosphere? He shrugged it off and wished the guys luck under his breath.

They entered the small town of Fayetteville with the jeep rolling at a slow crawl, their weapons drawn and eyes on every corner and shadow. They parked near the town center. There wasn't much to Fayetteville: a few houses and even fewer stores or merchants. A shed nearby advertised tools for rent, and a saw-sharpening service. Oddly, another sign on the shed advertised bike tours: motorbike tour $25. Probably for the tourists at the Peak who might wander here by accident.

"You suppose that $25 is per person, or per tour?" Sam asked. "I mean, could a family go out on bikes for that?"

Shane looked at his brother. "I don't know, dude. Why don't you hang around and look into that. I'm gonna check for supplies."

Jason chuckled. "Look at those crappy bikes, the seats

are all torn--"

"Hey!" Shane interrupted. "Let's focus. There's the drugstore. Let's check there first."

Sam and Jason saluted and followed him into Jim's RX, the town's only pharmacy. Its door was easy to break open, as the lock was a hundred years old. The shelves hadn't yet been picked over, which meant that no one here got the "end of the world" memo. The boys scooped aspirin, bandages, and antibiotics into their bags.

"Look for anything that ends in -ayacin, or -cin." Sam told them. "Those should be antibiotics. And try to find iodine for cuts."

Some snack items hung on racks near the front: peanuts, chips and cakes. They snagged those, too.

"I'll take these bags to the jeep," Shane said. "You guys keep rooting around for anything else we might need."

Shane turned and started for the door. His hand started to push it open, then stopped. Through the window, he spotted a black and brown lizard casually walking in the middle of the road. It was chewing on something, and apparently unaware of them as yet. At seven feet, this was the biggest one they had seen so far.

"Guys!" he exclaimed in a low tone. "Guys, look."

"Damn, they've got a lot of female drugs and stuff," Jason commented, oblivious.

"Shut up!" Shane tried to get their attention without raising his voice above a whisper. He threw a roll of toilet paper at Jason, who instinctively caught it. "Look out there."

"What?"

The lizard groaned and meandered across the street. It was foraging for food, rats, pigeons, anything.

"Oh... lovely..."

"Be quiet, you idiots."

"We could shoot it from here," Jason offered. "Easy shot."

"But who knows what else we'll wake up! We shoot that one, and a hundred more come down on us?" They only had guns – the bow was back at the jeep.

"Wait for it to get further away," Sam suggested. "It's heading up the road anyway."

"We have to hit the grocery store, though. It's about a mile further down. We'll need to drive."

"We start that jeep, it's gonna hear us."

"Hey," Sam snapped his fingers. "That reminds me. Load up on cologne and perfume. There's a whole shelf of it. Fill up this bag."

They sprayed themselves generously with men's cologne first, then loaded the rest of the bottles into a large knapsack. A bottle slipped out of Sam's hand and crashed on the ground. It shattered loudly and spun into a dozen pieces in all directions.

The boys froze, waiting to see if the sound had caught the lizard's attention. The air filled with sickening sweet smell of cheap perfume. After a moment, they ventured a few steps, and the glass crunched under their sneakers like popcorn.

"Dammit," Shane cursed. "Why don't you two ring the friggin' dinner bell?"

Sam shrugged apologetically. He tip-toed around the glass, and Jason followed him.

Outside, the giant lizard was gone, now completely out of sight. Where it had wandered, they could only guess, and hoped it had moved up the street to find food.

They left Jim's RX in a hurry and put their bags in the jeep. Sam gently placed the cologne and perfume bottles on the back seat, careful not to rattle them further. Any noise could attract predators.

But it didn't matter, anymore. They had been found.

Sam heard the *cha-chink* of a shotgun being cocked. He turned and faced a pistol and a shotgun barrel just a few feet from his head. Shane and Jason already had their hands up.

Two men in their thirties, large and burly, now trained guns on the boys. The men wore leather jackets, dew rags on their heads, and chains hanging from their pockets to their belts. Tattoos covered their arms and necks. They hadn't shaved in days.

"Welcome to Fayettville, boys," the man with the pistol said, though it sounded more like Feet-ville. "You aimin' to steal from us?"

"No Sir. We're just getting supplies," Sam explained. "From the pharmacy, that's all. We didn't take anything else."

"Well, you see, son, that pharmacy belongs to us. Those things are ours. Matter of fact, this whole piss filled town is ours."

The two men laughed. One of them whistled, and a truck came around the corner, revving its engine unnecessarily. It bore a large incongruous smiley face on the side, painted in yellow, and was driven by a man with a missing tooth. He pulled up to the group and spit a disgusting wad of tobacco through the window. Another man with sunglasses and a beard sat in the passenger seat and stared ahead.

"What you find, Mitch?"

"Couple of thieves."

"Well, get to it then. Put 'em in the back."

The boys steeled themselves to resist. Jason reach down for his gun, but the shotgun-man stopped him. He moved the barrel to within an inch of Jason's chest.

"No stupid moves, guys. Just do what you're told, and you won't get shot."

"Not yet anyway," Mitch said. All three men laughed. "Listen up, boys. Put your weapons on the ground. Now."

The boys complied, dropping their pistols and bow.

"Now grab your stuff, that now belongs to us, and get in the back of the truck."

Shane glared at the man, but Sam put a calming hand on his shoulder. He stepped onto the truck bed with his bags of supplies, and his brother followed. At first Jason looked like he would make a move against the armed men, but then he relaxed his muscles and jumped into the back of the smiley-face truck.

Mitch collected their weapons and threw them into the front seat. He snickered and made a comment about Jason's long hair.

"Who are you?" Sam asked.

"Me? I'm nobody," the shotgun-man informed them. "Our people, well that's a diff'ren story. We been preparin' fo' this a long time. And we are called the Grinners." He bowed slightly. "Nice tah meetchya."

Doom preppers! Great! Sam sighed to himself. *Crazies waiting for the world to end. Why do only the wishes of lunatics ever come true?*

Mitch laughed as he lit a filterless cigarette. "Doesn't make sense, does it? 'Cause we don't make people smile." He leaned in and blew smoke in their faces. "But nothin' makes sense no more."

The driver spat again, and complained, "Let's go! Stop jabberin' with these pups."

Mitch and the shotgun-man got into the back and kept their guns trained on their captives. The truck started up and did a U-turn with much more gas and fanfare than was needed. They skidded their tires and sped up the road.

Sam rubbed the palms of his hands together. He shared a look with the other two boys. Shane knew what Sam was thinking, and shook his head. *Not now, you'll get one of us killed.* After a tense moment, Sam backed down and leaned against the pickup's railing.

"I got a feeling we're not invited to dinner," Jason said.

"No. I think we're screwed six ways to Sunday, as my Mom would day," Shane said, for the moment resigned to his fate. "But stay frosty. We'll get our chance."

"We should rush them now, before we get to their camp. Might be too many of them there."

"Just wait. We're still outgunned here. Be cool."

They headed toward the opposite end of town in a pick-up that lacked any semblance of shocks. Despite the ruckus, the lizard did not reappear.

CHAPTER 8

THE sight of only two more men at the campsite filled the boys with hope. They had feared they would meet a gang of ten or twenty. And then they heard the men talking about taking them to "the compound" that night, and they realized this was just a checkpoint.

"So how big is your compound?" Sam asked.

Mitch smacked Sam in the face, but it landed wrong. It was less of a punch, and more of a slap.

"Shut up, for the last damn time. Shut up, or I'll shut you up." He put his gun right to Sam's temple.

"Easy now," Shane said calmly, his hands raised up in surrender. "We're not looking for trouble. We just want to know what's going on."

"Well," said the shotgun-man. "Trouble is what you found. And how do you know *we* aren't lookin' for trouble."

Mitch snorted and smiled. "Trouble is his middle name."

"Alright," the toothless driver cut them off. "We'll take 'em to Dexter tonight. He'll decide whether we kill 'em or not. Or if we're gonna use these ones to get the box out."

"Yeah. Send these bitches in there. Why should we risk our skins to get it."

Get the box out?

Sam wondered what was going on. If these men needed something, chances favored it wasn't a box of roses from a church chapel. The million dollar question was: what and where?

"We'll need these pups to make supply runs, too" the man reminded them. "Thanks to Bill, we don't have any more boys to send out. And those girls back there aren't worth a damn for supply runs."

"They got their own purpose," said the shotgun-man, smiling and looking into the distance. "Oh yeah."

The boys sat on the ground where they were told, and kept their eyes on the six men around them. A fire burned twigs inside a ring of stones, and the men were roasting some kind of meat over it. Sam didn't want to think what it might be. Had these men taken the dead lizard carcasses?

The men gave the boys a small bottle of water and a small portion of whatever meat they had cooked. It looked like chicken, but was probably pigeon. Sam was hungry, and didn't focus on it too much. They ate in silence.

In the afternoon they all loaded into the truck again, and headed out on a dirt road. The boys guessed they had driven twenty or thirty miles east, when they came upon a large compound. It was surrounded by broken down cars, stacks of tires, and part of a makeshift wooden wall. It was heavily guarded by at least a dozen gruesome looking men with no humor on their faces. Only scars and tattoos.

Inside the walls, the compound looked like a military base. Over fifty men and women went about chores with guns strapped to their belts or backs. The few women there were big and scary. They passed a cage with two younger women inside, maybe in their twenties, scarcely dressed in torn clothing. They looked sadly at the boys, as if they knew something bad was in their future.

The boys were taken into in a building that served as the gang's command center. They were forced to sit down in wooden chairs at a large oak table.

Here they met Dexter, the leader. He wasn't at all what they had expected. Dexter was a small, slight notion of a man in his early forties. He looked more like a square insurance salesman than the leader of a gang of psychos. Unlike his troops, he was clean shaven, and had no visible tattoos or piercings. Teaching a math class would suit him better than this setting.

"Welcome, gentlemen," Dexter said. He shook their hands. "My name is Dexter. I run this wonderful place. It's safe here, so you can relax. And your names are..."

The boys introduced themselves warily, first names only, and shook his hand. Dexter was a little too creepy to fathom.

"I hope my men have treated you well." he continued. He examined the bruise on Sam's face. "Sorry about that. Sometimes they get too spirited."

Sam just glared back.

"Well, anyway. Let's get to business." Dexter unrolled a map in front of them. "I need something from here."

He pointed to a place on the map. It meant nothing to the boys. It looked to be a few miles from the compound, based on the labels in black marker, but they didn't know it.

"What is it?" Shane asked.

"It's a house. And it has a box of things that belong to me," Dexter said. "Weapons, explosives, and a couple other things you do not need to know about. It will take two of you to carry it. You and you," he pointed to Shane and Jason. "Sam, you'll stay here. And if these two don't come back with my box by tomorrow, I will cut off your hand. If they're not back by the next day, I will cut off your head."

He said this all as a matter-of-fact, the way you'd explain how milk comes from cows. "No hard feelings. But I will give Sam the most horrible death. Trust me on this, my new friends."

He snapped his fingers and a guard stepped into the room. "Oh. Of course, we'll give you some guns, and your bow. Can't let you get eaten before I get my box."

"How nice of you," Shane said. "And why don't you just send a dozen of your own men in to fetch it?"

"That simply isn't possible. The people living in that

house have lots of gun power, and they hate me. They would not like to give anything to me. You see, they know me, and our hatred is quite mutual."

Dexter paused for effect.

"And the area is filled with hell hounds. Creatures. That's what we call them: hell hounds. So, it's a little dicey getting in there and then back out. If we make a lot of noise going in there, all hell will break loose. Chaos. If you know what I mean. Probably both sides will lose a lot. But these people don't know you. They'll welcome you with open arms. No shots, no sounds, no problems. And in the night, you two will sneak out with my box. Bring it here by tomorrow noon." He looked up from the map. "This will work, guys, trust me. I can't send my men in, it would be a blood bath. And well, not because I like my men; I just need them. I don't need you. If you get killed, I will put an end to Sam here, and we will find another crew to help us out. Got it?"

"Got it," Shane sighed. He saluted Dexter with two fingers and resisted the urge to give him the middle one.

"Don't those people guard their house at night?" Jason asked. "How are we supposed to just go walkin' out with your box?"

"You'll figure it out," Dexter said. "You're smart guys."

"What the hell is in this box of yours?" Shane pressed. "The One Ring? Your precious?"

Dexter laughed. "Funny. Yeah, it's something like that."

Dexter poured four shot glasses of whiskey, and sat one in front of each of the boys. He raised the fourth glass. "Drink to success, gentlemen."

They drank. It burned Sam's throat and he coughed. He wondered what Tina and Ken would do when the three of them didn't return to the lodge tonight.

Dexter described the box in detail, and where it would be: in the basement. Then Sam's hands were tied behind his back, and he was thrown into the cage with the two women. Jason and Shane were given two handguns and a bow. Then Mitch and another man put them in the pickup and drove out of the compound.

Sam watched them go, and turned to the girls. One had dark skin, Hispanic, very pretty. The other was milky white, and looked like she'd never seen a day of work, sunshine, or hardship in her life. Until now.

"So. You come here often?"

"That supposed to be funny?" the Latino girl asked. "This isn't a club, you know. These men aren't playing around. They kill all the men and boys who come through here."

"Sorry, I'm just nervous. Let me start again: my name is Sam."

The Hispanic girl eyed him head to toe before answering: "I'm Camila. This flower puff here is Lucy."

The other girl cowered in the corner with her hands against the bars, and didn't say a word.

"Last couple of days, they've been bringing in a lot of

men," Camila explained. "But those men never leave alive. They use them for supply runs, then kill 'em."

"But the women get it worse," Lucy said. "It's awful." Her eyes looked forward with the emptiness of a stuffed animal's button-eyes.

"Damn," was all Sam could say. He tried not to stare at their bodies, naked except for underwear and torn shirts. Camila was especially beautiful. Her torn shirt couldn't contain her ample form, but this was not the time for that; so he cleared his head.

"Your friends..." she said.

"My brother, actually, and a friend."

"What are they doing? A supply run?"

"The leader wants some box of stuff. In some house."

"Dexter. He's a bastard," Lucy said. "He thinks he's gonna rule the world now."

"Doesn't matter if they get it," Camila said. "These men will kill you even if your brother brings them the supplies, or whatever they want."

"What about the creatures?" Sam asked. "You see many of them?"

"The scalies?"

"The what?"

"That's what they call 'em here. A couple of those things attack the compound almost every night. Sometimes more come. But the men shoot them down. This place is pretty well guarded."

"Thank God for small favors." Sam muttered.

"God does not visit this place," Camila said, dead serious. "He has forgotten us. Only hell comes to see us here."

That was too deep for Sam. He had no answers for them, so he slipped to the ground and rested, his hands still tied behind his back. He wasn't worried about the ropes. When the time came, he could burn them off. That much he could do. But he couldn't pass these steel bars. He would need an escape plan for that.

CHAPTER 9

JASON and Shane were dropped off about a mile from the house in question. The truck drove away and left them alone with a warning to be back by tomorrow at noon ...with the box. When the pickup was out of sight, they crouched down and surveyed the grounds from behind some bushes. Their target was a medium-sized house of two stories that badly needed new paint. It stood alone on the side of the road, no other houses for miles. It was quiet. Nothing moved, save for a man sitting on the porch in a rocking chair, rocking leisurely and smoking a pipe.

Jason made a plea to change course. "Let's go back and rescue Sam. Then get back to the lodge."

"Against fifty men? Look, I want to rescue my brother more than anyone, but we have to be smart here."

"Look. Even if we do somehow get into that house and back out with the box, you think he'll let us go?"

"Of course not. He's already planned our executions."

"So... what's the point?"

"The point is that whatever is in that box might be

good for us too. Think about it: that Dexter guy really wants it. It must be really important for him to go through all this to get it. I get the feeling we're not the first guys he's sent out here to fetch it."

"You mean, like it has potent magic? Voodoo dolls? A ring of power?"

"No. Yes. Maybe. I don't know." Shane shook his head in frustration. "Maybe it's a doomsday device. Whatever it is, we can't let this Dexter prick get it."

"I hear that."

"So, we should get it out of there and take it to the lodge. We get Ken to come, and then we rescue Sam. We can pretend to trade it to Dexter for Sam, if it comes to that. But we're not giving any more weapons, explosives, or voodoo dolls to that maniac."

"Whatever it is, we can probably use it against him. As a weapon or as leverage."

Shane smiled. "Now you're thinking."

"And about Sam," Jason was hesitant to ask. "Can he help? You know, with his... super-sparks? Whatever that was he did before?"

"Sam can take care of himself until we get back. Don't worry."

But he was worried. Everything was turning sour, including his lunch. That mystery meat wasn't settling well in his stomach. Either that, or his nerves were making his stomach ache.

"The enemy of my enemy is my friend," Shane said. "Maybe those people in the house will help us."

Jason nodded. "They don't seem to be Dexter's best friends."

They devised a plan to go inside and meet the people of the house, all in the open. They wouldn't mention Dexter right off. They wanted to look at the box first. They needed more information. After they knew what the box held, they could move forward with a plan.

With casual ease, they stepped along the road to the house. No weapons drawn, and purposely nonchalant in their advance. When they reached the porch, they raised their hands, palms up, and greeted the man in the rocking chair. He hadn't acknowledged them yet, or made any movement other than slowly rocking. The chair now creaked to a halt.

When the old man finally spoke, his voice was thick and hoarse, the voice of a lifelong smoker. "Come on up."

"Hello Sir." Shane introduced Jason and himself.

"Jake Thompson," the man said, continuing to puff on his pipe, but no longer rocking back and forth. He looked like a man in his late sixties, a bit scruffy, but not menacing. His beard was long, gray, and needed a trim, and his faded overalls sported a million pockets, most likely for a variety of tools, screws and tobacco.

"We're walking the countryside looking for shelter. Hoping you might let us stay here a night or two."

"Yeah," Jason added hesitantly.

"Is that so?" The man stood up and opened the

screen door. He motioned for them to go inside. Shane was surprised he hadn't asked for their weapons, or any assurances of peaceful intent.

Inside, a group of four men and two women sat at the kitchen table. They were pouring over stacks of papers: manuscripts, charts, and drawings. Some of the pages had scientific calculations on them. These people all wore glasses and looked like stereotypical academics. It was an odd incongruity considering the situation. Had Dexter not realized? His thugs could have just walked in here and taken his precious box without a fight.

A tall thin man stood up and shook their hands.

"Walter Feynman," he said. "Can I get you two gentlemen a lemonade?"

A woman was already pouring them each a glass. She looked more like a doctor than a housewife. It turned out she was in fact Walter's wife, and a professor of physics.

"So," Walter went on, "you're the two he sent in."

"Pardon?" Shane sipped the lemonade. It tasted bitter with no sugar.

"Dexter. He sent you two to steal something from me."

"What do you mean?" Shane feigned ignorance, but had a feeling it was pointless.

"Don't do that," Walter said impatiently. "We can pretend not to know, but it just wastes time. I do know that Dexter is trying to get something of mine. Of ours." He made a gesture toward the others with his left hand. "And this has his handwriting all over it. He sent you two in here to get something for him."

Jake spoke up, "It's a little suspicious the way you just walked up here. You didn't wave any guns in my face. Was it because you already knew something about us?"

"Well, no... you see..." Jason sputtered.

Shane cut him off with a look. "All right. Here's the deal. Dexter has my brother. He plans to kill him if we don't bring back this... box, or whatever. He wants some box."

"The formulas," Walter explained. "He wants the formulas stored in the vault."

"Okay." Shane said. "He didn't tell us that, but whatever. We have to take it to him, or he'll kill my brother."

Walter took off his glasses and cleaned them with a tissue. He replaced them on this face and looked directly at the boys. "Not a chance in hell."

"Sir...?"

"Do you know what the formulas are, son?" Walter explained, "They are the means to create weapons, biological weapons. Highly targeted to a specific genome. He intends to target a virus at those creatures out there, and destroy them."

"I'm not seeing a down side to that," Jason said.

"The down side, son, is that it could wipe us all out." Walter raised his voice for the first time. "Dexter is reckless. We know him a bit better than you. He used to work with us, until we kicked him off the team. He always thinks he's doing what is right, but he rarely ever does. Those biological elements could easily strip the Earth of *all life* – not just those lizards out there."

Walter's wife put her hand on his shoulder, and he calmed down and lowered his voice again. "And there are several different species of mutations out there. He may not realize that. Not all the creatures share the same genes."

Another man stepped into the room. This man was big, muscular, like a human tank with a crew cut. He had guns strapped to his back, belt, and boots, and carried an automatic machine gun in his arms.

"Everything okay in here?" He asked Walter.

"It's fine, Sergeant."

Is that a title or a name? Shane wondered.

"Impressive guns there, but you've only got one man?" Shane asked. "Dexter has fifty or more. Aren't you afraid he'll come busting in here anyway? Regardless of what we do?"

"We have more guns," Walter said. "And more creative weapons."

"Look, just give us something to take back. He's gonna kill my brother!"

"He would spot a fake formula, and kill you just the same," Walter told them. "And there is no way I will ever let him have the real ones."

Shane looked helplessly at Jason, who was lost for words or ideas.

"He'll kill you either way," the Sergeant said.

"I am sorry," Walter added. "It's a hard pill to swallow,

but you must consider your brother dead at this point. There is nothing I can do to help you. At least the two of you can walk away from this alive."

Jason finished his lemonade, and sulked in silence. Shane paced to the window, then back. "So why did you even bother to let us in?"

"To see if Dexter has a personal message for us," Walter said. "Actually him sending you here is a message. He's telling us he's coming for it. He knew you couldn't succeed, but this was his way of warning us that he's serious. Still, I was hoping for a more personal message, maybe a note he gave you."

Shane shook his head. "No. No message. He just told us to steal some box you have here."

"Ah. A pity. I had hoped to get something more from him. After all, I can't just check his Facebook page anymore. If you know what I mean."

Two men at the table chuckled.

Shane shrugged. "So what now?"

"Well, that's up to you," said Walter. "You can go back and try to rescue your brother, or you can move on. But you cannot stay here. And you cannot have what you came for."

"This sucks," Jason said. "You're supposed to be enlightened. I can see you're not just some gang of thugs here. So you should help us."

"Dexter's day will come," Walter promised. "But not today. We'll deal with him later."

"Do you even know what's happening here?" Shane

asked. "Any idea why all this crap has fallen on the world?"

Walter drew a breath and smiled the way you smile when you tell a child he can't have another cookie before dinner.

"No. I'm sorry. I don't have any answers for you. I do, however, have a message for Dexter – if you should decide to go back to him." Walter took a moment, then said: "Tell him the DNA strings are not the same. There are at least two different species of creatures, so his idea won't work. Also, I want to meet him, just the two of us. He'll have sanctuary to come speak to me. Here. He has my word."

"I'm not your messenger," Shane spat. He was in no mood to be helpful.

"As you wish, son. You have nothing but choices left in this life. Your past choices led you here. Make sure all your future choices in life you take you to where you truly want to go."

There was a pause, as the boys tried to think of more words to plead their case.

"It's getting late," Jake said. "You should get going before dark. It's not safe after dark."

"Go where?" Shane asked, incredulous of the emotionless demeanor these people displayed.

"As I said, that is up to you." Walter turned to his wife. "Can we give them something for the road?"

"I have some sandwiches in the fridge," she said kindly. "And we can spare a couple bottles of water."

"Fridge? You have electricity?" Shane just then realized he could hear the sound of it running.

"We are highly resourceful," Walter explained. "For years, we've been prepared to go off the grid. Since our work is sensitive, we can't risk an outage."

"Work? You have a lab here?"

"We have," Walter said simply.

His wife put the water bottles and sandwiches in a plastic bag, and handed it to Jason.

"I hope you understand," she said. "Good luck to you both." She squeezed Jason's arm, and patted Shane on the back, then left the room. The others at the table remained silent and pretended to read the charts in front of them.

Walter opened the door for them, and extended his hand. Shane shook it hesitantly and walked through the doorway.

"Gentlemen. It was good to meet you," said Walter. "And I wish you luck in this brave new world."

Like zombies, disbelieving of how quickly they had been turned away, the two boys walked back out onto the porch, followed by Jake.

"Here, you might be able to use these," Jake said in a gravelly voice. He reached into one of his deep pockets and produced a handful of cherry bombs, then added a pack of matches. He shoved them into Shane's hand.

"Be careful," he said. "It's a jungle out there. More than ever." He puffed his pipe and repeated: "More than ever."

The two boys ambled down the road. Shane tucked the cherry bombs into his pocket, and turned back once to look at the quiet house. Jake rocked in his chair again.

The sun started to fade, and the world ahead did not invite them in. Friends and allies seemed few and far between, while enemies waited just about everywhere. They hoped none of Dexter's men were watching the house. They guessed not, as Dexter seemed to want to keep his distance from Walter's team.

"Remember before when I said we were screwed?" Shane said, his voice shaking with frustration.

"Yeah."

"Well, I'm getting tired of that. Tired of being slapped around."

"Yeah. I hear that."

CHAPTER 10

KEN paced back and forth in the watchtower, waiting and watching for signs of movement on the road. Tina brought him a water, and noticed how fast the sun was setting these days.

"Anything yet?" she asked.

"I thought they'd be back hours ago. I haven't seen or heard anything out there."

"Night's coming, maybe they'll shoot off a signal flare."

"They have those?"

"I saw some in the jeep," she said and smiled. "Don't worry. They're experienced hunters."

He looked through the binoculars again, for the millionth time: nothing.

"Are you more scared for them or us?" she asked.

"Both." he replied honestly. He hadn't expected her to pick up on that. "I don't think we can survive without them. We barely made it this far. We're not... you know."

"We're not like them. It doesn't mean we're not

survivors." She hugged him and kissed his cheek.

"So if they shoot off a flare, what does that mean?" he asked. "Seriously. We go rescue them? Do we know how to do that?"

"I'm not sure. Do we have another car?"

"Not one that runs. But that town isn't too far. There are bicycles in the club house. We could try to bike it."

"Let's wait and see the flare first. I... I was just guessing."

A brief flicker of movement on the open road caught Ken's eye. He peered through the growing shadows, and again thought he saw something stir. A small animal, maybe. It was the first sign of life he had seen all day. In the failing light, he couldn't be sure if it was real or a trick of the eye.

"What is that? Is that something?" He got his rifle ready and aimed through the scope.

Tina took the binoculars. A creepy silhouette approached them, small, with a furry arm... or a fuzzy object in its arms. Skirting the shadows, it shuffled up the road and headed for the lodge gates.

"Ken. It's a child. Don't shoot, it's a small child on the road."

The figure plodded forward on tiny legs. It followed the dirt road, but seemed aimless or drunk in its approach. It wobbled as it tried to walk, right up to the front gate. Ken exchanged the rifle for a pistol, and they ran down to meet it. He didn't trust anyone or anything anymore.

They opened the gate just enough for the child to walk through. It was a little girl of about six or seven years of age. Her long stringy hair was unwashed, her face smeared with dirt. She stumbled into their safe fortress and collapsed on the ground.

Tina rushed to her, and lifted her head. "She's dehydrated, get me a bottle of water."

Ken pulled one from his jacket, and handed it to her. Tina dribbled some water on the child's mouth and forehead while Ken struggled to close the gate by himself. It thudded shut, and he triggered the lock. Then he knelt next to Tina and the little girl.

The child's eyes opened. She drank more water and coughed. Her left hand gripped a stuffed animal, a green fur-lined frog, as if it meant everything to her. Her yellow dress was dirty and torn, and she wore sandals on her small delicate feet, both of which were scratched and bruised. This child had clearly seen a little piece of hell and managed to get out of it alive.

"Marky," she said. Her creaky voice was almost too weak to be heard.

Ken picked her up and carried her into the hotel lobby. He laid her down on the couch, and Tina cleaned her face with a wet rag.

"What's your name, sweetie? Where are you from?"

"Marky," she squeaked again. She closed her eyes, exhausted.

"Is she trying to say Marky or Mommy?" Tina asked.

"I don't know. Let her sleep a bit," suggested Ken.

"I'm going back to the tower to see if anyone else is coming. You stay here with her."

The cat showed up and nuzzled the child. Ken had forgotten the cat was even in the hotel. Now it curled up next to their new small guest and purred. Then the girl and cat fell asleep together as Tina looked on.

Ken watched the road for more unexpected guests.

An hour later, the girl woke up. She reached for the bottle of water and drank it. Tina was slicing up apples and heard the child cough. She brought her a plate of the sliced fruit.

"You hungry, sweetie?"

The girl timidly took a small apple slice without answering. She bit into it and stared at Tina. Her other hand reached out and took the frog back in her embrace. She squeezed it close to her body. The cat woke up and took off, suddenly remembering it needed to be somewhere else.

"What's your name, honey?"

"Lily," the girl said meekly.

"Where are you from? Where is your mommy or daddy?"

The child pointed outside.

"Last night you said Marky."

The girl jumped up, excited. "My brother? Is he here?"

"No, sweetie, I just heard you say his name. Marky is your brother?"

The girl nodded her head up and down emphatically.

"Where are they?"

"Outside," she pointed to the door. "But... the bad men, they took mommy. And then Marky said to walk away. He made me go." She lowered her voice to a whisper: "He's gonna save her."

"How old is your brother?"

"Eleven and a half." She held up ten fingers, then closed her small palms and flashed one. "Older than me. My mom sings, you know."

"Can you wait here, Lily? I'm going to get my boyfriend."

Lily nodded without conviction.

The cat returned, and Tina put it in Lily's lap. "Just pet the cat, honey, until I get back."

"What's his name?" the child asked.

"My boyfriend?"

"The kitty. What's his name?"

"Oh," Tina scrambled for a name. "Snowball. You keep Snowball company, and I'll be right back. I promise."

Lily petted the cat, and ate the rest of the apple slice. She hardly seemed real. Her long curly hair was tangled and dirty, but more striking was her expression of dull apathy. She seemed more like a long-forgotten doll one might find at a garage sale. The child had seen too much horror for such a young age.

Tina ran up to the tower, and found Ken using the rifle scope to scan the outside. It was fully dark now.

"How's the girl," he asked.

"She told me her mom was taken by 'bad men' out there. And, her eleven-year-old brother is trying to rescue her."

"Really? Tough kid, if that's true."

"Ken. We should help her."

"We are helping her. She's safe in here."

"I mean we should go out and help get her mother and brother."

"Babe, we can't even find our own people. What can we do? If the guys come back, I promise we'll go out and find her mother. But we need Shane and the others first. Our group needs to be whole again."

Ken still felt insecure with just the two of them. He didn't want to be a leader, ever. He wanted Shane here to make the decisions, and Sam and Jason as back-up. Tina was stronger in this, and that embarrassed him a little. He steeled himself to be brave, and kept the scope trained on the road below.

"We need to stay put for now." He turned away from the scope and kissed her lightly on the cheek. "Someone has to be here in case the guys come back, honey. And what if this kid's mom and brother come here? She found us. They might, too."

"I understand," Tina conceded. "Who do you suppose the 'bad men' are?"

"Well, bad men do exist," he reminded her. "You have to imagine what kind of people survive this kind of thing. The strongest, the scariest, and the worst in humanity. Those kind take to an apocalypse like flies to honey. I can only guess what's out there, worse than the creatures."

"Worse?"

"We see the creatures coming, babe. But, bad men... they can hide so easy."

The child had climbed the stairs on her own, and now surprised them in the watchtower. She still had her fuzzy frog, and the cat followed her.

"Hey sugar," Ken smiled.

She waved at him with one hand. "I was scared down there. Don't leave me alone."

"Sorry, Lily. I won't leave you again. Hey, this is Ken. He's nice, isn't he?"

Lily stared at him, but didn't reply.

"Lily," he said. "Wow! What a pretty name. It's a flower, you know."

She nodded. She knew.

Ken knelt down next to her, and asked, "Lily, how many 'bed men' are there? The ones who took your mommy?"

The child shrugged.

"Can you guess? Two. Or a hundred? Many, a lot, or just one or two?"

"A lot," she said, certain. "Maybe a hundred."

Ken looked at Tina, the fear on his face mirrored hers. This situation might be worse than expected. A hundred men could come here and get in. An army could break the gate and take over their little safe haven.

"So how is your brother going to rescue your mom?"

She shrugged again. "I don't know."

"We should stay together," Tina said. "I'll get the apples and water. Let's all stay up here in the tower. Lily can sleep on the floor."

"My mom's a singing star," the child announced. "She's a singer. Everyone loves her. She sings pretty."

"That's great, honey." Ken said, but he wasn't listening. His attention was drawn to movement near the gate. A shadow darted from the grass to the wall.

"Hey, what is that?" Tina whispered. "What the hell is that? Is someone climbing up the wall?"

CHAPTER 11

SAM watched the sun fall. As darkness enveloped the compound, more fires were lit inside stone pits of varied sizes. Dexter's men and women roasted meat, changed guard shifts, carried sacks of supplies, and still performed their chores. There was a flourishing nightlife in this place.

His hands were still tied. He looked around the cage, examined the lock.

"I don't suppose you ladies know how to pick a lock?"

"Maybe," Camila said, "If I had a pin. But I don't."

Then he noticed the roof was just a piece of plywood laid over the top of the cage.

"Hey is that bolted down? Can one of you try to lift it a little?"

Camila jumped up and hit the plywood with her hand. It raised an inch and fell back.

"Even if you do push it off," Camila said, "you've got to climb up and out. Then you're just in the middle of this . . . hell. These guys just want an excuse to stab you or bludgeon you. They take days to kill their captives.

They enjoy it."

Lucy finally spoke. "Dexter can't protect you if you escape."

"Dexter!" Sam snorted. "Just a psychopath. You want to trust your fate to *him*? That's a bad mistake. I'm getting out of here."

"Take us," Camila urged. "Please, we can help you."

Sam furrowed his brow. "I never planned to leave you. Can you climb over that?"

"I can," Camila said. "I'm not so sure about the princess here."

"I'm sorry," Lucy pleaded. "I've never done anything like this before. And I haven't had a drink in a week. I mean, I don't need one, I'm just scared. I can't function... like this."

Oh good, Sam thought. *An alcoholic soccer mom who's never broken a fingernail. My odds of survival keep improving like a swimmer with cement shoes.*

"Well just imagine there's a case of whiskey on the other side," Sam said. "An alcoholic housewife's dream."

"I'm not a housewife," Lucy said. "Or an alcoholic! I'm a singer in the Honeybees. The band."

"Oh wow! Really? *Fill My Glass Full of Love*, I remember that song. Hey! You are her. Nice pipes. Nice hit."

"It's just called *Glass Full of Love*," she said derisively.

Whatever. I really hated that song, he thought. But now might not be the best time to mention it.

"Well, I met someone famous before I died. How

about that!"

"This is a charming fan club meeting," Camila interrupted. "But can we get back to an escape plan? Please."

"My kids are out there," Lucy told them. "My son and daughter. She's only eight. I made them run and hide."

"Smart," Camila said. "These assholes here are not good with kids."

"They can't be alone out there," Lucy whined. "Lily will get scared. And Mark will try to do something stupid. He will try to save me. I know him. *Gawd!* I need a... I need an aspirin!"

"Easy there," Sam said. "If you told them to run and hide, they're probably safe. And my brother will be back soon. We'll get out of here. Trust me."

A stumpy man passed the cage and slammed a baseball bat against the bars. "Shut up in there, you be-atches!" He walked on.

Another creepy man stopped for a moment and looked them over. The man reeked of both bourbon and dirt. His stringy hair hadn't been washed in weeks.

"After chores, I'm gonna enjoy you, a long slow time," he said to Lucy. "Maybe even pretty boy here." He laughed and flicked his cigarette at Sam, then walked on. The still burning cigarette butt bounced off Sam's chest and landed on the floor. Sam stamped it out.

"Charming," he said. "I really love these guys."

It was a clear night. The moon was nearly full and gave them some much-needed light. The late-night breeze turned chilly, and the women shivered in their underwear and torn shirts.

Mitch joined them at the cage. For the first time, Sam noticed the man was missing a finger.

"Don't worry, pumpkin," Mitch leaned against the cage. "I'll keep you warm tonight. I think I want you." He pointed to Lucy.

Other men had ravaged Camila with kisses the night before – *thank God* that Dexter didn't allow more. She shuddered at the thought, and spat at him. But the men were more talk than bite. Dexter would never allow them to do more than lightly touch or kiss the girls. It was a carrot he dangled cleverly to keep the men happy.

"Easy my little burrito," he told her. "Don't be jealous. I'll get back to you another time. We've got nothing but time these days."

"I'm gonna shove my knife up your *culo, perro sucio*," she cursed in Spanish. She wasn't afraid. Anger had long ago replaced fear as the dominant force in her life.

"Oh yeah, baby," he said and walked on. In the distance they heard him snicker. "Oh yeah, baby." Then he started humming the tune to *Glass Full of Love* by the Honeybees. He crossed the compound and walked out of sight.

"Okay, he gets my vote for most adorable prom king," Sam announced. "I like him!"

Lucy started to cry, and sank to the floor.

"Oh hey... hey..." Sam tried to console her. "I was just joking. We're gonna get out of here. Tonight. I promise."

"You've got to pull yourself together, lady," Camila said. She undoubtedly had lost patience with the weaker woman these past few days. "This is not a gig at the Roxy. This is real life. Get it together, and be strong. Stop being a damn victim."

Sam agreed, but kept silent.

At that moment, an explosion sounded at the other side of the compound. A second explosion, then a third. The men dropped what they were doing, picked up their guns and ran in the direction of the blasts. Someone started shouting orders.

And then the creatures came. They were attracted by the explosions. One of them jumped the make-shift wall of the compound and was quickly shot down. All of this was happening at the other end of camp, a good distraction. Sam recognized this as their cue to escape.

He generated an electric burst and sizzled the ropes off his wrist. He jumped up the bars and shoved the plywood off the cage. Then he jumped back down and lifted Camila. In an instant she was up and over the bars. She fell back down the other side, recovered and stood ready.

Sam lifted Lucy, who struggled to climb up the bars. He literally pushed her over, and Camila tried to catch her. They both fell back to the ground. Sam was up and over the bars in two seconds. He had always been as agile as a tree monkey.

The girls regained their feet, and all three of them turned to run for the wall. They were stopped short by the barrel of a gun. Mitch and another man stood in their way. The other man raised a machete, and Mitch levied his shotgun at point blank range – three feet from Sam's chest.

"Oh I thought you'd try an' run," he said. "What an incredibly stupid thing to do."

He raised his shotgun, and fired.

Sam flew backward and felt his shoulders hit the ground hard. An unnatural warmth flooded his chest, and he thought: *Oh, hell! That's a first.*

CHAPTER 12

"WE can go on back and get the box from Walter's house," Jason said. "They only got one guy with a gun."

"No." Shane rubbed his eyes; they were tired and troubled. "I don't trust him. He was too calm. He's got something up his sleeve. And Dexter knew we couldn't steal anything from there. Walter was right: Dexter sent us as a message to Walter. He's coming for them."

"So what's our plan?"

"We go back and get Sammy. I think I've got an idea."

They trudged back the three miles to the Grinners' compound. At least they still had their weapons, and now they had four cherry bombs, as well. The plan was to create a distraction at the opposite end of the compound, farthest from the cage. While the men were busy at that end, Shane and Jason would scale the wall and get to Sam.

He knew Sam would take advantage of the commotion and make a move of his own. Hopefully, the cage would be clear of any guards by the time they got to it. The three boys could climb back over the wall, run for the cover of the woods, and then home.

"Are we planning on taking the women with us?" Jason asked. "We can't leave them there."

"If they can climb the wall, they can come."

"And if they can't?"

"I guess... they can still come. I don't know. Let's take this one step at a time. First, get Sam."

They crept as close to the compound's edge as they dared. Thick bushes provided temporary cover, and they crawled under and through them as best they could. Shane spied two men standing on top of the wall. He fished three of the four cherry bombs out of his pocket.

"How's your throwing arm?" Jason asked.

"We're about to find out."

"You've got to get them right on the wall, or over it."

"I know."

Jason struck a match and lit the first cherry. Shane hurled it at the wall. Without pausing they lit and threw the second one. Then something happened that they hadn't counted on. The guard on the wall saw and instinctively caught the cherry before it landed inside the camp. If a baseball is thrown at your head, some people will just catch it without thinking; this man was one of those people. In an instant, it exploded, taking off the man's hand and sending him flying back over the wall. The second bomb followed his body over and exploded inside the camp.

The other guard panicked. After seeing his comrade's hand explode, he jumped down and yelled for help.

Shane threw the third bomb, and it bounced on the wall and went off just this side of it. Shards of a car's window blew out with the blast. These were no ordinary cherry bombs. Jake must have made them himself. They carried a lot more force than the boy had expected.

Shane and Jason scrambled backward and made their way as fast as they could to the other side of the camp. They heard men cursing and shouting inside. Lizards started screaming out of the woods, heading for the wall where the blasts occurred. The noise must have shaken the bowels of purgatory itself.

The boys crawled, ran, and scrambled through the end of the woods, just out of sight from any wall guards.

When they reached the other side, there didn't appear to be anyone guarding the walls at that end. The commotion on the other side of the compound had intensified. Someone had set the wall on fire at that far end, where they had set off the bombs. Maybe the fire was meant to keep the creatures out, Shane could only guess. But instead it was attracting more.

The two of them climbed over the rubble that constituted the wall, and reached for the top. No one challenged them. They kept their heads low and peered over the side.

"The cage, look!" Jason pointed.

In front of the cage, the two women and Sam faced an armed Mitch and another man with a blade. Three other men ran to join Mitch, and raised their guns toward Sam and the women.

In a split second, too fast for him to react, Shane saw Mitch aim his shotgun at Sam and fire it directly at the boy's chest. Buckshot scattered out. Sam flew backward and hit the ground hard.

My God! He's dead. Shane wailed inside.

But Sam was not dead. Electricity crackled around Sam's upper body. He had instantly created a shield and repelled the blast. This was new, something even Shane had never seen before.

"Son of a bitch," Jason whispered, somewhat amazed.

There was no time to think. The man with the machete ran for Sam, swinging the weapon in a wide arc. Shane drew an arrow and shot it straight into the man's neck. The fat man fell hard to the ground next to Sam, who was still unable to move. The wind had been knocked out of him.

The other men aimed their rifles at the three captives, and at the same time, a lizard came rushing up the wall. Shane knew time was too short to fight on both sides. Jason shot one of the men in the head, but the other two still aimed their guns to shoot back. Camila grabbed the machete from the dead fat man and rushed one of the gunmen. She buried the blade in his chest, just as the other gunman shot Lucy in the upper thigh. Jason put him down with a bullet to the skull.

Just in time, Shane reloaded and turned to repel the lizard. An arrow sank deep into its eye socket, and it rolled back to the ground.

Camila helped Sam to his feet, and they half-carried

Lucy up the wall. Blood gushed from her upper thigh. Shane and Jason reached down and helped her up onto the wall, then to the other side. All five of them crawled down to the grass below. Jason and Shane had to carry Lucy, and the group hastened up the dirt road with all the speed they could muster. It wasn't fast enough.

Two giant lizards scrambled onto the road in front of them. Sam was still stunned, and without a weapon. Camila only had a knife, and Jason and Shane were carrying Lucy.

The lizards were fast upon them, giving the group no time to react. The hell hounds bared their fangs and made an attack run. Camila held her knife in front of her, but it wouldn't be enough.

In that instant, a shot rang out, and then another. The two lizards slumped dead to the ground. Their bodies skidded forward from the force of their running assault, but they were dead. Someone had shot them both in the head.

Jason and Shane looked over to see a pre-teen boy positioned in the tall weeds about twenty feet away. He was holding a revolver out in front of him with both hands. It seemed amazing that a young kid this small could even shoot a revolver, let alone aim it and hit something.

"Son of a bitch," Jason whispered again.

CHAPTER 13

LUCY'S leg was painted red with blood, even after they tied a piece of Shane's shirt around it. The wound forced them to carry her gently, which meant: slowly. Shane felt like they were snails inching their way up the road, with a pack of wolves on their trail. They would need to speed up soon and cover more ground.

At least Sam was fully awake now and back to himself. He and Jason took the guns and guarded their long march back to the jeep while Shane and Camila helped to move Lucy. And of course, there was Mark – the boy who had saved them.

Mark was Lucy's son. He was not afraid to carry a gun or shoot. As a matter of fact, he didn't seem afraid of anything at all. Sam admired the kid. In any disaster, most people wallow in pity and fear, while a rare few rise and stand up. This kid was one of the rare few.

They got off the road, and moved through the thick brush along the west side. This made the going even slower, but they feared a Grinner posse might be on the road at any moment.

"It's at least another mile," said Jason. "And those

men are gonna rev up their trucks and come after us sometime tonight."

"I know," said Sam. He knew, but their options were few.

Shane tried to sound more positive. "The creatures are keeping them pretty busy. They might not come for us tonight."

"That Dexter," Camila said, "he has a drawer full of fingers. Cut from hands of other people. I've seen it." She shuddered. "He's coming for us. You can bet on it."

"If we stay off the road, we can hide when we see them," said Sam.

"Mom, are you okay?" Mark asked in a reedy voice. He looked up at her with wide, hopeful eyes.

"I'm okay, baby," Lucy lied. She needed a drink more than ever.

"Are you angry at me?" He asked.

"Honey, no. Angry? No. Why?"

"Because I didn't go with Lily. You told us to run away, but I didn't. I made her go alone."

"Oh honey, it's all right," Lucy said. She was out of breath, and struggled with the words. "You did good, baby. Real good."

Sam thought Mark looked sad, but not just because his mother was hurt and his sister was lost. He looked like he wore that sadness often. *Left behind while she partied after her shows?* Sam wondered. *Always drinking, always drunk?* This wouldn't be the first rich and famous mother to let down her kids, Sam supposed.

"You did great." Sam put his arm on the boy's shoulder and walked next to him. "You saved us."

"Yeah," Mark said with some pride.

The kid wore a Pittsburgh Pirates t-shirt and a thin jacket. His jeans were dirty and torn at one knee, and there appeared to be a deck of cards in his back pocket. One of his sneakers seemed to be perpetually untied. He would stop every hour or so to tie it, but somehow it was magically loose again an hour later. The boy reminded Sam of himself when he and his brother went hiking and fishing in much younger days. Sam liked Mark a lot. Hell, who wouldn't love a kid who can aim and shoot dragons like that?

"Which way did your sister walk?" Shane asked.

"Up this road. Same as us," Mark told him. His voice cracked, but not from emotion; it was from total fatigue. "But I don't know how far. I don't know where."

"We'll find her," Shane assured him. "After we get back to our camp, we'll help your mom, and then go look for Lily."

"Okay."

"You'll like our camp," Sam said. "It's a castle, and a fortress. It has lots of warm beds. And it's safe."

"There's no place safe," the youth corrected him, looking down at the road. "Not anymore."

"We'll make it safe," Shane said. "Trust me. The boogeymen can't get into our castle. No friggin' way."

"I'm not worried about the boogeyman."

"Well..." Shane didn't know how to respond to that.

"Well, we'll make it safe from everything else."

Mark looked up and said, "Okay," but didn't sound convinced.

Jason had jogged ahead, and now came running back. "Just over this ridge, I can see the town. Not far to go. But the jeep is at the other end, remember."

Then Jason saw something and froze. He held up his hand to motion for everyone else to stop. He made a "stay quiet" gesture with a finger to his lips, and pointed to the grass across the road. A cougar, close to five feet long, crouched in the grass. It prowled sideways along the edge of the road.

"That's a damn big cat," Shane whispered.

Up in these mountains, wild cats were common. But this one was bigger than most. Its eyes glowed in the darkness, reflecting the moonlight. With a low growl it acknowledged the group of humans, and continued pawing forward. It studied the them closely, but took no aggressive action. After a moment, the big cat slunk into the taller grass and disappeared in the opposite direction.

"That was cool," Mark said under his breath.

"You like cats?" Sam asked. "We have a cat, back at the castle."

"Like that one?"

"No. It's smaller."

"Cool."

They continued into the night. Eventually they entered Fayetteville again, this time avoiding the main street. They skulked through the alleys and made their way toward the jeep. Lucy was very weak, so they sat her down on the ground in the alley between Casey's diner and the Bait Shop. The group rested while Sam and Shane ran to get the jeep.

Twenty minutes later, Sam came back alone.

"Problem," he said. "Those pricks took out two of the spark plugs. We need to find replacements."

Jason exhaled a tired sigh. "Town like this, there must be a mechanics shop. How about that motorbike tour place?"

"Come on," Sam said, but Mark jumped up and started to follow. "Hey, little man, you stay here and guard the women. Can you?"

Mark looked at him with defiance. "Of course I can." He held his gun firmly with both hands. "I'm not afraid."

Sam squeezed the kid's shoulder. "I know, buddy."

He and Jason ran up and down the street looking for car parts. They hit the jackpot: a gas station not far away. Sam identified the two spark plugs they needed, grabbed them and ran back to the jeep. Shane was still scanning the drugstore for car accessories and supplies.

"Got them!" Sam tossed the plugs to his brother.

"I'll get the jeep running." Shane kept his voice down. "You two start filling bags again with supplies. We need antibiotics for Lucy, and anything else you can find. Medicine, food, anything. And hurry. When I get the jeep started, we need to pick up the others and head for the lodge. The faster, the better."

It was just after the spark plugs were installed and the

hood shut, that he heard the low hum of an engine coming down the street. He looked up and saw two sets of headlights: a truck and a car.

He ran into the pharmacy, where the guys had already filled two bags with medicine.

"Guess who's back?" He pointed to the back door. "They'll look for us near our jeep, so we need to move further down."

The guys took the back alley until they hit a dead end. The only way from here was up. They scaled a flimsy metal fire escape to the roof of a three-story brick building. It was the town's bank, permit office, and mayor's office, all in one.

From the rooftop, they were able to see the truck and car drifting through the streets. The vehicles stopped every few yards while the men inside the cars examined the buildings and alleys with flashlights. The truck and car engines idled in low gear, but few of the men spoke. A couple words floated here and there in low tones, but the boys couldn't make out the words.

The men spent extra time around the jeep and the front of the pharmacy. After some debate, now in louder voices, they decided to leave two men to watch the jeep.

"Their camp won't be far," a voice said. "We'll find it. Not many places to hole up in these parts. Not for *wussies* like them."

Two men jumped from the pickup, and then the truck and car moved on out of town... up the road, where they would ultimately reach the Peak Castle Lodge. The two men who had remained behind – both with assault rifles – started to patrol the area around the jeep. It didn't take long for them to get bored.

Sam whispered, "We have to get rid of those two. Then get to the lodge before those freaks do."

"I'm on it," said Shane. He produced an arrow and notched it in the bow. He drew back hard and aimed down at the man closest to them.

Jason said, "Wait, that one's going into the bar. Wait till he's gone."

The moment the man entered the building and the door slammed behind him, Shane let his arrow fly. It plunged deep into the other man's chest, right through his heart, and the Grinner dropped to the ground. His hand clutched the arrow for a few seconds, then went limp. His dead eyes stared straight up at them.

The second man came out of the bar with two beers. He started to toss one to his friend, then halted in mid throw – his comrade's dead body a yard away. The man dropped the beers and took his rifle in both hands.

Shane let another arrow fly, and it struck the man's chest, right on target. But this time it had no effect. The arrow had landed in a bullet-proof vest. It hung there a moment, before the man snapped it off with ease. He looked up at the boys on the roof and fired his rifle. His aim was bad; the bullet grazed the edge of the rooftop. Chips of wood splintered into the air.

The three boys stepped back out of the rifle's line of sight, and Shane reloaded.

Jason had an idea. "If he keeps making noise like that, a lizard is bound to show up and take him down. Then we can deal with the creature from up here. I'm sure *it* won't have a vest."

"Or a dozen creatures could show up," Shane warned. "I think it's better to just shut him down fast."

"If he keeps firing, he's gonna attract a lot of attention to this place," Sam agreed with his brother. "Not the least of which is those psycho Grinners. If they hear it, they'll turn back."

The man below fired another shot. It took a bigger chunk off the roof corner. This man was decidedly a fool. Each shot gave his position away.

"Come on down," the man growled. "And I won't kill ya. Just need to take ya back to Dexter."

"What an idiot," Jason said. "He's in the middle of the damn street, telling us he can't kill us."

Sam smiled wryly. "Dexter wants us alive. This guy can't kill us."

"He wants one of us alive, not all," Shane said. "He might only want to hear what Walter said to me and Jason."

"Who?"

"It's a long story. Anyway, be careful. He might not need you alive."

Shane stayed on the roof with his bow. Jason and Sam crept down the fire escape, softly making their way to the bottom rung. They needed to find another way back to Mark, Lucy, and Camila, while Shane tried to keep

Chuckles busy – that was what they nicknamed him: Chuckles, the clown with a gun. With Chuckles wearing a flak vest, only a shot to the head or neck would stop him. That's not easy with a longbow.

Jason and Sam couldn't see any way back to the others, except by going right in front of Chuckles. Instead, they sneaked back to the drugstore, and formed a new plan to distract this man, so that Shane could take him out. This plan required quiet moves and finesse.

They heard Shane's voice from the rooftop.

"If you make some more noise, a few lizards might take you down for us."

The thought hadn't occurred to the nitwit gunman, but now it did. He looked around at the ghost town, and lowered his voice. "Just come down peaceful-like. Dexter just wants to talk to you."

Shane sent an arrow down in response. It landed in the man's left arm. Not a deal breaker, but it hampered the man's ability to shoot. He cursed softly to himself, and backed onto the bar's porch, so he couldn't be seen from the roof.

As Jason and Shane crept out the front door of the drugstore, broken glass crunched under their feet. They stopped, but the man hadn't noticed them. He was focused on his bleeding arm.

"Wait here," Jason mouthed.

Sam waited, and wondered what was happening. Jason disappeared in the shadows and was gone. Another arrow came down from the roof and nearly pierced the gunman's right boot. "Dammit," the man said and backed away further toward the end of the porch.

Just then, Jason popped up and shoved his knife under the flak vest and into the man's side. He dug the blade in deep. The man turned and they both fell off the porch in a roll, right in the middle of the road. Jason pulled the knife out and pivoted his body on top of the man, then slit the Grinner's throat. Blood pooled around them in the dirt.

Sam ran to help Jason up. "You can do that? I mean... how did you learn to do that?"

Jason shrugged. For a long-haired loser, he still had a few secrets. They gathered the supply bags and hopped into the jeep. Shane climbed down, and the three of them drove to get the others.

Lucy was unconscious when they arrived at the alley, but she was alive. They put her in the back with Mark and Camila, and headed out of town. They hadn't collected all the supplies they wanted, but that wasn't the priority anymore. They needed to reach the Peak before the Grinners found it.

They diverted from the main road, shut off the headlights, then veered across a flat field. They crept along the back roads like rats scurrying around the baseboards in the dark, avoiding the house cat.

CHAPTER 14

KEN studied the vehicle advancing on the road. Still an hour before the sun would start to shed any light, the morning was misty and dark. In his mind he begged the sun to hurry its rise; he desperately needed some illumination. The road was far too dim to guard, and strange things were happening again.

They had already confronted one unexpected guest tonight, now dead in the garden, and he wasn't sure he had the stomach for more. This new movement on the road had him on pins and needles.

"Something's coming," he told Tina. "But I can't see what. It's some kind of car."

He switched from binoculars back to the scope on the rifle, and aimed it at the vehicle fast approaching their gate. Tina grabbed the binoculars, pressed them to her eyes and prayed it would be their friends. She was in luck.

"It's the jeep!" she cried. "Come on. The gate!"

This time Shane drove the jeep through the gate and parked inside the walls. The courtyard wasn't meant for vehicles, but he barreled across the lawn anyway and found a space over a flower garden.

Lily ran to her mom. "Mommy!"

But Lucy was still unconscious. They carried her into the lobby and laid her on the red couch. Tina and Ken examined the wound. The bullet had gone all the way through, which was incredibly good news. Ken applied iodine and antibiotic ointment to the open wound, and Camila wrapped it up tight with gauze. The bleeding had stopped, for now.

"When she wakes up, she needs to eat and take these." Sam held out a bottle of antibiotics from their supply-run bag.

"What's wrong with mommy?" Lily sobbed. She craned her neck and stared up at the tall Sam as if looking up at the top of a redwood tree.

"Mom's tired," Mark told his sister, holding her tiny hand. "After she sleeps, she'll be okay."

"Is that her daughter?" Shane asked.

"Hey, is that Lucy Loop?" Ken wanted to know, stunned and a bit star-truck. "From the Honeybees? Wow. It's really her."

"She's a singer. I told you," Lily said, wiping a strain of tears from her cheek.

"That you did," Ken remarked. "That you did."

"She's gonna be fine," Mark whispered in his sister's ear, even though he wasn't so sure. Lying for his mom was a big part of his job as big brother.

As the morning unfurled, they introduced each other

and ate a breakfast of peaches, apples and carrots. They also had more prepackaged snack cakes lifted from the drugstore, and water was passed around. During their feast, they got Ken and Tina up to speed about the Grinners and Walter. The new world was getting crowded with enemies, in some ways worse than the big lizards.

Mark carefully sorted his deck of cards, which turned out to be Magic: The Gathering, and explained to Tina that "*No it's not like Pokemon!*" with some indignation.

"More like D&D, or kinda Game of Thrones," Sam explained to her, casting a wink to the kid.

Mark smiled knowingly, as if he had just shared a private joke with the older boy.

"Lizards can't climb walls, but Grinners can," Shane said. "Now more than ever, we need a guard in the watchtower *at all times!*"

"Starting now," Jason agreed. "My turn. I'll be up there if you need me." He grabbed a rifle and an apple and headed up the stairs.

Lucy still slept. Lily climbed onto the couch and napped next to her with the fuzzy frog in hand.

"We have another problem," Ken said darkly. "A new problem."

"What?" Shane asked. *What now?*

"We had a new guest last night, sneaked over the wall. Here, follow me. I'll show you the body."

Ken led them outside and into the courtyard. The sun was up, round and full, unfettered by even a single cloud.

The garden looked beautiful, approaching surreal. He pointed to the ground next to a row of orange and yellow marigolds.

A giant hairy spider had been crushed into the grass, impaled by a hunting knife. Its legs stretch out at least three feet long, and the body itself was almost a foot in length. A cross between a fishing spider and a wolf spider, it was a horrifying sight – even to those who are not gripped by arachnophobia. It looked like it might eat small dogs for lunch.

"They've started coming out of the west woods, over there," Ken pointed to the treeline. Up until now, everything scary had come from the east side. "And unlike our lizard friends, these spiders can climb walls. They can get in."

"Awesome," Shane said in his trademark tone of sarcasm. *We're screwed.*

"That might be what carried the dead carcasses away," Sam speculated. "Spiders eat meat. Usually insects, but at this size... they would need larger prey. They might have taken our lizards."

"What, to their web?" Camila shuddered.

"I think wolf spiders don't spin webs," Sam explained. "They make nests. They'll carry their food back to the nest. Of course, these are mutated types, so... yeah, maybe they do spin webs."

Ken said, "We saw maybe half a dozen outside from the tower, but only this one came in. I shot it first. The knife was... later."

"Wow, good shot."

Mark joined them, and was very impressed by the spider. "Cool," was all he said. He stared at it, mesmerized.

Jason spotted the spider from the tower and shouted down at them: "Dudes. That is so messed up." Shane gave him the thumbs up.

Snowball had followed Mark and now rubbed against Sam's leg. He meowed at the dead eight-legged intruder, but soon lost interest. *Cats only like things that move*, Sam mused. But it was more than that; Snowball didn't seem threatened by it.

"Hey, we've seen a couple cats. And on the road back there we saw a cougar," Sam reminded them. "And birds are everywhere. So I guess cats and birds are immune to whatever is mutating everything else into lizard creatures."

"And dogs and other animals are not immune," Shane said. "Humans, most humans, are not. Those of us outside the city escaped the mutation, but not many others did. And Walter said there are multiple strains of mutations. That they don't all have the same genes. Is this what he meant? I thought he meant different lizards, but..."

"Maybe the spiders and lizards are both mutations, different kinds." Sam guessed. "And I have a hunch more types of creatures are hatching, or will hatch, out there. Either now or later."

They let a moment of tense silence pass on that scary

note, as they stared at the grass.

Then Shane said: "Awesome!"

Lily and Mark spent the morning helping Camila and Sam fill the bird feeders in and around the courtyard. They also spread seed out on the grass. Seeds were in good supply, as huge bags of bird seed lined the garden's storeroom. Birds had been an attraction for the resort's guests, and today it was a positive distraction for the kids, as well as the adults. Hundreds of birds came down to eat. Blue jays, cardinals, finches, larks, orioles... large crows also bullied their way in.

Snowball seemed uninterested. He didn't chase any of them. He just lay on the grass and basked in the sun's warm rays.

"It's a long shot," Sam said. "But the birds might help protect us. Warn us about invaders, the spiders and such, if any come over the wall."

Camila didn't sound convinced. She pulled her long black hair behind her head. "I don't know. At night that won't really work."

"I said it was a long shot. But they might at least be able to warn us in the day – if we see them scatter."

"Regardless, I like the birds. They just fly about as if the world hasn't changed."

Camila was at least five years older than Sam, but he noticed how beautiful she looked in the light of day. Her tan skin and ample form, barely contained in her tight shirt, her smile – tantalizing to any young man.

"So how long have you been able to... you know..." she asked?

"Oh. Uh, I passed puberty years ago."

"What? No, I don't mean... I mean... the electricity thing."

"Yeah, I know what you mean." Sam smiled. "Well, my whole life. But I didn't start to control it till I was eight or nine. By fourteen, I could do some more things with it."

"And now? Looks like now, you can really pump up the volume." She stopped spreading seeds and touched his chest. "There would be a hole right here, if not."

"Sometimes I can do things," Sam said. "But only on instinct. Like a protective mechanism. It's not so easy to just do it by will. I can, but not so much. I don't like to talk about it."

"You mean you can't do it now, to show me?"

"It's not a magic trick." Sam sounded perturbed, but he wasn't.

"No. I know. I just asked."

"Besides, it drains me. I get tired afterwards. I need a few hours to recharge the batteries. No pun intended."

She laughed. It was a nice laugh.

Shane had noticed her, too, and joined them in watching the birds. "Sammy, why don't you go inside and help with Lucy and Lily. The adults will handle the birds."

Sam could take a hint. He made a gun with his thumb and forefinger and clicked it at Camila. "See you later."

"Later? Why is he seeing you later?" Shane asked.

"I think it's just an expression," She said with a wide, honest smile. There was no guile in her heart. "So you're the handsome older brother."

"In the flesh. Let's get these sweet little birds fed, shall we?" His flirting was never very smooth.

The group worked all afternoon stringing empty cans and pieces of tin on wire to form a fence around the perimeter. They hoped it would serve as a warning bell against unwanted guests. Most likely the spiders could crawl under it, but the lizards would surely set it off. Men might set it off, too.

The watchtower guards were doubled at night. Two people from midnight to six, and one guard during the day. Shane knew that Dexter would be coming. He was surprised no attack had come yet; he thought they would have heard from the maniac by now. If Dexter's men had actually found them, one or two men might be watching the lodge now from a distance. Dexter was a shrewd man. Whatever he had planned, it wouldn't be good for Sam and Shane's group in the Peak Castle Lodge.

It will be bad like a jilted woman with a six-string guitar, he thought, echoing one of his dad's old sayings.

"We need to watch the back, too," Shane told Jason as they sat in the tower.

"Yeah, we gotta walk the wall, all around. Regularly. But the back is hard for anyone to reach. I think it's the front road he'll have to use, or maybe through the woods."

"We also need more weapons," Shane said. "We'll have to try St. Marks. We need a lot more guns and arrows for what's coming our way."

Jason nodded and silently agreed. He watched the night descend and wrap itself tightly around them. Nowadays he hated seeing the sun go down. It meant darkness, and darkness was not their friend.

And then a light, bright orange and red, streaked across the sky, someplace off in the distance. They watched it sail in an arc, glowing and beautiful like a small bit of fireworks, and then it dissipated and let the black sky close back in.

"Is that a signal flare?" Jason asked.

"Yeah, I think so. But it's pretty far off." Shane watched the sky until the signal faded, then stared at the place it had been. "Might be a trick. Dexter's men trying to lure us out. Or it could be other people... good or bad. Regardless, we're not going out there to find out."

"I hear that."

Sam walked halfway up the staircase and shouted to them, "Hey, come down and look at this!"

They briefly went back down to the lobby, where a light was on. Except for Lucy, who was sleeping again, everyone gathered around the single light bulb.

Ken flicked a switch, and another light went on. "Solar panels," he explained. "They're installed on all the roofs, even on the clubhouse. They charge batteries connected in here to a circuit board. I flipped the circuits

ROD LITTLE

on today."

Sam clicked the light off, then on again.

Ken continued, "We should have enough power for hot showers, cooking, and lights... *if* we are careful and ration it. On sunny days the batteries should be able to recharge all the way. Cloudy days might give us half a charge. My guess is that the resort was getting a third of its power from solar. And being so far from the grid, I'm sure it came in handy during winter outages."

"Sweet," Jason said. "If we can cook again, I'm all for it. I'm getting so damn tired of raw apples."

Ken nodded. "As long as we ration it. Don't overuse it. Just the essentials."

Shane was still worried, and it showed on his face. "No lights on the second floor and higher. Okay?"

"Why not?" Tina asked. She did not favor darkness. It allowed her mind to conjure up too much thought: guilty memories of her family, her days in the hospital. She loved that no one here knew anything about her past. Even Ken knew very little.

"Because we don't want to attract attention. Until we get more weapons, we need to stay hidden. This place needs to look like it's empty. Our best protection right now is to be invisible. No lights on at night, except here on the ground floor. The walls should hide any light down here. I think."

"Makes sense," said Ken.

It was a relief to have electricity. It was a comforting connection to the old world they once knew.

Tina picked up a can of Ma-Made brand stew. "I'm willing to try cooking this. Anyone else up for eating it?"

Shane snapped his fingers, pointed to her and winked. He never turned down hot food.

While they ate, the wind howled against the castle walls like a wounded ghost. The windows rattled, but held firm. And as the night wore on, the group talked, drank, and no one paid any attention to the ghosts outside. No one, except Sam.

PART II

"...Against such forces as have been loose tonight... Even with a modern rifle it would be all odds on the monster."

— Arthur Conan Doyle, The Lost World

CHAPTER 15

BOHAI Chen was the sole survivor of a plane that crashed *en route* from Toronto to Pittsburgh. It met the ground in an underpopulated area near the Pocono Mountains, so sparsely populated that no one was around to witness its fiery demise. The jet separated into three distinct pieces, intact, except for the tail section, but the force of impact killed everyone on board – everyone except one. By a miracle of fate, or luck of the draw, Bohai lived and only suffered a wrenched back and neck. The sole survivor was able to climb from his section of the cracked plane and stumble onto the side of the mountain to live another day. And to view the horrors of the wreckage around him.

Originally from Taiwan, his parents had moved to Toronto when he was just three years old. He moved to Los Angeles at eighteen for his undergraduate studies, and then three years ago moved to Pittsburgh to continue studying robotics at Carnegie Mellon University. He had nearly completed his graduate degree, when this tragedy happened.

Coming back to school after a weekend trip to see

Mom and Dad, he took the usual red-eye out of Toronto. A short flight, only an hour and four minutes in the air, he had taken this exact same flight two dozen times in the past three years. *Sooner or later, fate is gonna get ya,* he thought.

"A plane crashes every day," he used to remind everyone. He knew how unsafe it was up there, never mind the crap about how it was supposedly the safest form of travel. "Safer than riding a bike," people use to say. *Those people are morons,* he thought.

"Safest form, my ass," he now muttered, looking over the smoldering wreckage. He could make out pieces of the engines, the tail, a window or two... but not much more. Unfortunately, he could also discern body parts among the mess. He called out, and hoped someone would answer. Only the crackle of the fire replied.

"I don't remember my bike ever killing a hundred people!" He screamed in frustration at the dead bodies. None of the dead argued back.

After a failed attempt to find any survivors, he wanted to get far away from the revolting amalgam of twisted metal and bloody corpses. The sight of some of the victims made him stop and close his eyes, sick and dizzy. For an hour he hunkered down in the snow and held his knees to his chest before moving on.

His phone had been busted in the crash. He cradled it longingly, ran his fingers over its cracked screen, then tossed it into the blood-stained snowbank.

"Not likely to have a signal up here anyway," he said

aloud to himself. "No worries." He might have searched the bodies for another phone, but the thought of it repulsed him, and he doubted he'd find one still intact, anyway.

He wandered down the mountainside for over a week, surviving on two power bars mashed in his shirt pocket. Melted snow was his only source of water. Sleeping outside under the trees with only leaves for cover, it was cold and uncomfortable, but he was alive.

Eventually the snow gave way to dirt and rocks. It was warmer down at the lower altitudes. This also meant fruit trees. He was starving, hungry enough to consider eating worms and caterpillars. He had even eaten a few smashed acorns. They tasted bitter, but he ate them anyway and relished them.

Now the sight of ripe pears on a tree brought tears to his eyes. He shimmied up the tree trunk and picked one immediately. As his teeth bit into its green skin, he thought he might pass out. Clenching it in both hands like a precious gem, he ate it to the core, unconcerned with anything else around him.

A handsome boy, he always boasted an active social life. This was uncommon among grad students in robotics and computer science. He was the exception. His straight black hair and witty charm led him to enjoy almost every hot girl at his school in California, and in Pittsburgh he had been plowing his way through CMU when he fell in love. That didn't stop him from screwing around, it just slowed him down. The romance ended a week before this trip, and he thought seeing his family would help to clear his mind. It had cleared more than his mind, it cleared his whole damn schedule.

You never know when your next take-off is your last take-off, he remembered hearing someone say at the airport. *So be good to your loved ones.* He laughed now at the irony, but not cruelly. It *was* that lady's last flight.

Oblivious to the changes in the world, he still expected a rescue. He had taken the flare gun from the plane. It had two flares left. He was saving them until he got closer to civilization. He would shoot one off tonight. He hoped a town or ski lodge would be near enough to see it.

Bohai found a ranger station, but it was unmanned. The only help he found there was a large hunting knife. He took it. Up until now, he had been using a long sharp stick as a weapon. Now he used it as a walking stick, but sharpened one end of it with the knife.

A stream ran strong through the next pass, and he followed it for at least a mile. At a shallow point, less than two feet deep, he waded in and scanned for fish. He doubted he had the skill to spear one, but maybe he could net one in his shirt. So far he only spotted minnows and tadpoles gliding under the surface.

After several attempts, he managed to snatch a small minnow in his hand. He took a deep breath and popped it in his mouth; then swallowed it whole. For an instant, he thought he might throw up. But he concentrated, took deep breaths and kept it down. He focused on math problems to calm his mind. *That wasn't so bad.* But he would not eat another. That would have to be enough protein for today. He could survive on his bag of pears.

At that moment he looked up from his fishing spot in the middle of the stream, and was face to face with a large mountain lion, a cougar. It drank from the stream, then lifted its head, looked straight at Bohai. The boy did not move.

He wasn't afraid of this cat. Bohai always had a good rapport with animals, and he swore he could actually understand them, communicate with him. It was hard to prove this to others, but he knew it to be true.

The cat stared at Bohai with pity, as if to say *I'm sorry.* But it wasn't like: *I'm sorry for your plane crash;* but more like: *I'm sorry for your human race. You're in trouble, my friend.*

The lion lapped up one more drink of water, then turned away. It bounded off into the tall grass and disappeared.

In that moment, Bohai felt truly isolated and lonely. He waded back to shore and continued along the stream, his walking stick in hand, the backpack slung over his shoulder. It contained his only remaining possessions: an extra change of clothes, the pears, knife and flare gun.

As evening neared, his legs ached. Tired, both mentally and physically, every part of his body hurt, but he feared that if he stopped he would never make it to a rescue point. He tripped and fell into the stream with a loud splash. His hands scuffed on the rocks, and his wrist began to throb. He scrambled to get up, then sat back down in the water. Wet and tired, he refused to get back up. Resting there on the rocks, he let the slow, cold current wash over his legs.

Then something else splashed. A dark shape entered the water and swam rapidly toward him. It looked like a giant lizard or small crocodile, but he knew it couldn't be – not in this part of the country.

The lizard emerged from its underwater swim and climbed up onto a rock, its head and shoulders agleam with dripping water. It snarled at him and bared a set of unnaturally long fangs. Bohai could not sense anything from this animal, he could not communicate even with empathy. This was no ordinary creature.

For the first time in his life, Bohai was afraid of an animal.

This is no animal, he thought. *It's a demon. An alien. A freak of nature.*

The boy scrambled backward toward shore, his arms and legs beating through the water, and the lizard dove smoothly back into the stream without a splash. It headed straight for him. The head rose again to hiss at him, anticipating its meal to come. The rage coming from this creature was palpable.

Bohai stood up and held his sharp stick in front of him. He was trained in Bō stick fighting, but had never before taken on anything so big. As the lizard reached him and lashed out, Bohai swung the stick around, used the momentum and sent the creature rolling to one side. The stick cracked – it wasn't strong enough. He dropped it and hunted frantically in his backpack for the knife. All he could feel were pears. He grabbed one and threw it hard at the lizard's head. That made it hesitate for only a split-second before it lunged again. Bohai braced himself for the pain of a bite.

Suddenly something jumped over Bohai, knocking him to the ground, and raced to meet the lizard head-on. It was the cougar. It made contact and sank its teeth into the lizard's neck. Another cougar leaped from the grass and jumped on the reptile's body, ripping open its stomach with sharp feline claws.

The lizard was subdued in seconds, and dead within minutes. The two giant cats pulled meat from bone, and feasted on its carcass. A smaller cougar, or maybe it was a bobcat, joined the meal, and they all quietly devoured their prey. One of them turned and looked to Bohai as if to ask if he wanted any.

"I'm good, thanks," he declined. The cat went back to gnawing the fresh meat.

Bohai sat there in the last minutes of daylight, hoping to dry his jeans, but the sun was gone all too soon. He was scared now. Not of the cats, but of the rage in the lizard – a monster that doesn't belong in North America. Something wasn't right here.

Night wrapped itself around him, and he sat there alone – alone in human terms, anyway. The cats still remained with him. He thought he saw a spider clinging to the side of a tree, but it was at least two feet long. That wasn't possible. A trick of the darkness, he thought.

Whatever it was, it crawled back into the woods.

Eventually he stood and fired the flare gun. The cats looked up at the spectacle, as it painted the sky orange and red. They looked at him again with pity and confusion, then went back to eating.

The cracked walking stick was useless. He picked out another one and took a few minutes to sharpen the end, then continued back on the path downstream.

There was a momentary soundless discussion among the three big cats, then the largest one followed the boy. After a few hundred yards, it was walking right next to him.

"Thanks, buddy," he said. "I need the company."

After midnight, he collapsed on the ground. He could walk no more. Every muscle ached. He just lay there on the rocky ground next to the stream, head resting on his backpack, and fell asleep.

The cougar lay next to him and kept watch.

And then a small eight-legged creature reached out to him in a dream, and told him a strange tale of the world ending.

CHAPTER 16

IN the morning, Jason and Shane took the jeep out to siphon gas from derelict cars. They also needed to look for a new vehicle – one that wouldn't be recognized by Dexter's men, and one that would provide shelter from rain and from any creatures they might meet along the way. The roofless jeep was no longer practical, despite its four-wheel drive.

It was an odd oversight, but no one had yet gotten rid of the big dead spider. Sam decided it was a good project for Mark. The two of them took it out back and buried it where no one could see.

Before noon the jeep came back followed by a dark blue van. It had tinted windows, fully blacked-out, looking very much like a serial killer's vehicle of choice. In any case, it offered better protection than the jeep, and had plenty of room in back for supply runs. It also had a working heater, a vital component for winter looming just two months away.

The boys had found it easily, not far away, but hadn't found much else. They had filled a few cans with gas, stole an extra car battery and some flashlights from the glove compartments of abandoned cars. An old '74 Vega had a case of candy-bars in the back seat, melted. Food was food, melted or not; so they took the box.

"We need to think about a supply run to St. Marks today," Shane said. "It's almost forty miles, but it's a paved road. Takes less than an hour to get there."

"How's Lucy?" Jason asked.

"Awake, and begging for a drink. Something stronger than water," Sam said. "And yes, we hid the beer and wine."

"Good." Shane patted his shoulder. "We don't need any liabilities inside our fences. Keep an eye on her."

Mark bounded onto the grass and inspected the van. He climbed inside and said, "Sweet." Kids could sum up small parts of the world with the greatest sincerity in the fewest words. His shoe was untied again.

Lily sat near the garden and petted Snowball, who batted the top bloom of a purple violet back and forth as if it were the most fascinating plaything on Earth. Content, the little girl hummed and wove a bracelet of long grass. It was as if her whole life had been filled with bad times, so she knew how to make the best of it. Perhaps this experience was no big deal to her. Most days her mom was either gone or drunk. The child seemed incredibly unfazed by their current situation.

"We should go now, if we want to get back before dark," said Sam. "We've got about seven hours of daylight left."

Shane squinted and made the calculations. "An hour

to get there, an hour back. That gives us a few hours to loot the town for what we need."

Jason drove the van, Shane rode shotgun, and Sam rode in the back with Ken. Camila and Tina stayed behind with Lucy and her kids. Camila was a strong woman; Sam trusted her to be able to handle what comes their way. She waved from the watchtower as the guys drove off.

The trip was bumpy, but easy. They sped down the road at over 70 mph for the better part of the route. Nothing blocked their way except for a single dead car that forced them to swerve into the grass. They nearly hit a tree, scraping a few shards of bark on the door handles, then retook the road and moved on.

Jason parked just inside the town of St. Marks in a parking lot behind the diner. They would go on foot the rest of the way. The hope was that the van would look like any other abandoned vehicle and be ignored by anyone coming this way, especially the Grinners.

They stepped onto the main road of St. Marks and identified the grocery store further up. The vacancy of the small town magnified the sound of their shoes scuffing the road. This was not a serene setting. It was deserted, but not at peace. Not even birds landed in this place; it was a true ghost town.

St. Marks was only marginally bigger than Fayetteville. It sported a population of barely two thousand, mainly serving hunters traveling through and an occasional mountain tour. This would work to their advantage, as the town might have a kick-ass sporting goods store filled with guns.

Jason and Shane headed out to look for weapons while Sam took Ken grocery shopping. The first place they hit was the ALL GROCER-EE, according to the broken sign.

The store stank of rotting vegetables and produce. Spoiled meat had attracted flies in the back, and the boys could only imagine what rodents lurked there. They steered clear, and focused on boxed cereals, vacuum-packed products and canned goods. In a small toiletries section, they picked up rubbing alcohol, cotton, bleach, soap and shampoo. Then Sam remembered the perfume, and he scooped up the last four bottles of it left on the shelf. Clearly not a big seller out here in the sticks.

Jason and Shane hit the jackpot in the Fish & Sporting Goods store. They gathered twenty-two rifles, two handguns, three longbows and about two hundred arrows. Shane also took a sturdy crossbow and slung it over his shoulder. They filled several bags with bullets and ammo. Jason also took three fishing rods and some lures, nets, and gear. Fish might be their best source of food in the future, after the cans run out.

They looked around for something bigger, a military grade weapon, but there was nothing here.

"We need to find a military base," Shane suggested. "Also, grab some maps. Maybe they show police stations and military depots."

Of course, St. Marks didn't have a police station. Towns this small relied on the State Police. However, they were betting most of the homes had guns in them, stuffed behind the couch, hidden in the cellar, or even mounted on the wall. Up here in the mountains, everyone owned a gun.

"We need a Caterpillar tractor, or an army tank," Jason said. "Drive right through Dexter's front door. Right down his throat."

"We need a lot of things. I don't think tanks are sold at the Quickie-Mart here. Come on, let's start loading the van."

Outside, a lizard crept through the streets, licking and smelling the sidewalk. It had picked up their scent. Shane watched it for a second, then pulled back hard on his bowstring. He sent an arrow into its head. It squealed and thrashed about for several seconds, then collapsed and stopped moving.

Jason walked back and retrieved the van. He drove it around to the ALL-GROCER-EE and helped the others load the groceries and toiletries into the back. Shane carried several loads of weapons to the sidewalk, and waited for his turn to be picked up. He killed another small lizard as he waited. When the van finally picked him up, there was barely room for everything they had taken. He squeezed as much as he could in the back, then put a few items up front. The lot wouldn't fit, so they would need to return the next day for the rest.

More lizards started converging at the other end of the street, about half a mile down, still quite far away. Sam spied a giant spider on the roof of a barber shop across the street. It simply waited there, not moving. Watching for dangers, perhaps. At this distance it posed no immediate threat.

"We should go soon," Sam said. The congregation of lizards at the edge of town was making him nervous. Today the creatures looked more coordinated, less chaotic. *Like an army planning an attack,* he thought, although guessing it was just his imagination. A group of them broke off and headed toward the humans, straight down the middle of the street.

"Where's Ken?" Shane asked. "Time to go."

Ken had decided to try the local pharmacy for more drugs, antibiotics and such. It was a dozen buildings further down the street.

Shane whistled. "Ken! Let's go!"

There was no reply, and they couldn't see or hear anything from the pharmacy.

"What the hell!" Shane was irritated. "I'll go get him."

But at that moment, Ken came flying out of the pharmacy with a lizard right on his heels. It had been inside the store. Now Ken ran, and another lizard came out from under the porch and snapped at his leg. It managed to get a bite on Ken's foot, but lost its grip. Ken stumbled, his arms thrust out and caught himself as he spilled onto the ground. The aspirin and medicine bottles in his arms went flying in all directions and rolled down the street. A lizard swallowed two bottles of ciproxin in one gulp.

Ken's shoe was still clamped in the first lizard's mouth – the animal chewed it apart with the zeal of a starving man entered in a pie-eating contest – but Ken was free. He scrambled to his feet again and ran on one sock and one shoe toward the others.

"Start the van!" Sam yelled. "Start it!"

By now over a hundred lizards teemed into the streets from side alleys, burrows, and open garages. One scrambled out from underneath a rusted car. Ken was surrounded, and the first lizard dropped his shoe and bit down on his ankle. He fumbled for the gun at his belt.

This all happened within seconds. The group watched helplessly, as their friend was dragged down.

"Go!" Ken yelled, then turned and fired a gun at the lizard on his foot.

The others fired their weapons into the melee. Bullets and arrows took down lizard after lizard, but more kept coming. It was a swarm of black death. The boys backed into the van, and Jason revved the engine.

"What do I do?" he yelled. He didn't know if he should hit the escape pedal, or back up to try to get Ken. But backing up meant backing into hundreds of angry jaws.

Desperate, Sam shot an electric bolt into the crowd of reptiles. It sent a couple rolling, but couldn't stop them all; it barely made a dent in their ranks. He tried, but couldn't put a force-field around Ken. There wasn't much Sam could do at this distance; he wasn't used to using his powers this way.

The throng of lizards devoured Ken. Hundreds jumped on top, and now their friend couldn't even be found. All they could see was a mob of lizards massing on the road, and a pool of blood forming around them. Tails lashed back and forth in excitement, furor. They tore into Ken wildly, and some of them now turned their attention back to the van.

Over three hundred creatures now streamed into the street, and more joined in the distance. Jason hit the gas pedal, and the van pulled away, spitting gravel from its wheels. Shane closed the back doors and lost his balance from the forward momentum; he fell backward on a stack of bullets. Both he and his brother were stunned. They all were.

"Dammit!" Jason said. "Dammit!"

Those words were all he could say, and that was about all Sam could think. The unthinkable had just happened, and it wasn't over yet.

Up ahead only a couple lizards had made it this far and tried to block the way. The van sped past them, and ran over the tail of one unlucky beast. In the rear view mirror, Jason watched a sea of black fill the streets. It looked like a flood of dark water, a bubbling tsunami. It consumed Ken and came roiling after them to sweep them away, too.

Jason sped up to 60 mph, a risky move on this rocky stretch of the road. The dragons were fast, but ran out of breath quickly; they couldn't follow for more than three or four minutes. Eventually they stopped, breathing heavily, and glared longingly at their fleeing prey. By the time the van reached the first bend, there were no more lizards following in the rear-view mirror.

Sam and Shane watched the town disappear, a dark writhing mass of chaos still moving in its streets. Ken was back there. His body was, anyway. Winded, all the creatures lurked at the edge of town and snapped at each other. Their pursuit had petered out, but not their rage.

"We're okay now," Shane said.

Sam slumped against the back door of the van. His words were barely audible. "No. We're not."

CHAPTER 17

AT age nine, Sam had childlike suspicions about his father, and his brother shared some of them. Soren Jayden Summer was a secretive man. Though he was a caring soul who always made time for his sons, he rarely discussed his work, and often lied about it. Never saying exactly what his job was, he gave the impression that he worked for a pharmaceutical company. A laboratory of sorts was built into the basement of their home, strictly forbidden to the boys; but Sam got an illicit glimpse of it on more than one occasion. His father seemed to be cataloging thousands of plants, bugs and soil samples. The best explanation was the search for a new drug somewhere in the deep forest.

For years Sam fantasized that his dad was a secret agent for the government. Then he came up with the idea that the man had taken one of his own experiments, a secret new drug, that caused new abilities in humans, and that was why Sam had inherited the sparking ability. Another theory was that pills had been slipped into the boy's morning cereal, and that *he* was the experiment. But as he got older, Sam realized these were ridiculous ideas.

All of his theories until his teens had been fantastic and ludicrous — the product of so many sci-fi books, movies and Star Trek reruns that he enjoyed with his brother.

"We're all born different," Shane used to tell him. "Some people are strong, some are missing a leg, or blind. Some are tall. Everyone is different. You can spark up. It's just you. Don't be thinking too much about it, Sammy."

That was the final theory they accepted by age thirteen. Dad wasn't a mad scientist; he was just a man who worked for a drug company. He hadn't created any "spark" drug.

But back when he was nine, Sam remembered a singular day when the basement door had been left ajar. His dad had run downstairs in a hurry and forgot to lock it. Sam crept down the steps, as he had done once before, except this time he got more than a passing glimpse of test vials and computer screens. This time he saw a strange object, copper color and cylindrical. It looked a bit like the tire pump he used on his bike. His dad touched it and ribbons of light flared orange on both sides. Sam watched his father extend a glass vial to the cylinder, after which a small opening appeared and accepted the vial. The lights changed color to blue, then purple. Though he knew nothing about this mechanism, Sam got the impression it was testing the contents of the tiny glass container.

Just then his father noticed Sam and became extraordinarily angry, sending his son running back upstairs. That was the only time Sam had every seen real anger in his father's eyes. The man was furious, and later questioned Sam about what he had seen. Sensing this was a real problem, Sam lied and said he had seen nothing. In a few days the event passed, and his dad was back to normal, carefree again. He took the boys fishing, and made as if Sam's transgression had never happened.

But Sam never forgot that day, and a small part of him always wondered what his father was up to. Shane convinced him to shake it off.

"Dad makes a good amount of money," his brother told him. "Enough to keep us happy. You don't get money for nothin' in the way the world works. Whatever he does, he does it for us."

Shane was okay with the notion their father was plundering the forest for a drug that would be over-priced down the line. If that indeed was his job. Sam was not so okay with it.

Very different, his mother was an open book. She was happy in her role as the mom of the house, almost to the extent of a 50s television show. When she wasn't baking or cleaning, she was planning picnics or outings for the family. Her only flaw was that she complained incessantly about small details: Sam's hair was too shaggy, Shane didn't wear a jacket in the rain, Dad shouldn't ride a motorcycle, and a plethora of concern for every minutia that might threaten their safety. Looking back, Sam realized this was all part of her umbrella of concern.

"You don't need hair like Mr. Wham or The Bon

Jovis," she used to say. That sent both boys howling on the floor in laughter. "It's not *Mr.* Wham, mom, and I'm not a big fan." Mom would roll her eyes and claim her preference for The Partridge Family or David Gates of Bread. One day Sam looked them up on the internet, and pointed out that Mom's pop singer had longer hair than his. "You're not a pop singer," Mom would always reply. "Get a hair cut. Be like your brother."

These were fond memories, despite concerns over Dad's job. He could scarcely recall a day when Mom didn't wear an apron.

When his parents died, so did his misgivings. The only thing he could remember now, was that he missed both of them greatly. He especially missed talking with his mom.

Some days more than others.

A heavy mood suffocated every corner of the van on the long ride back to the lodge. They drove in silence. Sam thought about the dead businessman's rolled-up note, back by the lake. It seemed so long ago.

I saved another bullet in my pocket for you.

He wanted to say something, but found no words. After a minute he gave up and kept quiet. Sam didn't want to be the first to speak after the loss of their friend. How would they tell Tina? And if Lily asks: "Where's Ken?" Would it be enough to say: *he's gone, and not coming back?* Sam wished somebody would speak. The silence of the lonely road at dusk made it harder to stifle the memory of Ken's screams.

Ten minutes and six miles later, Jason slowed the van. He thought he detected movement on the road ahead. A shadow cast by something taller than a creature crossed into the road. Jason took his foot off the gas pedal and let the van roll to a full stop.

"Guys," he said. "Get up here. What do you think?" He pointed up ahead at a figure a dozen yards in front of the van. It looked like a boy with a dog.

A young Asian man in his early twenties came out of the bush and walked along the roadside grass. Stepping into the headlights, they could see how tired and worn he appeared. He shouldered a tattered backpack, and held a crooked stick in his hand. A big cat walked next to him, not a dog. It looked like a mountain lion, a puma or cougar, but – like the cougar they'd seen the day before – it didn't seem to be hostile. The powerful cat walked next to the young man in the docile way a dog might follow a boy.

"A trick?" Jason asked.

"He doesn't look like a Dexter goon," Shane said. "He doesn't look too good, either. A big wind could blow him over."

"Looks banged up."

"Maybe he escaped from Dexter."

"It could still be a trap."

Shane shifted in his seat. "Let's find out."

He slid the side door open and stepped out of the van

alone. With his bow drawn and ready, he took several steps toward the young man and halted.

"Hey. Stop where you are. Who are you?"

The young Asian man put a hand up. "Easy. I'm not armed."

"Where are you from?" Shane kept his weapon aimed at the man's feet. He could hear Sam and Jason whispering behind him, and the click of Jason's rifle being cocked.

"You're the first person I've seen in two weeks, maybe longer," the young Asian man said. "My plane crashed up in the mountains. I... I'm just trying to get rescued." He looked back at them, then to fill the awkward silence, added: "My name is Bohai Chen. I'm not armed."

Shane studied him for a moment. The guy seemed genuinely confused by their reaction to him. He seemed to have expected a warmer reception.

"I've been walking... looking for help," Bohai said in a thin, weary voice. He looked drained, spent, as he added, "Seeking rescue."

Shane lowered his weapon and relaxed. "Rescue? Who do you expect to rescue you?"

"I don't know. Rangers? Cops?"

"There's no one left. You know there's no rescue crews left, right? The cities are... empty. Sort of. Do you know what's happened?"

"No. But I guess something's not right" Bohai said. He looked down at the cougar waiting patiently next to him. "Something went wrong I guess. I thought someone would come to the crash site by now. But... anyway, I saw a big lizard. That didn't seem right." He stopped talking, realizing how ridiculous his words sounded. Subconsciously his right hand ran through his strong black hair, pushing it back in a nervous gesture. It was getting too long, he thought.

"It isn't right. But it's true," Shane said. "We've seen lots of them."

Sam and Jason got out of the van, and Bohai told them about his plane crash and his days wandering through the woods. On another day, it might have been an unbelievable story. Shane summed him up quickly, and didn't think this guy was with Dexter. He looked like hell, torn and scratched, but his story made sense.

"Come on," he said. "You can come back with us."

When they got back in the van, the big cat made as if to jump inside, and Shane stopped him.

"He's safe, I promise," Bohai assured them. "He comes with me. I want him to."

It was close quarters in the back of the van, loaded with supplies and now a 200-pound cat. Sam watched the great feline, but it didn't care; it closed its eyes with indifference and went to sleep. Bohai looked relieved. At long last, he had been rescued.

CHAPTER 18

THE scene inside the Peak Castle Lodge was dramatic and briefly chaotic. While Camila attended to Bohai's wounds, Tina broke down and wailed at the news of her boyfriend's death. Everyone had questions about Ken, about Bohai and the lion, and about what to do next. Mark and Lily watched through small round eyes; they watched as the level of anxiety climbed like the scream of a woman on fire and bounced off the walls of the lodge. Eventually Lily also started to sob.

The cougar slept in the shade on the far side of the courtyard, giving the humans room to get used to him. Snowball did not seem concerned about the bigger cat, but was agitated by the flurry of human activity and hid under the lobby couch. Both cats knew how and when to practice the fine art of discretion.

Sam started the task of unloading the van, careful with the guns and ammo. He stacked some of the weapons inside the lobby, and some in the watchtower. Meanwhile, Shane, Camila and Lucy tried to console Tina. Lucy was no stranger to loss; for the first time the former rock star was actually helpful. Pain, she understood.

"Come help me, Mark," Sam suggested. He wanted to distract the kid. "Give me a hand outside."

Mark helped him move the food and toiletries into the kitchen and pantry. It took several trips, but his small arms were capable. Though he strained with the bigger boxes, the kid refused to complain or rest. Sam admired his strength of spirit. In times of turmoil, kids often rebounded faster than adults. This boy seemed especially resilient.

After Bohai's wounds were doused in iodine and bandaged up, he ate some carrot slices, then helped Sam and Mark. He was tired, but felt alive. He only half believed the story he had been told about the creatures mutated from humans, even with confirmation of strange happenings from the cougar. He didn't want to believe. For sure, something was wrong with the world, but the stories these people were telling him seemed almost too far out. The stories he was hearing from the animals were even more far-fetched, but animals didn't lie or exaggerate.

"Quite a fort you've got here. I'm looking forward to a bed."

"We're trying," Sam said. "Where are you from, originally?"

"Before here? Canada. I came here to study at CMU."

"I mean..."

"I know what you mean," Bohai said. This was not his first time answering that question, but something in him refused to answer it directly. "My parents are Chinese. Taiwanese."

"Just wondering, it doesn't matter."

"If it didn't matter, why ask it?"

"You're right. I was hoping for a Korean."

Bohai laughed. There was something he instantly liked about Sam. He couldn't pin it down, but there was something honest and natural about the guy.

"So, I hear you're the other freak," Bohai said. When Sam shot him a dark look – not quite offended, but not quite welcomed, either – he immediately cast a disarming smile. "I didn't mean that the way it came out. I'm the freak of my own home town. And I heard you're different, too. You can do things. Strange things, with electricity."

"Yeah. Sort-of. Who told you that?"

Bohai didn't answer. "I have... different abilities, too."

"Which are...?"

"Sometimes I can understand animals. Some animals. Not all of them."

"You talk to animals?" Sam snickered.

"No," Bohai said patiently. "Not talk. Communicate. I understand them. And they empathize with me."

"Really?" Clearly Sam didn't believe him.

"Come here," Bohai walked out to the courtyard.

Sam told Mark to keep unloading the van, then followed Bohai to a large tree in the side yard. Bohai reached down in the grass and picked up one seed. He held it in his hand and looked up. A sparrow lighted on his palm and ate the seed. It stayed there and chirped without any concern for the boys.

"They tell me you can knock a lizard off its feet, with a shock."

"This little one told you that?" Sam snickered again.

"Not this one. Others told me."

"So why is it that you can talk to animals?" Sam asked bluntly. "Why you?"

Bohai shrugged. "Why can Pavarotti sing and Rembrandt paint? Figure that one out and get back to me. We've all got our talents, right?"

"I guess so. And what does the big cat tell you?" Sam teased, but he was starting to believe. And he was actually feeling relieved that he might not be the only *different* one here.

"He told me a lot of things," Bohai said. "But that's not the real news. The most interesting thing I've been told this week is from a different source, out there."

The sparrow flew off, and Bohai reached up into the tree. He extended his hand, and two baby tree spiders crawled down the branch and over his hand. One crawled around his knuckles and into his palm.

"It's what these little guys have been telling me," Bohai said with a more serious stare that chilled Sam. "What they told me this morning. That's what's really interesting."

The group gathered around the table in the lobby while Jason and Camila cooked their second batch of canned stew. Even Lucy was up on her feet now and poured water for everyone. Tina silently stared at the table. They told Bohai all they knew about Walter, Dexter and the Grinners. He listened, and then shared his own story.

"I have strange news from the outside world," Bohai said. "You can believe me or not, but it's something we have to consider."

"Go ahead," Shane said. "I'm all ears."

"There are three factions of mutations," Bohai told them. "You've already seen the lizards." There were nods and groans around the table. "There are also spiders, and bats."

"Haven't seen bats yet," Jason said, listening from the stove. "That's messed up. I mean, they can fly. Could be a problem."

"We've seen big spiders, though." Shane shuddered, and added, "Totally creepy."

"Those are the three types," Bohai continued, "at least in this part of the world, in North America. There might be other creatures in other parts. I don't know. The lizards are the biggest faction, by far outnumbering everything else in this region. Then the spiders, and the bats are the smallest group."

"Small bats?" Camila asked. "Or small groups of giant bats."

"I, uh... assume it's the second one," Bohai guessed. "Anyway, the three of them have formed their own armies, and are getting more organized. Those three armies are getting ready to go to war against each other. It won't be nice and neat and clean, you understand? It'll be a bloodbath. Like any war."

"And we're caught in the middle," Shane said.

"The middle of a war that doesn't involve us," Camila added.

Sam disagreed. "That's not true. It does involve us. It's probably the reason the war is being set up. To ultimately wipe humans out."

"He's right," Shane conjectured: "Think about it. If you wanted to get rid of the people in this country, on this planet, or whatever, but keep the infrastructure, the best way is to make the inhabitants kill and eat each other. Bring us down from inside. So you mutate them into three different types of creatures, mortal enemies, and send them after each other. When the war is over, all you have to do is take out the winners, who've already killed two thirds of your problem. And the buildings and infrastructure all remain whole, not damaged. You take over all the cities and homes, and populate them with your own people."

He crossed his arms, proud of his deduction and ready for his much-deserved applause.

"If that's true," Camila asked, "who is doing this? Is it another country? Or terrorists?"

"Or something of a more alien kind." Shane winked as he cast his presumption. He was enjoying spinning this tale. Years of watching old science fiction movies, was finally paying off.

"This genetic technology might not be beyond the scope of a country here on Earth," said Sam. "It could even be a mistake of our own government. An escaped virus. It could even be Walter!"

"Damn right!" Jason pounded his fist on the counter top. "Government cover-up. I've been telling you."

"Or aliens," Bohai said. "My friends think it's something from the sky. From space. But they don't know for sure. No one knows."

"How do we live through that kind of war on Earth?" Camila asked.

"We keep our heads down," said Shane. "We bunker up in here. Close the windows and stay inside. Let them kill each other out there. Let them wipe each other out. Then we'll deal with the winners."

"Which will probably be the lizards, based on the numbers," Sam said, "and then we're right back where we started."

"It's more complicated than that," Bohai interrupted.

"Why?" Lucy shrugged. "It makes sense to stay out of it."

"Maybe," said Bohai. "But we have a decision to make. The spiders want to ally with us."

That brought a cold silence to the room.

Even Jason stopped stirring the stew. "What the hell, man. You serious?"

"The lizards outnumber everything, by far. The spiders want to team up with us. They'll protect us here, if we help them in the war against the lizards, and —

eventually – the bats."

"That's crazy," Lucy said with a stony face. She stared out the window, and it was hard to tell what she was thinking.

Camila raised one hand like a traffic cop, then lowered it. When she had everyone fixed on her, she said "Waking up and finding that everyone you know is gone: that is crazy. Seeing your next-door neighbors mutate into reptile things: *that* is crazy. This business here, this is just common sense. And I'm on board."

Sam guessed she would have made one helluva wife, mother, or soldier – take your pick. They were all the same job, someone once told him. He liked her strength. She could probably hold her own against any man... or creature.

"It does make some sense," Sam said. "In a way. If they don't have the numbers to beat the lizzies, then they need us. And we certainly need them! An army of eight-legged soldiers on your side, that sounds pretty good right now. Up until this moment, it seemed it was us against the world."

"And when the war is all over?" Jason asked. "What then?"

"Then," Bohai said, "they side with us against the powers that started all this. We take back our homes."

"Aren't spiders too small?" Mark stated more than asked. No one had even noticed him until now. "I mean, too small to help against those big monsters?"

"Some have gotten bigger," Bohai said. It was an

understatement, but he didn't want to throw too much at them at once.

Jason blushed. They may have killed one of their new allies in the night. At that moment he was grateful that Sam and Mark had buried it and hidden the evidence.

"I love a good fight," Shane yelled, and slammed his fist on the table. He sounded excited again. "What the hell. Let's go to war, people." He raised his glass and drank.

"Damn government siding with aliens," Jason rambled, as he dished out the stew. "I told you! They've been doing it since Roswell."

Bohai ignored him and continued, "We have access to explosives and weapons the non-humans can't operate. That's why we'd be a useful ally to any side."

"But we need to think about this," Sam said. "We'd be siding with an unpredictable army. With spiders. That doesn't seem creepy to you?"

"Sure. But if they protect us against the lizards," Shane held up his hands. "How is that bad?"

"I don't know," Sam shook his head. "What do you think, Bohai? You're the one who... talked with them. What's your take?"

"I can hear them, that's a positive for starters. I can't hear the lizards. I feel nothing from them. We'll never be able to get along with that side, with their reptile army. But the spiders are smart, and peaceful. They won't attack you without reason."

"Actually... we killed one," Jason admitted. He decided

to come clean, and tried to sound sincerely apologetic. "It came over the wall, but I guess it didn't really attack us. It was just here. It startled ...some of us... a good bit." He didn't want to say Ken's name aloud.

"They won't strike against us," Bohai promised. "But, if we want their protection, we need to form an alliance with them." He gathered his thoughts and tried to explain: "And they are different from the lizards. The spiders have feelings, are empathetic. The reptiles are not; they're just blank to me, almost insane. Mindless and insane."

"Can a spider really take on a lizard," Shane asked. "I mean the weight difference... those lizards are huge. They're raptors!"

Sam couldn't erase the image of Ken being devoured by the writhing throng of lizards earlier that day.

"The tarantula venom is potent," Bohai said with confidence. "One bite can kill a being ten times its size. Small tarantulas eat rats and mice." He paused, and added: "Nietzsche said the best weapon against an enemy is another enemy."

Shane was convinced. "They got my vote. I'm in."

The group voted. It was unanimous, except for Tina who didn't vote. Staring down at the table, she silently ate and listened to the debate around her. Occasionally she touched her many bracelets, a nervous habit that was increasingly a part of her. Camila reached across the table and comforted her by touching her hand, but Tina did not react; she was not yet ready to climb out of her emotional spiral.

Bohai nodded. "Tonight I'll go out and tell them."

"Well, that doesn't seem too weird," Shane said. He was trying to be funny, his trademark defense mechanism, but he just sounded worried. He was dealing with a mixture of both fear and excitement at the prospect of a battle plan. Everything sounds better before it becomes a reality.

"Can you come with me?" Bohai asked Sam.

"You want me to go with you?"

"Yeah. It would help. You don't need to be scared."

"Okay. Sure, if you need me. I'm not afraid, anyway." But he was afraid.

I'm going out with Bohai to talk to the spiders. What's to be afraid of... besides the freaking spiders? And everything else!

Shane returned to his sarcasm, which summed it up best: "Well, that doesn't seem too weird, either."

CHAPTER 19

DEXTER had not stopped making plans to get into Walter's lab, but now he was more distracted with thoughts of revenge on the boys, and on getting Sam back. He had a special interest in the boy with the extraordinary powers, and he needed the women back to keep these asinine backwoods men busy.

One of the few who actually saw the amber-green fog come down from the sky, Dexter knew what had happened in the cities. He had told no one, but he knew. He knew *everything*. Or at least he suspected he knew, but he cared less for that than for his own selfish revenge.

For the past nine years, anger and the desire for retribution had been festering in Dexter for a number of reasons, not the least of which was his brother's rejection of him. He had been kicked out of the family, disowned and sent away for his political views. Anger had become a way of life for him. Now far away from his childhood home, he missed it. He missed a lot of things, and that only served to anger him more.

Dexter had several personality disorders, and his temper was but one of them. Since his teen years, he had always lacked the ability to let go of insults, slights, or anything he felt had embarrassed him. He punched a teacher once for disparaging one of his physics theories. That was in high school.

Now, much later in life, he had not softened or matured. If anything, each year made him angrier and more sullen.

He leaned back in his chair and twisted a Rubic's cube in his hands, which he could usually solve in 33 moves. When his henchman walked in, he glanced up and threw the cube on the desk.

"We've been watching their camp," Mitch told him. "They go out back to get water every day. Usually just one or two of 'em. We can capture two of their group, easy, I'm sure."

"No," Dexter said. "No more fun and games. This ends now. They took off Harry's hand, and killed four of our people. And that doesn't count the casualties from the lizards. That was all their fault – setting off those explosions. And God knows what deal they struck with Walter!"

"You don't want them alive anymore?"

"Only the boy with the magic tricks, and the two girls." Dexter said. "The rest are dead to me already."

"So what's the plan, boss?"

"We're driving straight down their throats."

"The bazooka?"

"Take fifteen men. Drive two trucks up to their gate and ring the doorbell with the M1 cannon. You blow it away. Blow their door to hell. Once inside, you kill everyone except the boy. And if you can, get back our two princesses. The men need a distraction; they're starting to annoy me."

Mitch pulled out a cigarette but didn't light it. He knew Dexter didn't like the smell of smoke. He was a little afraid of the smaller man. "And if they have more chicks?"

"Take them if you want, I don't care. But I want all the boys killed, except that one, the one who can miraculously survive a gun shot. Bring me the heads of those other two bastards I sent to see Walter. I want those trophies. I know they struck a deal with Walter and his precious team of yes-men. Where do you think they got those little bombs? They are terrorists. Bring me their damn heads."

"You got it, boss," Mitch grinned. He was antsy and itching for something to do, anything away from the compound. Dexter gave him the creeps, as did many of the other men, for that matter.

Dexter pulled out a new list of chemicals he wanted. His laboratory was built, but needed to be stocked. He had accumulated almost everything he required, but he still lacked some of the information for what he was building, the dark cloud spinning in his mind. Holes needed to be filled, and Walter had the key that might fill in the gaps.

Walter is next on my list, he thought. *After those kids, Walter's head will be on my mantle.*

Dexter's hatred for Walter was heated and stoked on a daily basis. It bubbled in his brain like a witch's cauldron of porridge set way too high. It was actually anger at his brother displaced on poor Walter. Hatred of the whole world was close to spilling over into every part of his life. It was only a matter of time before he might even turn on his own men. Insanity resides in the most inhospitable of vessels, and lunacy is the hardest intangible to contain.

He handed over the list of chemicals. "These are the rest of what I need."

"We may have to go into Pittsburgh for this stuff," Mitch warned. "Unless you let us take Walter's lab."

"He won't have these, and I told you it's not time yet. Stop asking me."

"Sorry, boss." Mitch backed off. He didn't want his head on the back wall, too. "It'll maybe be a two-day trip if we go to the city. But at least we can get some good supplies while we're there."

"You can go tomorrow." Dexter scribbled something on a piece of paper. He was always writing illegible notes to himself. "Tonight you take the Peak. Take that lodge from those kids."

"Okay, boss."

"At midnight. Exactly at midnight." For some reason this was always an important point for the obsessive compulsive scientist. Everything had to be at very specific times, usually even numbers.

Crazy freak! Mitch thought.

185

"Then tomorrow afternoon we'll get back to building the lab. Take the men on the overnight run tomorrow."

"Tonight at the Peak, after they're dead, we'll take all their supplies, too," Mitch assured him.

"No need. We're taking over their place. We'll make it an outpost for our expansion." Dexter still thought he would take over the world someday. "Leave a few guys there."

"Good idea, boss."

"And Mitch."

"Yeah, boss?"

"Trophies. I want trophies."

Mitch glanced at the back of the room, where the heads of two people floated in giant jars, preserved in a solution. There were fingers, too. The skulls of lizards and humans also lined the back wall. The side wall held an array of empty test tubes, not yet built into a lab. It was a tapestry from Frankenstein.

"You got it, boss." He headed out quickly. He was dying to light that cigarette.

CHAPTER 20

AFTER dinner, Bohai took Sam on a quick hike into the woods, twenty minutes deep into its murky recesses. At a clearing, he stopped and spoke to a small spiderling, then sent it on its way through the dense growth of trees. The two boys relaxed against a maple trunk and waited. Nights were getting cooler up here, and a crisp breeze rattled the leaves. There were no crickets or moths – nothing but a quiet forest.

"Can I see you do it?" he asked Sam.

"Do what?"

"You know what."

"It's not a carnival act or a card trick."

"I know, Sam. But I showed you what I can do."

Sam couldn't argue with that. "Fair enough."

Extending his arm, hand out and palm up, Sam generated a small sphere of electricity about the size of a quarter, then increased its size ten inches. Purple and blue, it looked like a novelty plasma ball, the ones sold with the black lights and Halloween posters at malls. Except this one had been produced from thin air. Against the closing darkness, it glowed bright. A few giant spiders came out of the shadows for a closer look. Sam hadn't even realized they were there. He raised the ball higher into the air, then exploded it, and the sparks faded into nothing – like mini fireworks. Other than a brief crackle, it had made no sound.

"The spiders are impressed," Bohai told him. "That's important."

"Thanks. I guess."

"I'm sorry you lost someone today. I heard about it."

"Ken. Yeah. He was an alright guy. It was pretty awful. Happened on the supply run, before we found you. Pretty bad, pretty gross." The image of the sea of tormented lizards still haunted Sam. He tried to downplay his grief.

"Sorry." Bohai squeezed Sam's shoulder, then turned his attention to movement in the dark forest.

The spiders began moving away, giving a wide berth to the clearing. At first Sam thought they were leaving, but then he realized it was to make room for something else.

What approached them next took Sam by surprise. It impressed and terrified him at the same time. He thought about how he might describe this later to his brother, but words would never do it justice. Some things in life have to be seen in person.

Crushing wild brambles and bushes as it crawled forward, a colossal tarantula entered the clearing. The size of an elephant, it moved slowly and deliberately. It towered over the boys and raised itself up on eight hairy legs, each one longer than twelve feet. Its two shiny black fangs tucked under its head were the size of rhino horns. Beautiful, if a frightening being can be described as such, its hairy legs and abdomen sported orange and yellow stripes along an otherwise velvet back body.

When it reached the boys, it lowered itself to the ground, and tucked its legs in close to its abdomen.

"He agrees," Bohai said.

"He said that to you?"

"I feel it. I can feel his words and meanings."

Bohai looked up at the behemoth, then bowed slightly and turned to go. "We're done here. Let's go."

Sam didn't need to be told twice. He was more than happy to get away from the furry mammoth and his army of hairy, creepy giants.

As the boys walked back to the lodge, most of the spiders dispelled. However, two of them followed the boys back to the Peak's gates, keeping a distance and staying as hidden as possible in the tall grass.

"Our bodyguards?" Sam asked.

"They'll watch over our home for us. A couple more might come and go, and keep an eye on the lodge."

"I guess that's comforting," Sam smirked. "In a weird way. So, was that their king?"

"No. I doubt we'll ever meet their leader. The one we met is more of a General."

"I'm not afraid of him."

"He knows. He likes that about you."

"He likes me?"

"It's you they want, you know," Bohai said, closely watching Sam. "The spiders want you on their side. That's why they sided with us humans. It's about you. They think you're the next savior of the planet."

"I hate to disappoint them, but I'm not."

"You don't practice enough," Bohai scolded. "You need to try more. Your power is like a muscle. You need to workout every day, and make it stronger."

"I don't like using it at all."

"That's your problem. It's a new world, Sam. You'll need it – *we'll* need it. We'll need all our abilities to survive. It's not like back at school when you were teased and made fun of."

"How did you know?" Sam asked.

"You don't think I experienced the same? I talked to mice and birds. You think that was considered normal? And once I got someone expelled for cheating. A mouse told me – how's that for a pun inside a pun? He ratted on a cheating ring. Two other students got suspended. And I got my ass kicked for a week."

"People always say they loved high school, but high school was hell," Sam said, his tone bitter.

"If one is different, one is sure to be lonely. I read that somewhere once. You know?"

"I think so." He actually had never read that, but it sounded right.

"It's over, man. High school and play-time are over. And now you need to get stronger. We're going to need your power. It has to get bigger. We both have to grow up."

Twigs and brush crackled under their feet until they reached the road that led to the front of the lodge.

"And another thing," Bohai said. "The spiders won't help us against those men, the ones who had captured Camila and Lucy."

"Dexter's men? Why?"

"Because their deal with us is to protect the humans against the lizards and bats. We're human, and those men are human. It's an internal fight for us to handle. We'll have to deal with them ourselves. The spiders won't get involved in our internal conflict."

"Politically sensitive spiders," Sam mused. "Who would have thought?"

"I told you – they're smart."

After a long pause, Sam confessed something to Bohai. "You know, when I was fifteen, I almost killed a kid."

"Seriously?" It wasn't the worst thing Bohai had heard this year. He and Sam didn't stop walking, but slowed their pace.

"Yeah," Sam said. "There was this kid, Billy Morksi, a total *jagoff*. He'd been in trouble a lot, and even with me and Shane, and once he tried to kill us. Years before. But anyway, that's not important here. This one day he showed up at a weekly card game my brother used to play in. I was fifteen and Shane was seventeen. They sat across from each other at the table, about six guys were there, and I watched from the side. So anyway, there was this one hand with big money on the table, like two hundred dollars. That was big for us. There was an Ace on the table and two Jacks. I see this kid Jepp has an Ace in his hand, and he raises the bet. We called him Jepp, even though his name was Jeff, I don't know why. Anyway, everyone else folds, but Billy calls and raises, and keeps re-raising. It's over three hundred dollars by the time the final card is shown. That last card is a 5. It's useless to both of them. You know how to play cards?"

"Yeah, I know how."

Sam continued, "So Billy smiles and lays down his two Jacks, three of a kind. He's ready to take the money, but then Jepp lays down his two Aces: a full house. The look on Billy's face, I'll never forget. It wasn't disappointment, it was anger. I've never seen anyone so angry. So anyway, he accuses Jepp and the others of cheating, then splashes the pot. That means he throws the money across the table, I think. He pulls out a big hunting knife and grabs me from behind, puts the knife at my throat. He said he'd kill me, if the others didn't confess to cheating and hand him the money. Billy wasn't very smart, wasn't good at cards, and didn't always think things through."

"Sounds like an a-hole," Bohai said.

"Exactly." Sam continued, "So he has this knife right at my throat, and he's got his arm around me, almost choking me. I'm scared that Shane is going to do something crazy, or one of the others might, so I want to get Billy off me as soon as I can. I figured I could just shock him and he'd let go. Except I was all pumped up with adrenaline, and I never shocked anyone actually touching me before. So I hit him with too much juice. It ran into him and he fell clutching his chest. He had a heart attack right there."

"Damn. What did you guys do?"

"We called 9-1-1, of course," Sam said. "They took him to the hospital, and blamed the heart attack on the buffet of drugs he was taking. I knew it was me, though. I tried not to ever use it again, my power, after that. Billy was a freak, but I didn't want to kill him."

"Is he still alive now?"

"Well, probably not." Sam shrugged. "Unless he's alive as a lizard. But last I heard he was messed up, in a mental hospital. I wonder if I'm part of the reason why he's there. Or was there."

"You can't analyze the past, Sam. It's fluid. Sounds like this kid Billy was on a bad path, with or without you."

"Fluid? I don't know what that means. But here's the rub: Jepp did cheat. He was good at magic tricks and he brought that last Ace from his sleeve or something, from out of nowhere. He had one Ace, not two. I knew he'd cheated, and I didn't say anything."

"Damn."

"Yeah. I still feel bad."

"Let it go, man. You can't control everything in life. And things are different now. You need to practice, because we need your abilities. Your power is about the only advantage we've got."

"Really?" Sam laughed. "I thought a truck-size tarantula was the best thing we've got."

"Yeah, that too."

Shane had the night shift in the tower, so Sam sat with him for an hour to keep him company. The two boys cleaned their guns the way they had been taught by their grandfather on hunting trips, years earlier. They also serviced some of the other guns that had been fired. This was more of an attempt to keep busy than a real necessity. Afterward, they practiced with the new crossbow, shooting a target on the grass between two trees outside the wall. Sam's aim was rusty, but Shane was sharp as ever.

He told his brother about the big tarantula and the walk into the woods. Shane didn't say much; he just nodded a lot and kept adjusting his crossbow. Perhaps he thought his little brother was exaggerating. Certainly he had mixed feelings about the arachno-human alliance.

"I tried to talk to Tina tonight," Shane said. "I think she'll be okay. She's strong. I gave her a shot of whiskey for a nightcap. She'll be better tomorrow."

"Speaking of whiskey, how is our alcoholic rock star?"

"She's a pip. Not the best mother I can guess. I've hidden all the booze, but she'll find it. She's persistent."

"The kids?"

"Lily's in another world. But I guess most kids are, at eight. Mark is strong, though. A tough little kid."

"What do you think of Camila?"

"Same as you, Sammy. She's hot as hell. Damn." He motioned as if to cup big breasts.

Sam smiled and shook his head.

As the night wore on, Sam went back to his room and tucked himself into bed. He tried to think about the giant spider, their impressive new ally, and their new hope. But instead, he couldn't stop thinking about Ken being drowned in a sea of lizards, buried under a black throng of killers.

The living will never be as strong as the dead. They alone have the power to reach you wherever you are.

One of his teachers had said that once. The context was different, talking about case solving in crime labs, but the words meant something different to him now. The last two years had taught him the effect of death on the living.

Lying back on his soft bed, he closed his eyes. His tired body quickly drifted off. Sleep was the best medicine tonight for both mind and body. Unfortunately, tonight's sleep was short.

Footsteps and commotion in the hallway woke him up at a few minutes past midnight. Jason threw open the door. "Somebody's coming up the road, and fast! Get your gear."

CHAPTER 21

REVENGE comes at midnight. It always comes at midnight. Sam didn't know why, but he felt it.

At midnight Shane heard the sound of car engines and loud voices approaching from a distance. Through the binoculars he spotted two pickups barreling up the road, heading straight for the front gate. Their headlights appeared like the wild eyes of a charging bull. The first truck hit the tin can wire fence and brought it with them, trailing cans in a loud cacophony along the way. The nine-fingered Mitch could be seen at the front.

This was Dexter's men!

Shane ran down the stairs into the second floor of the resort and sounded the alarm. He banged his hand against the wall and shouted for everyone to get up. At that moment he realized: *we need an actual alarm bell.* Too late now, he made do with shouting and clapping.

Jason ran shirtless into the hall, struggling to pull a concert t-shirt over his head. "What is it?"

"Dexter's goons. Lots of firepower. Get everyone up!"

Sleepy and confused, the others stumbled out of bed

196

and into the hall. Jason passed the news on and grabbed for his guns.

Shane ran back to the watchtower and loaded his new crossbow. He didn't need the binoculars anymore, the trucks were no more than seventy-five yards away. They stopped in the middle of the road, headlights on high beams. He counted eight men in the first truck, and six or seven in the second.

One of the men in the truck-bed of the first pickup hoisted a big bulky gun onto his shoulder. He leaned over the front and rested the huge barrel on the cab roof.

"A bazooka!" Shane whispered. "Oh my God!"

Jason joined him with his sniper rifle. He saw the big gun, too, and took a knee to get a good aim. His knuckles were white from their tight grip on the barrel.

"Take out that cannon first!" Shane yelled. He aimed his crossbow and let an arrow fly. It sailed into the right arm of the bazooka gunner. A miss – he had been aiming for the head or throat. The gunner shouted a curse into the air, but didn't let go of the gun. His eye squinted as he took aim at the gate.

And then he fired the rocket. The boom was deafening.

At that exact same flash of time Jason shot the man in the eye, and the gunner fell back. The bullet entered the gunner's brain, instantly killing him, and his gun flew out of his arms. The blast hit a tree and exploded it into pieces, its bark and branches flying in all directions. The tree trunk burst into flames.

Another two men scrambled to lift the bazooka again, and plopped the cannon back onto the cab roof. One of the men took the gun in hand, but he hadn't been trained with it. His partner took a good minute to get it reloaded, and steadied him with his hands.

By now Sam was poised in the second watchtower, which had not been manned until now. He started shooting a rifle at the men in the truck. Jason and Shane also fired from their tower. They peppered the trucks from both sides, but only took out two men, the wrong two men – the bazooka was still on target.

The big gun fired again, and had more buck than its gunner had expected. It fired high, but this time it did hit the stone gate and blew the top half of it off. The courtyard was partly exposed.

The clumsy gunner and his mate reloaded the bazooka, while the rest of Dexter's men fired their guns at the two towers and kept the boys pinned down.

Two minutes passed. Bullets flew in both directions. Even Mark helped; he joined Sam in the second tower and did his best with a small pistol. Although he couldn't hit much from this distance, he did manage to shoot out one of the truck's tires.

The men had one final load left for the bazooka, but that's all they needed. They loaded it and fired. The third blast instantly destroyed the rest of the front gate on impact. It collapsed inward, sending pieces of stone flying across the courtyard. A few chunks rolled out onto the road. A huge gaping hole now presented itself where the gate used to be – a hole big enough to drive a truck through.

The first pickup revved its engine and raced forward. Jason shot the front windshield out, then shot the driver in the head. The pickup swerved and crashed into the right side of the gate opening. It now blocked the second truck from driving in. The men got out of their trucks and fired their guns. A bullet hit Jason. Three men climbed over the front truck and got inside the lodge.

"They're inside!" Sam cried. He told Mark to stay in the tower and keep shooting. He turned and took the stairs two steps at a time.

Bohai was the first to confront the three men, and he fired his revolver twice. He was skilled at hand-to-hand combat, but not experienced with guns. His aim was off, and he only managed to hit one man in the shoulder. Another man shot Bohai, who fell to the ground. Barely conscious, he lay on top of stones and rubble blown from the wall, his blood draining out onto the grass.

The cougar sprang up and knocked the shooter off his feet. Its jaws clamped down on the man's neck with incredible force and bit down, crushing his windpipe. Shooting Bohai would be the man's last bad deed in life.

Shane had to put his bow down to help Jason, who had been shot in the arm and neck and was bleeding out fast. Shane wrapped a piece of torn shirt tightly around his friend's arm. He tore another piece of cloth and used it to apply pressure to Jason's neck. Blood still gushed out.

"Just nicked me, nicked my neck," Jason told him. He took the cloth from Shane's hand. "I can hold this myself. Get back to your gun, man!"

Shane didn't know what to do. Jason looked bad.

Sam reached the courtyard in time to see a large bald man aiming his gun at Camila's head. She stood frozen, a knife in her hand. Lucy appeared behind her and screamed.

"No, we take her alive," his wounded partner shouted. He aimed his gun for Camila's leg and fired. It missed.

Lucy cried out again and pulled Camila back.

Sam slammed the wounded man in the face with the butt of his rifle, and the bald man spun around toward Sam. The brute stood only two feet away; he pulled out a hunting knife and lunged for Sam's heart. Sam sent the man headlong to the ground with a bolt of electric shock. Baldy was stunned but not hurt. Sam still always instinctively pulled his punches. That was a mistake. Baldy got up and knocked Sam to the ground with one blow from his musclebound arms.

There was no more shooting from the towers; even Mark was out of bullets. Sam only heard gunfire outside. The crisscross of bullets sounded like Dexter's men were either shooting at each other or shooting at the walls.

Shane looked down to see one of Dexter's men sink to the ground. Another one ran off into the east woods. Their shadows and silhouettes moved in the glow of the headlights like phantom stick figures. He looked closely around the trucks. Then he saw a man slip through the gates with a rifle. One of them was inside the courtyard! Shane ran downstairs to stop him, but he was too late to stop the man from shooting.

Sam raised his head to see the bald man who had punched him, now with a gun aimed straight at his face. Sam was drained, and had dropped his rifle in the scuff. Helpless, he looked up at the silhouette of the bald man, back-lit from the headlights of the trucks. Another man came up from behind and also raised his gun. Sam was sure he and Bohai were about to enter the world of the dead.

Instead, the man in back aimed his gun at the bald man's head and fired. Dexter's man collapsed.

Dizzy and aware that his head was bleeding, Sam raised himself on his elbows. The silhouette approached, still holding his gun. The boy thought he heard someone say his name and struggled to see who it was. He spoke four words before passing out.

"Stu? Is that you?"

CHAPTER 22

STATE Patrolman Stu Reese had been watching Dexter's men since he first realized they were the ones who had built the road barricade a few days earlier. He already knew most of these men by name, and had arrested at least half of them in the past decade. They were anti-government survivalists, sometimes called "doom preppers," who built cabins in the mountains and prepared for the eventual collapse of the government. They weren't smart survivalists – they stocked more beer than bullets or food – but they were determined.

Stu was also familiar with Dexter and Walter, but to a lesser degree. He realized there was a University lab in the hills, or so they claimed that's what it was, but rarely had occasion to visit the house. The scientists were more law abiding than the rougher men in the survivalist pack.

When he saw two fully loaded trucks head out from Dexter's compound this night – with an M1 2.3 inch cannon, he decided to follow. He trailed them at a safe distance on his motorcycle, its headlight off. Hugging the roadside a mile behind them, he arrived at the Peak Castle Lodge right on time to see the M1 cannon destroy a tree. Before he could position himself to start shooting at Dexter's men, the second rocket took out part of the gate.

The lodge, where those kids were headed. He wondered if they had ever made it here.

Stu knelt behind his bike, and aimed his rifle, but something stirred behind him in the high field grass. He turned to see two lizards ambling through the brush toward him. The cannon noise had attracted them, and Stu was to be their first meal.

Dammit, he thought. *I don't have time for this.*

If he shot the lizards, it would give away his position to Dexter's men, and he was counting on the element of surprise. He pulled out his Taser, hoping it would repel the beasts without too much noise. He didn't need it, though.

A huge spider spun down from a tree and sank its fangs into the first lizard. The poison instantly paralyzed its victim and started liquefying its organs from the inside. The lizard writhed and convulsed, then went limp. Seconds later, two more spiders descended on the other lizard. Almost soundlessly they dragged the two bodies back into the woods and out of sight. Only the crunching of leaves and reeds could be heard. They disappeared after the heavy bodies were hauled away.

Damn, Stu thought.

He turned back to the chaos at the lodge. He witnessed the front gate rupture under the force of the rocket. Now he was sure the kids were in there; he could see them in the towers, and Dexter's men were starting to drive toward the hole in the gates. Stu aimed and shot one of the men. Someone else shot the driver, and the truck crashed into the wall. More men were filing out of the trucks and climbing inside the wall. Stu picked them off one by one from behind. No one had realized yet that he was behind them.

He saw a couple of men who managed to avoid his bullets and now were clambering over rubble, going inside. Two others remained on his side of the wall. He shot one, and the other slunk away into the woods.

Stu ran for the gate, and climbed up over the broken stones. He got inside just in time to see a big bald man punch Sam to the ground. The burly man now aimed his gun down at Sam. Stu took out his handgun, his favorite Double Eagle Glock, and shot the man directly in the head. The man fell over with only half his brains intact.

"Sam?" Stu bent over to see if Sam was all right.

The boy uttered Stu's name and passed out.

Shane came running down the steps and the look on his face shifted from horror to confusion, and then to relief. He smiled widely at Stu, and looked like he might want to hug the man. Instead he settled for one strong pat on the shoulder and said, "It's about time the cops arrived."

Tina shook herself out of her misery and jumped into action. She had been a student nurse, and so now was officially promoted to Castle Doctor. They had three serious patients laid out on tables in the lobby, and she was pressed for time to take care of them all.

In triage, Bohai was made first priority. He had been shot between his chest and right shoulder. The bullet needed to be removed – something she'd only seen done on video. She used Betadine and tweezers to pull it out, while Camila and Lucy assisted her with extra lighting and lots of alcohol, iodine and gauze. The bullet trembled in her hands. She dumped it in a bowl and then stitched him up. That much she could do – she was good at sewing wounds shut. Still, she had no idea if Bohai would live, if she had done it right, or if he'd ever wake up.

Meanwhile, Shane and Stu doused Jason's wounds with alcohol and iodine and got him bandaged up. The bullet had gone straight through his arm, and the neck wound had merely grazed the skin. Luck had been on his side, as it had missed the carotid artery by a centimeter. They gave him a shot of whiskey for the pain. Later Tina would complain they had wrapped the bandages wrong, but for now it seemed to be doing the job; he was able to rest and start recovering.

Sam wore only bruises and scratches on his face and body, nothing serious. He had passed out from the punch to the head. Mark put a cold wet towel on his forehead, and Lily held his hand. Snowball helped by purring.

After the patients were well under the control of Dr. Tina and her staff, Stu and Shane walked outside to survey the damage to the wall. Their front gate was wide open, now a giant hole that exposed them to the outside world. Dust still swirled in the air. One of the trucks had been driven off by one of Dexter's men, but the front truck was still smashed up against the wall. Stu reached in and turned off its headlights.

Large chunks of the stone gate were littered everywhere, making it hard to walk around without tripping. The rubble had stirred silt and dirt into the air. Everything stood quiet again. All this damage had been done in the shortest blink of time. It was a stark reminder of how razor thin was any protection or safety in this new world.

The cougar had started dragging the dead bodies of Dexter's men out into the woods. They had no idea what for, but were glad to get rid of the dead. Stu's experience with dead bodies was that they're just not fun to have around, and start to smell bad after a few days.

"The cat? Dangerous?" Stu asked.

"No, I think he's okay," Shane said. "He's okay. He's with Bohai."

"That the Japanese kid in there on the table?"

"Chinese. And yeah. I hope he makes it."

"I hope he makes it too," Stu said. He noticed one of the kids missing from their first meeting, but didn't bring it up. He could guess what had happened.

"Look at this gate, Stu."

"Yep. That's not gonna be easy to rebuild."

"That was our best defense here." Shane picked up a

small stone and held it in his hand.

"You're still on high ground," Stu remarked. "Still in a good spot. Just need to get this hole closed up."

"Have you been out here alone all this time, Stu?"

"Yeah. Been following the Grinners."

"You know them?

"Oh yeah. For years. Not the best company to keep."

"You'll stay with us now, right?" Shane pleaded. "You shouldn't be out there alone."

"Yeah. I'll stay a bit." Stu lit a cigarette and walked out around the truck. "For now let's move this pickup sideways and block the entrance."

"Right. Good idea." Shane was glad to have Stu on board, someone else to help shoulder the burdens of leading this group. "Good thinking."

Sam woke up and found himself lying on a table. He lifted himself off it and stood on shaky legs. It wasn't fully light yet, but was trying to get there. He guessed it might be 6:00 am. Mark was sitting on the lobby couch, where Jason was teaching him how to clean a gun. Jason's arm and neck were wrapped up. Bohai slept on the next table, his chest completely wrapped with gauze.

"He okay?" Sam asked.

"Don't know yet," Jason said. "I hope so. Time will tell, man. Are you all right?"

Sam had a headache and a black eye. "I'm fine. I need a drink of water."

"There's water in the jug over there, and some hot water for instant coffee or hot chocolate in the kitchen. The whiskey has... uh, disappeared." He gestured toward the back of the room, where Lucy and Lily were sleeping on sofas.

If Lucy took the booze, that wasn't going to be good for anyone, but especially not for her.

"Where's everyone else?"

"Sleeping, I guess. In their rooms. Stu is on watch."

"The cop, Stu. That was really him?"

"He saved your ass, man. Maybe saved all of us. He took out five or six of those bastards."

"Those bastards," Mark repeated, as he polished his gun.

"Language, little man!" Jason scolded. "Be cool."

Mark shrugged and eyed his gun, pretending to know more than he did about it.

"I'm going to make some coffee." Sam rubbed his eyes and walked toward the kitchen.

Jason held up a bullet to the light, then slid it in a chamber. "This one – it's for Dexter. Damn if it ain't."

"Dam if it ain't," said Mark, and Jason pointed a warning finger at him. Mark just giggled.

Sam made a mixture of hot chocolate and coffee for himself, and a pure instant coffee for Stu. He carried the two mugs carefully up to the watchtower without spilling a drop. The morning air was fresh and cool up at the fifth floor. A spirited breeze played with Sam's hair.

"Sorry, no milk," he apologized to Stu. "We need to look for instant powder packets on the next supply run."

"Thank you, and black is fine, Sam. You feeling okay?"

"I'm fine. Anything happening out there yet?"

"It's quiet."

Stu sipped his coffee, and gazed out over the countryside. It was maybe the best coffee he'd ever tasted. That was perhaps because it was his first cup in over a week. He always said that coffee was the best of life's simple pleasures. It wasn't complicated or expensive, didn't cause a hangover, and wasn't acquired at the expense of drama, like women. Coffee was perfectly simple and good.

"They'll need to regroup," Stu said. "I doubt they'll send anyone else after us for at least a few days. If they were smart, they'd attack again today, while we don't have a gate. But I know most of those guys. And they are not smart."

"Dexter is, and he's running the show over there."

"Yeah, that could be a problem. But he isn't *tactical* smart. He's book smart, but I bet he doesn't know how to fight a battle or win a war. I'm guessing he needs a few days to make a new plan."

"I hope so. And on that subject... what is our plan?"

"Well, I'm not in charge," Stu clarified. "But I'd say rebuilding the wall is job one. Get everyone back to good health, and then reinforce these towers with extra weaponry. Then we need to go out and find better guns.

You kids need some automatic weapons. Those revolvers aren't good enough. And we need some silencers. Right now your brother is the only one who can shoot a bow worth a damn, and so he's our only silent shooter. We need silencers for the guns."

"Okay," Sam agreed. "And it would also help to get some big guns. Ones like that rocket launcher that brought the gate down."

"Smart thinking. You'd able to remove any big threat before it gets up the road."

"Any idea where we can find that kind of stuff? Big firepower?"

"Yeah." Stu sipped. "I got a few ideas."

For now, the smashed and dented pickup truck would be their gate. They would have to climb over it to get in and out. Not very convenient, but it would have to do as a temporary measure. Because it takes a few minutes to climb over and get in, the theory was that the watchtower guard would have time to shoot any trespassers – or so they hoped.

They explained to Stu about the spiders, not to shoot any, as they were their allies. He only partly believed their story, but he couldn't deny the eight-legged critters had saved him the night before. If it was true, it was good news, because now they could focus their attention on Dexter. And that was going to be a full-time job.

Stu told them about a friend of his who used to collect used military weapons. His house was about fifty miles away, and not easy to find, but the man would certainly have some heavy artillery, and maybe even some equipment they could take.

"He's a good man. If he's still alive, he'll help us out," Stu said.

"And if he's not?" Shane asked.

"Then we help ourselves."

CHAPTER 23

LATE the next morning they set off to find Stu's friend. They took the dark van, this time with Stu driving. Sam and Shane went along, but everyone else stayed to guard the fort. Jason and Bohai needed to recover. Mark wanted to come, but Sam gave him a watchtower assignment to convince him to stay behind.

As they pulled away, Shane saw something in the rear-view mirror, which jumped onto the van roof. He noticed several long legs pull up and out of sight: an was an eighteen-inch wolf spider.

"Sam, there's a spider on our roof. On our frickin roof." Unlike his brother, Shane wasn't comfortable around spiders, snakes, or even insects.

"Well... it's for our protection, I guess," Sam said. He tried to sound reassuring, even with his own mixed feelings about the arachnids. "Just ignore it and help Stu navigate."

Shane turned back to the front and muttered to himself. He unfolded the map and plotted their location, then realized the map was upside down.

"I don't need a map," Stu said. "I know exactly where

we're going. Never needed a map; don't need one now, mind you."

Sam sat back and enjoyed the bumpy ride. He thought about Bohai's advice to practice his art more, so he relaxed and balanced a tiny spark on his fingertip.

The house was hidden at the end of a back road. This was more like a secluded road just off of a back road. You couldn't get more remote than this. The old shack barely passed for a house, dilapidated and unpainted since 1953. An M198 Howitzer sat rusting in the front yard, and an even more completely rusted 1967 El Camino with two flat tires was parked in a patch of grass on the side of the house.

"I haven't been here in almost a year," Stu warned. "You two better stay in the van. I'll go in alone."

Stu stepped out of the van and called his friend's name. "Frank, you there? Frank, it's me Stu."

No answer. The woods were quiet, except for the rustling of leaves. Even the birds were gone, probably scared off by the spider.

The front door creaked open, and an old man appeared. He looked to be 100 if a day. His scruffy white beard ran up to sideburns and then faded into a bald head. He held a shotgun in his hands, surprisingly steady, but lowered it when he saw his friend.

"Stu, you old son of a bitch." His voice was hoarse, but loud. Years of being half-deaf had given him a habit of yelling.

They shook hands and spoke for a moment about nothing, idle talk. The boys couldn't understand much of the man's slang expressions, despite the yelling. Then the two men disappeared into the house.

"I guess his eyes are bad," Shane noted. "Or he probably would have wondered why we have Cujo up there on the roof."

"I doubt he even knows what's happening. Look at this place. It's in the middle of nowhere. Edge of the world, and then turn left."

"Good for him. Better to die not knowing I think."

"Maybe," Sam murmured absently. He was still examining the house and yard. "How could anyone live alone like this? We should take him back with us."

"Uh, you saw him. Any chance he would come back with us? Sam, if a guy like that wanted to be social, he'd live on the grid. He wouldn't have a Facebook page, but he'd at least be on the grid."

"Good point."

"I doubt he even has a radio or TV. Wonder if we can take that Howitzer."

"It's rusted through," Sam laughed. "Probably blow up in our faces if we tried to use it."

"True that."

The woods got quiet again. It was spooky.

"I feel like I'm in a horror movie," said Sam. "This is like where every serial killer movie was ever filmed. Kids in a van parked in front of an old house..."

"Yeah. Look at that shovel over there, sticking in the

ground. What do you think is buried there? Or who?"

"I'm sure there are some bodies buried here," Sam mused. "Probably all the way back to the sixties."

He peered out the tinted windows at the creaking weather vane on top of the shack. The wind had picked up, and the vane was now moving and squeaking. A shadow moved across the sky.

"What the hell? Did you see that?"

Shane had been looking at the ground, but he did see a shadow pass over it. "What was that? A bat?"

"No, it was like a plane," said Sam.

"I didn't hear anything."

"It was really high up, and didn't make any noise. Maybe a glider?"

"I don't think gliders can fly very high. Maybe a drone?" Shane suggested.

"Maybe Jason is right. Government conspiracy? Spy drones?"

"Or it could just be Walter."

"Or Dexter!"

"Oh crap. He might be spying on us. I hadn't thought of that."

"Hurry up, Stu," Sam willed their friend to come out quickly. They looked up at the sky again, then back at the front door of the house. The flying object didn't return. Nothing moved on the ground either. Nothing happened for a long ten minutes.

At last, the door burst open, and it startled Sam. Stu walked out carrying a duffel bag, and was laughing.

"That's a good one, Frank. Sorry I don't have time for more. See you soon. You take care of yourself."

Frank didn't come out, but waved from behind the screen door. An eternal hermit, he wasn't climbing out of his shell just for the end of the world.

Stu got back in the van and dumped the bag in the back seat next to Sam. "This was all I could get. All of his big guns are too old and rusted through."

Sam opened the bag and found a dozen hand grenades, two automatic pistols, a silencer and a small grenade launcher. There was also a box of shotgun shells and some matches.

"That's it?"

"That's a lot," Stu countered. "The silencer alone is worth its weight in gold. To us anyway."

Sam snapped his fingers. "Hey, I got an idea. Stu, we need to make a detour on the way back."

The detour took them on a bumpy road, and the word "road" was being generous. This was the back way into the town of St. Marks.

"You sure about this?" Stu asked.

"I'm so stupid, I should have thought of this sooner," Sam said. "I saw it in one of the windows last time. A shop sells remote camera drones to tourists, to take photos of the mountains from high up. If we can get one, and get it to work, we can spy on Dexter. And on Walter, for that matter."

"I guess so." Stu shook his head. He had never even

owned a cell phone; only a ham radio. "I don't know anything about drones."

"I've got it covered," Sam assured him.

They entered St. Marks and eased up the main road. Sam half feared they would see Ken's skeleton, stripped to the bone. Thankfully there was nothing but an empty street. All the lizards were gone. The spiders were obviously doing their job.

"There!" Sam pointed to a camera shop, and they pulled up to its facade. As promised, a camera drone was displayed in the window.

The door was locked, so they broke a window to get the door open. They were cockier about making noise, now that they had acquired protection, but Sam didn't want to push their luck. He kept the volume of his voice down.

"Find one still in the package. We may need the instructions."

They located two camera drones, still sealed in the box.

"A thousand bucks!" Stu whistled. "You kidding me?"

"The good ones aren't cheap. But they have a lot of features we'll need. Besides, I have good credit here."

The second model was smaller and cheaper in quality, but they took it, too, as a back-up. Next they drove up the street to the drugstore for more antibiotics, this time cleaning out the shelves. Finally, they hit the grocery store and loaded up again on canned goods, coffee and bottled drinks. The back of the van was packed full. Stu took a carton of cigarettes and threw it on the front dashboard.

They ate beef jerky and pork rinds for lunch. *These things will last for decades*, Sam thought. He popped open a can of soda. The pop and fizz carried across town and echoed back. He couldn't wait to get out of this deserted death town once and for all.

He walked along the street. The scuff of his sneakers on the pavement sounded singularly loud. It was hot for this time of year, so close to fall, and scarcely any breeze moved the still air. His eyes fixed on the bar that Ken had burst out of just before he was eaten. The porch railing was busted, but there was no other sign of the struggle that had occurred. This ghost town now had real ghosts to deal with, tenants who would not pass on.

Sam stood for a long moment and bathed in the disgust he felt for this place. Then he heard Stu and his brother talking.

"Last chance, guys," Stu said. "Anything else we need? We may not be back here for a long time."

"Cement," Shane said. "What about cement to repair the wall."

"Hmm. Don't see anything like that here."

"There's a hardware store, take a look."

Stu and Shane crossed the street to a combination hardware and auto body store with building supplies. They searched and found two bags of ready-mix concrete. It might not be enough, but it would help get the rebuilding started. They loaded it into the back seat.

Sam took a few more steps. He held up his soda can and electrified it. It became hot, and the soda boiled inside. It didn't hurt his hand; he didn't even feel it. After a few more seconds, he stopped it and sent the can flying down the street with a bolt of electricity. The hot projectile landed three hundred yards away and bounced to the side of the road, then began to roll. He watched it spin down a sewer grate.

"Come on, Sammy." Shane called out.

With the van packed wall to wall, Sam had to put the concrete bags on the floor under his feet. He sat back and closed his eyes.

At last, they drove out of St. Marks and started back home. By now it was late in the afternoon, and they had another forty miles to go. Stu tried to go faster, but the roads twisted and turned, loaded with potholes and rocks. It was hard to drive above 40 mph, especially with the van fully loaded. They took the journey in silence, watching the landscape pass.

Suddenly Shane clapped his hands together and broke the lull: "Devil Girl from Mars!"

"Beg your pardon?" Stu asked.

Shane turned to Sam. "Before, remember, I said *Demon Girl*. But it's *Devil Girl*. That's been bugging me all week."

Sam tried to get comfortable with his feet propped up on the bags of concrete. "Glad you could get that off your chest."

"Hot damn," Shane shouted, extremely pleased with

himself. "I knew I'd remember it."

But Sam couldn't get so excited about the simple pleasures anymore. He thought about Bohai's words: *They think you're the next savior of the planet.*

Sam did not feel up to that bold challenge. He'd be happy to keep his brother and friends alive, and to keep his own life and sanity. But saving the world was beyond his scope. The notion overwhelmed him.

I saved another bullet... for you.

CHAPTER 24

WALTER stepped away from the window. His team had reported seeing aircraft over the past two days. Their altitude and lack of noise was astonishing. He had worked with the Pentagon before, and knew of only a prototype stealth bomber that could come close to this level of silent flying. He doubted this was it.

"That's another one," he said. "Any idea who's flying them?"

"Dexter, maybe?" Dr. Max Witherspoon suggested.

"The technology is too advanced. I don't think it could be him."

"Pentagon then."

"No. It's different. It's a new technology. It may be part of the Arctic project. Damn peculiar – it's a bloody mystery to me."

Walter had worked briefly on the Arctic project, Project Helium, before being pulled off for reasons unknown. It involved technology being developed under the shroud of secrecy only the Arctic pole could offer. What he had seen there would shock most people. He often suspected more was going on there than even he had been told. That was common with such projects, but this time he suspected its roots were more sinister. No one actually knew who funded it, or who ran it. At one point they claimed to have an alien pilot in detention, but then denied it. Everyone he ever knew who worked on Project Helium eventually just disappeared.

His wife entered the room. "Come get something to eat, Walt. You were up all night in the lab. Get some food, then sleep."

"Yes, dear," he said. He humored her, and ate the sandwich she provided. But then he would go back to work. No time for sleep, until either he or Dexter were dead.

The sound of a vehicle could be heard, wheels on the gravel outside. Someone had arrived. Max and Walter rushed out of the house to see the Sergeant and another man pull up in a jeep that carried a cage under a tarp. The Sergeant hopped out and met Walter and Max at the back bumper.

"It's getting harder to catch them," the Sergeant said.

"Been fully tranquilized?"

"Yes, Sir."

"You sure?"

"Down and out. I assure you. We used the elephant gun." The military man pulled the tarp off the cage to reveal a gray and brown lizard asleep inside. It was two and a half feet long, small compared to most of the others.

Walter was pleased. The smaller ones were much

easier to handle.

"Get it into the lab," he ordered. He turned to Max. "I want blood samples taken right away, and a saliva culture. You know the drill. Same as before."

He turned back to the Sergeant. "And get rid of the last one. It's dead."

Dexter was furious. Only two men had returned from the raid alive. One of them was Mitch, who now reported in, after being treated in their makeshift hospital for a bullet wound to the leg.

"You're all idiots," Dexter hissed. "You had a damn M1 cannon, and you still couldn't take their camp?"

"It's a fortress, boss," Mitch tried to explain. "We didn't really know how to use that gun. You said it would be easy. And you wouldn't let us fire any to practice."

"We only had three rockets! If I let you inbred fools practice, we'd have none. How hard can it be to point and shoot?"

Harder than you'd think, Mitch thought, but stayed silent.

"And you lost one of the trucks!"

"They had help, boss. Someone was behind us, in the woods. Les said it was the cop. He said he saw him."

"What cop?"

"A State Trooper, Stuart Reese. He's always busting our chops up here. Arrested Les twice! Once he confiscated two automatic rifles. Said they was illegal.

Damn nuisance cop."

Dexter pressed down on Mitch's wounded leg, and the man winced in pain. His leg and side were on fire.

Dexter leaned in close. "Get me the boy, the one who is *different*."

"I promise, we'll get him. Let me take a crew out now. They got no gate no more. We did take that down. We did that, boss."

Dexter backed away and walked across the room to his desk, shoved a stack of books onto the floor. His rage was blinding; he worried he might turn and kill the other man at any moment. Instead he picked up a letter opener and stabbed it into a stack of papers. He struggled to regain control of his emotions.

"No. We move on, and get back to them later. I want you to get me the rest of the chemicals and reactive agents I need. Get everything on that list. Take the men on an overnight trip."

"Sure boss."

"I need to focus on the real project. I'll get back to that peculiar boy, later."

He speculated he knew why Sam was different. Dexter knew more than he was letting on. "Those other kids will get their day of reckoning, and Walter too. But first things first. Get the rest of what I require."

"You got it," Mitch said. It hurt to put any weight on his leg. He took a step back, limped toward the door and waited to see if there was anything else. He never knew quite what to say to this strange little man.

Dexter was thinking: *I'm tired, I miss my home.* After a brief silent moment, he turned in a rage. "Now! What are you waiting for?"

Mitch hobbled quickly through the doorway and out of the room, trying not to bear down on his right leg. The men in the compound needed Dexter right now for many reasons, as he knew how to generate power and keep the place running. But Mitch knew that someday they would need to kill the mad genius. He also knew he was going to enjoy doing it.

CHAPTER 25

BOHAI awoke from his long sleep and managed to sit up. His head rang as if it had spent the night inside of a drum at John Bonham's last Zeppelin concert. His mouth felt dry. It took several swipes of his tongue to reassure himself he didn't have a mouth full of cotton.

Tina sat next to him and smiled down with that motherly expression she often wore. She brought him a glass of water, and he thought it tasted like cool heaven soaking every inch of his throat. She fed him some oatmeal and made him take his antibiotics. After he ate, she cleaned up his wound a little better and changed the dressing. As Tina left to sterilize her tools, Mark came in to check on the patient.

"That was pretty gross," he remarked. "I saw it, when she did surgery on you."

"I can imagine," Bohai said.

Mark poured him another glass of water, looking comically like a miniature adult taking things in hand. On his belt, the kid wore a pistol that looked heavy and incongruous.

"Does your lion cat have a name?" he asked. His small

high-pitched voice didn't match the years in his eyes.

Bohai relished the second glass of water in heavy gulps before answering. "He does. But we can't really pronounce it. I like to call him Zeus, for the mythical god of thunder."

"Cool."

"Speaking of which, where is he now?"

"I saw him dragging the dead bodies outside somewhere," Mark said.

"No kidding?"

"I'm glad. I didn't want to do it. You know, my mom and Camila are still washing brains off the front steps."

"Eww. That can't be fun. At least this got me out of that chore, right? There's a silver lining."

"Yeah, I guess so."

"I'm worried Zeus will scare the others, and they might hurt him. Can you send him in here, if you see him?"

"You want me to send your big lion in here? Are you crazy? I'm scared to go near it."

"He's actually a cougar. Don't worry, he won't hurt you."

"Can I touch him?"

"Maybe," said Bohai, wondering if Zeus would misunderstand the gesture. "Or maybe just send him in to me first."

"I guess. If you say so."

Bohai's headache softened, but remained a tiny prick of pain at the base of his neck. He drank more water and leaned back. "Where are the others?"

"Supply run."

"Already? Why so fast?"

"Get more guns, I think."

"Is anyone else hurt?" He hesitated to ask the young kid his next question. "Did anyone get killed?"

"Yes and No." Mark answered simply.

Bohai grabbed the kid by the arm. "What does that mean?"

"Some of those bad men got killed. A couple of our guys got hurt, but none of us got killed. We thought you might. Be killed, that is. But you didn't. I'm glad you didn't get killed. It's good you're alive."

Bohai was relieved. "Thanks, kid. Who got hurt? How bad?"

"Sam was punched out in the face, and Jason got shot," Mark explained. As an afterthought, he added, "...but they're okay now."

Tina came back into the room. She looked tired and overburdened. Her new hospital duties were weighing heavy on her.

"No more questions; you should rest. Sleep some more. And you," she pointed to Mark, "Go outside. Lily and your mom need help fixing the garden. There's a lot of rubble that needs clearing. But first take a water bottle up to Jason in the tower."

Bohai started to protest his confinement to the bed, but the pills and the headache were making him sleepy. He settled back and looked up at the ceiling. Only now did he notice the chandelier above his head. It was wildly ornate and beautiful. He stared at it until he drifted off to sleep.

The van arrived back at the lodge moments before dinner time. They put the wrecked truck in neutral and rolled it aside, so they could drive the van back into the courtyard. Everyone helped to unload the supplies, and Camila offered to cook dinner. She was excited to have a few new choices from the fresh supply of canned goods.

While dinner was being cooked, Sam tinkered with one of the drones. The task of flying it would be a lot more complicated than he'd first thought. The first obstacle was getting it turned on. Its batteries would need to be charged, and that might take all night with their slim solar power supply. If he used his powers, he might fry the circuits. Powering complex machinery with his abilities never turned out well. Best to wait for the solar panels.

"Here's to the sun," Stu said, raising a beer to the sky. Ironically, the sun was now going down.

Most of the lights were kept off to conserve power. Two lights were always kept on in the lobby, for emergencies. When dinner was ready, they ate with a single lamp at each end of the long table. Despite the dark corners and deep shadows they cast, the dim light gave the lobby cafe a warm glow.

Everyone sat at the main table for tonight's dinner,

except Tina who took her first turn in the watchtower. She couldn't shoot a gun, but she could shout if anyone came up the road. Since she was the house doctor, she didn't need to do guard duty, but she said she wanted the time alone. She would stand guard an hour until after dinner. The death of Ken had not finished torturing her. It would wrestle with her a few more rounds.

Even Bohai made it to the table, and snowball sat on Lily's lap. Only Zeus was not present, still missing since late afternoon. Bohai hoped the cat was still out tending to the dead, and not hurt in some way.

They feasted on canned tuna made into grilled tuna patties. They treated themselves to lemon tea made from powder stirred into stream water. As always, apple slices served as dessert. Sam thought he never before had enjoyed one great meal with friends around a single table. It felt nice. Stu was grateful, too. He had spent most of the last ten years eating fast food, and eating alone.

"We need to start fishing," Shane announced. "Get some real fish on these plates. That stream out back is full of trout."

"I'd like to fish," Stu said. "Haven't gone fishin' in years."

"You know chickens are birds," Camila reminded them. "So there should still be some around, since the birds were not affected by the mutation."

"True that," Sam said. "We could use them for fresh eggs. If we can find any hens."

"I'm on it," Jason said. He pushed his long hair back.

"We can check out some farms later on in the week." They wouldn't get the chance, but it was a nice idea.

"First we should fly the drone over Dexter's place," Sam said. "And see what he's up to. Tomorrow we should do it."

"Can we do that from here?" Jason asked.

"I wish, but no.... not exactly. We may have to get closer. The range is only five miles."

"How can we see what it sees?"

"It will broadcast to my phone. I know there's no actual phone reception anymore, but it can still communicate with the drone. I'll tether them to each other. We should be able to see whatever it sees."

"And if it gets shot down?" Shane asked. "I mean, that is a possibility. Dexter isn't stupid, he'll have guards all over. Can't they just look up?"

"Yeah, I haven't worked that out yet," Sam admitted.

"Fly it at night," Stu suggested.

"Hard to see. Video needs bright light," Sam explained, biting his lip. "But maybe we could fly over fast. Get some video of what they're up to, and fly it back quickly. In and out."

"Maybe we don't need to fly it over the compound." Jason spoke as if he were thinking out loud. "We just need to see if they're gettin' all ready for a bigger attack. Can we see enough from a distance like?"

"Not sure. We can try. We need to see if he has any other big weapons inside that compound of his. Any more rocket launchers."

Lucy came back from the kitchen with another glass of tea. Likely it was spiked. "Try is good. Can always try." She was getting drunk. The others exchanged looks, but didn't say anything. Tina made a mental note to hide the booze later.

"You should sing for us," Jason said. "You were in some pop group, right?"

"Yeah!" Lily clapped her hands. "Sing, mommy."

"I was the best singer," Lucy announced. "In the hottest band. Oh yeah, and I had the best roadies, let me tell you." She winked.

Mark got up and left the room. He'd heard all this before. Sam decided to go, too. He didn't need any more drama today.

After dinner, Jason began playing around with an acoustic guitar he had found in the recreation room. He started strumming one of the Honeybee's songs, and Lucy began singing along. Her voice surprised him, and he skipped a note, but then got back on track. She sang the words perfectly on key:

"Days become short forays,
and the rain falls in the red.
These times look bleak and frayed,
Taken lands all dry and dead.

Away to walk and disappear,
Stroll with the living dead,

Anger full, and empty heart,
Every single tear you shed.

Never turn nor look away,
Never shut your mind too tight,
Keep open your eyes wide,
In the end we'll make it right.

Time twists in tidal shifts,
Rips the world in three or two,
May we face it ever strong,
Maybe start anew."

Shane enjoyed listening. It was simple and sweet – one of the few Honeybee songs he didn't dislike. The song was about sadness after a break-up, but it fit well as a requiem to the loss of Earth.

"Almost makes me like her," he whispered to Camila.

Sam enjoyed it, too, but he didn't stay for the whole song. Instead he climbed the watchtower to relieve Tina. She looked pretty with her hair cut shorter. He wondered at what point that had happened. Her blouse fit snug as always.

"Hair cut?"

"Yeah," she said. "During surgery it was getting in the way. Afterwards I had Lucy cut it for me. Did you know she used to cut hair before she became famous? Anyway, short hair is easier this way, considering... you know."

"I guess so." He ran a hand through his own hair and

pushed it out of his eyes.

"She seemed happier cutting my hair. I bet she was a good person in her old life, before the rock star experience. I bet she was happy before she became rich and famous."

"Isn't everyone?" He smiled and shrugged. "Well, I like it. Looks good."

"Thanks. It's my 'end of the world' look."

"Very pretty. Now you should go downstairs and get something to eat. It's still warm."

"Thanks, I will. How's the black eye?"

"I'll survive." He subconsciously touched it with his fingers, not realizing how often he kept doing that. "I've had worse."

As she left, she kissed his cheek. It was quick and simple, and he tried not to read too much into it. He assumed it was a sisterly peck on the cheek, nothing to worry about. Yet in his mind, he fantasized that it might be more – even if only for a second. He wasn't looking for a girlfriend, and certainly not with the ex-girlfriend of a dead friend. Ken hadn't been a friend *per se*, but he had been a member of their group. Still, Sam harbored a million feelings that kept him awake some nights. After all, he was still human – an eighteen year old human male.

Still human. Thank God for that... he thought.

Bohai awoke to a faint thumping sound. He had been dreaming that crows were pecking on the window of his room back home. When he opened his eyes and lifted his head, he briefly thought he was there, back in his room at his parents' house in Toronto. Then he shook the sleep aside and remembered he was in a hotel room at the end of the world.

The thumping sounded again – ever so light – and he half-expected to see the crows from his dream at the large window of his hotel suite. But there were no crows outside his room now. Instead, a swarm of fireflies danced in the darkness just inches from the pane of glass. Like matches struck one after another, they lit a small corner the night with their glowing bottom parts.

"Liar, liar, pants on fire," he chanted quietly to himself. That was the rhyme his friends back home used to say whenever they saw fireflies at night.

He glanced at his watch: 5:15 a.m., then stepped to the wide window and lifted it open. The exertion on his arms caused the bandages to flex, and a burning ache shot up his side. He pushed a hand against his stomach and waited for the pain to ease. Although feeling much better, his chest and arm muscles complained with every movement. The headache was a bonus.

On the window's edge the fireflies careened in a circle over and around each other, their bottoms lighting on and off; but they were not frolicking. This was no waltz of joy. It was a dance of agitation. They wanted his attention and they wanted something more. He could hear their voice – and it was one voice, not several – speaking a single word: "Come."

After dressing quickly in the dark, he carried his shoes and stepped softly on socked feet, down the stairs and out the front door without making a sound. He slid his shoes on and crossed the garden, then slipped out the side door. At the front gate, he paused and waved at the watchtower. It wouldn't be good to get shot by his own side mistaking him for an intruder. Someone waved back, but in the darkness he couldn't be sure who.

Come.

Bohai followed the fireflies into the dense forest. He knew where they were leading him, and he knew what they wanted.

CHAPTER 26

WHEN dawn filtered into day, the war began.

That morning Sam woke to the sound of rocks hitting each other. He jumped out of bed and opened the closest window. Stu was gathering the stone pieces of the gate and stacking them into neat piles. Except for the rocks chinking together and the birds chirping, the morning was quiet. The air felt crisp, like any fall morning, and it smelled good, really good. If asked, he would have said that autumn was the only season you could really smell.

Sam went downstairs to the kitchen where Camila was cooking powdered eggs and instant coffee. It was 7:20, assuming the clock on the table still worked with any accuracy. He sat down, and Camila gave him a plate.

"Everyone else is still sleeping," Camila told him in a low voice scarcely above a whisper. "They were up pretty late. You feel okay?"

He touched his face again without realizing he was doing so. "I'm good. These eggs are great. Who would have thought? Powdered!"

"It's probably just because you haven't had real eggs

in weeks." She laughed.

He ate quickly, and reached for his phone to check emails. It was a habit that would not die soon. His phone no longer roosted in his pocket; it lay somewhere in his room with a dead battery. No emails, no news updates, no more Line messages. He missed all of them. Nothing to do about that now. He filled his coffee mug and went outside to check on Stu.

"The plan," Stu told him, "is to rebuild the gate with the pieces we still have. We'll seal it up with the cement we have on hand. But it will have to become a wall. Can't make it to open and close anymore. We'll have to seal it up as one big barrier. Try to make it strong."

"So how will we go in and out?"

Stu took him to the hedges on the side of the courtyard. He pulled the thick brush aside to reveal a door about six feet high, slightly smaller than a standard room door.

"I assume this was for the hotel staff," Stu said

"Sure, we can come in and out this way. But no cars. No vehicles. They'll have to be parked outside?"

"Yep, that exposes your van," Stu grumbled, toothpick in the corner of his mouth. He was trying to smoke less. "Someone could steal it or blow it up. But we got no choice."

"I understand. And we still have the guard in the tower. Anyone tries to steal it, we can see them, maybe even stop them. As for someone blowing it up... can't help that, I guess."

Stu agreed. "More important to have the front sealed off, if you get my point. And we need to check the rest of the wall. See if it's secure all around, even in back. Make sure there are no cracks. This is a big resort, so we should double check every nook and cranny."

"I'll look around now," Sam offered.

Sam took his coffee and wandered back through the resort grounds. He checked the wall for more doorways or for any cracks in the concrete, and pulled back the hedges for a better look at key points. The wall seemed solid, and no more doors popped up. He followed it all the way to the back, and then checked the other side.

At the rear of the lodge he noticed another watchtower, partly hidden by trees and vines. He had to pull hard to force its door open, stuck from months or years of disuse. Shorter than the front two towers, it stood about two and a half stories high, and its steps were cracked and dirty. He took them cautiously one at a time and rose up into the watch platform. A large blue jay had made its nest there. It sat calmly on its eggs and didn't stir when Sam appeared. *Tough bird*, he thought. Perhaps it was Bohai's presence at the lodge that put the birds at ease. Anything was possible.

A built-in telescope protruded on a stand at one end of the platform. This had once been a good place for tourists to do bird watching, but now suffered from years of corrosion. He cleaned the eyepiece with his shirt and peered through the scope. The rusty telescope swivel squeaked as he moved it. He looked down at the stream below and saw Zeus and a few other big cats drinking at the stream and catching fish for breakfast.

"Big Bro was right," Sam said aloud to himself. "Lots of trout in there."

He finished his coffee while enjoying the haunting, and yet peaceful, environs that only the back tower could provide. As the lodge sat on a hill, an embankment sloped down twenty feet to the stream. From here, he could see the top of the canopy of trees.

Sam thought about trying his spark – practicing the way Bohai had urged. He fought the temptation, at first. Too many years of denial were hard-wired into his system. Nothing about his special ability made him feel right. But after a bit of reflection, he gave in to it. He did not like to disappoint friends or family – and that was his greatest foible. He was too easily persuaded by loved ones. Sam too often did the wrong thing for the right reason. Now he prayed the use of his spark was not such a case.

First he looked in all directions to make sure no one else was around, then he opened the palms of his hands. He created a stream of electricity and balanced the ceramic coffee mug on it. Next, he built a sphere around the mug and moved it out onto the open air, out over the gully. He drifted it at least thirty feet from the ground and kept it hovering there, like a feather on air. It required almost no effort on his part.

He concentrated harder, and succeeded in spinning it. It whirled in mid-air, faster and faster. His control of his art was more impressive now than it had ever been. Losing restraint these past few weeks had done something to release it. Like releasing a demon, he wondered, or like unleashing power during a sprint? Either way, something had changed inside him. Every time he used his odd power, he felt corrupt, like a cheat. It was an uncomfortable feeling.

Now he raised the sphere higher, increased its size. It became a three foot diameter plasma ball and floated high over the stream. The cats decided to move on downstream away from it. He changed the spin direction, trying to control every axis, every point of its movement.

Suddenly the mug exploded and the sphere collapsed. The atmosphere crackled and sparked, as pieces of the ceramic mug fell into the water. They were so hot, they caused steam to hiss up into the air above the stream for a few seconds. And just as fast, the atmosphere stopped crackling, and the phenomenon was gone.

Like releasing a demon.

He took a deep breath. These sessions always winded him. It was as if he had run two miles, or swam five laps in a pool. His body was drained, but would regain energy quickly. He needed to sit down for a moment. The bird squawked but didn't fly off.

"Sorry about that," he apologized.

After a short rest, he left the tower and continued his inspection of the wall. Examining every stone, he made his way back toward the front. The wall appeared to be solid and without any new hidden doorways, cracks or weak points.

"No place for the demon to escape," he chuckled to himself. Not even he knew what he meant by that.

In the front yard, Jason and Stu had begun reassembling the gate. They had already added water to the concrete, and now Jason stirred it while Stu positioned the first stones. Sam helped spread the concrete and hold it in place. They didn't have the proper tools, but a spade found in the gardening shed seemed to work fine. Within an hour the wall was three feet high. It hardened fast in the morning sun.

"Let's go to four feet, and then let it set," Stu instructed. "We'll see how that goes, then shore it up with extra concrete tomorrow."

"But eventually we need to go all the way to the top, right?" Sam asked. He looked up at the twelve-foot high wall.

Stu shook his head. "We don't have enough cement. We can go about five feet I think, but that's all. At least it should slow down anyone who thinks of climbing over. And hopefully we can pick them off one by one from the tower. We'll go to four today, then add a foot on top tomorrow. We can lay some spikes in the concrete, sticking up. That should stop just about anyone from climbing over."

"Spikes? From where?"

"In the shed," Shane said. "We found a couple gardening tools with spikes."

"We can also break some glass bottles," Stu suggested. "Put the shards in the concrete sticking up. Anyone who thinks about scaling our wall will have to earn it."

"Yikes," Sam muttered.

"We need to protect this fort. Those men aren't playing games, and I don't think the lizards are either."

Camila came out and brought them some tea and packaged cookies. "Everyone's awake, and Jason's in the tower. His arm is healing. But Bohai is missing. He isn't in his bed."

"I didn't see him this morning," Stu said, "And I got up before the sun."

"He needs to rest, and heal. He shouldn't be outside."

"We'll go look for him later," Sam promised. "We need to finish this wall first so it can dry."

They set about bringing the wall to four feet, then took a break. Shane found some bottles to be broken and set in the top layer. They would add the shards and spikes tomorrow along with the last layer. Stu explained to them that an upright wall needs to harden in sections.

"I'll defer to your wisdom," said Sam, "since I know absolutely nothing about concrete."

The birds became flustered just then. Their warbling got noticeably louder and their movements more erratic. A flock separated from the trees and flew to the hotel roof. Snowball raced into the garden and stared intently at the sky, one paw raised as if preparing to run.

Something came out of the dark woods and approached the road: a hooded shadow. The figure stepped over the wire fence and tin cans, then approached the gate. It was Bohai wearing a hooded sweatshirt. With walking stick in hand and bandages peeking out of his sleeve, he peered over their new wall from the other side. He pulled his hood down.

"Good job, guys. But how do I get in?"

Sam motioned for him to go around to the side. When he opened the door, it occurred to him that there was no lock for it. They'd have to fix that later, and maybe even make some kind of barricade.

Bohai had been out hiking since early that morning, well before dawn. He didn't say much about where he had been, just that he had more news from the outside world. Even though his tone was light, a dark crease lived on his brow, and his eyes betrayed a deep worry. A great many things troubled him this morning, and he revealed only one of them.

"The armies are gathering," he told them. "Pittsburgh is overrun with lizards. They've started moving across the land. They're going from town to town, purging the countryside."

"Purging?"

"Weeding out the rest of the people. Killing and eating them – and anything else that's in their way."

"Damn." Sam handed him a bottle of water.

"The spiders are forming ranks and getting ready, but they're badly outnumbered. We should get ready here, because we'll have to fight soon."

"How much time do we have?"

"I think they'll reach us by tomorrow night or next day." Bohai gulped down the water. Eyes ringed with dark circles, he looked exhausted.

"Come inside and get something to eat," Camila said. "Get some rest. You're still banged up pretty bad."

Stu lit a cigarette. "New plan, gentlemen. Let this concrete set for a couple hours, then we get back to it. We finish it today."

"What about spying on Dexter?" Sam asked.

"Doesn't sound smart today. Let's stay close to home."

"We can fly your drone," Shane said, "But let's not go far. We'll go out a few miles. Stu, can you stay here and keep an eye on the wall?"

"Yep."

"Jason's in the tower, the others are inside recovering. It's you and me, Sammy."

Sam fetched the drone and gear and put it in the van. They left shortly before noon, and drove to a hill about five miles away. The drone wouldn't reach Dexter's compound from there, but it might be able to get a distant aerial view.

Sam positioned the drone on top of the van while Shane stood guard. He paced around the van with his crossbow ready in both hands. The lack of any movement made him nervous. There were no sounds, not even crickets out here. Their arachnid bodyguard hadn't come today, either. The spiders had disappeared altogether.

The drone had four sets of propellers installed on four wings, and a hi-resolution camera underneath. It whirred to life, and lifted precariously into the air. As it rose higher, it steadied; Sam was getting the hang of it.

The drone took off and flew over the trees, the valley, and quickly disappeared from sight. It was preset to come back to its GPS base if it ever got to the edge of its range. Right now it was three miles out. It could go a bit further, five miles max.

The brothers huddled around the phone and fixed their eyes on the screen. Thus far only trees and dirt appeared on camera. It was hard to discern any life through the small lens. Sam slowed the drone, so they could see more details. At five miles, they found Dexter's compound, but it was a distant image. The red light on the screen indicated the drone was at the end of its reach where its safety mechanism prevented it from going further. It hovered in that single spot, broadcasting its captured view.

They didn't see much around the compound. A tiny guard was barely visible on the wall. Something shifted in the trees outside Dexter's camp, but there was no way to tell what his men were up to.

"We need to get closer," Sam said.

"Can't you focus in?"

"Not much zoom, it's meant for wide shots. We should drive nearer. At least two miles over."

"No more high points between here and there,"

Shane warned. "It's all open field. We could be seen."

"Just for a minute. I can't see anything here."

Reluctantly, Shane drove the van off the hill and out onto the field. He was able to stay off the roads, but the grass-covered terrain grew increasingly rocky and hard to handle. Sam continued to monitor the six-inch screen. As they moved, the drone was able to move too. It got closer and closer to the compound.

"Hey. Stop," Sam said.

"Sam, we're in the middle of a field. Let's at least get next to the trees."

"Holy hell. Look!" Sam's eyes hadn't left the screen.

Shane leaned over and looked at the tiny monitor, but he couldn't figure out what he was looking at. "Stop shaking the phone, hold it steady. What am I supposed to be looking at?"

In the distance, gunshots were fired. They were barely able to be heard, but were unmistakable. Another shotgun fired.

"There," Sam pointed on the screen. A horde of lizards burst out of the trees and descended on Dexter's compound. His men were shooting rifles and shotguns at them as fast as they could, but the horde was massive. A swarm of at least a thousand reptiles climbed over each other to get to the front line. From the high-flying drone, it looked like army ants covering a hill or devouring a sandwich.

"Start the van," Sam said. When Shane hesitated, he smacked his arm and cried out, "Start the van! Get us out of here."

They estimated they had about twenty or thirty minutes before the horde would reach them. They were wrong.

They turned the van around and spun onto the open road. Before they even crossed the ridge, a different legion of reptiles barreled from the trees and headed directly for them. This was a smaller "side patrol," only forty or fifty reptilian soldiers, but it was enough to overtake the van. Sam had no doubt the creatures would be able to topple the vehicle, break the windows and get inside. He dropped the phone and got his pistol ready.

Several of the largest lizards reached the road and blocked their way. Sam rolled down his window and fired his gun. This wasn't helping – dead bodies are no easier to drive over than live ones.

Shane pulled off the road and headed across the field. He applied the gas, but the rough terrain came close to putting them on two wheels and spilling them. When he slowed down to keep the van upright, a lizard reached them and climbed up on the roof. Several more got in front and blocked them in. Shane stopped the van.

Within seconds they were surrounded.

"In the glove compartment, open it!" Shane yelled.

Sam opened the compartment and found another gun and a grenade.

"Give me the pineapple. The grenade!"

He handed it gently to his brother, and Shane tossed it out the window. The blast rocked the van; it felt like an earthquake. While the explosion killed five of the reptiles; it did nothing to slow the others.

One of beasts jumped on the front grate and glared at them through the window. Its eyes were glassy and red. It bashed its head on the front windshield; the strength of these creatures was amazing, and terrifying. A small crack appeared, which gave the animal confidence to try again. It reared its head back and smashed down one more time. The crack spread wider.

Sam and Shane sat ready with their guns pointed straight ahead at the windshield.

"When the windshield gives, shoot until you're out," Shane ordered. "Then grab that second gun, and shoot some more."

"Got it."

"Today their meal is not free."

After spending his bullets, Sam would use every ounce of power to electrify as many of them as possible. When that power was exhausted... well, it would be over.

The van rocked from the force of lizards banging against the side, and a few jumped on the roof. Their hissing and groaning was unbearable. At least one of the boys would be eaten today, and probably both, Sam thought. The back window splintered, but did not give way.

Like my brother said, you will pay dearly for this meal.

Sam aimed his gun for the lizard breaking the front windshield. That one dies first.

The creature pulled back and aimed its head for a final

thrust to burst through the glass. As it started to rear its head for the attack, its body slid backwards. Its eyes widened in confusion, as it was pulled back again by the tail. Something had hold of its posterior, and now heaved it roughly to the ground. It was a spider!

God bless the spiders! Sam thought.

Three giant tarantulas began tossing the lizards from the van, then smaller two-foot spiders paralyzed them with venom, liquefying the reptile organs from the inside. Through the cracked windshield, the boys saw an army of several hundred spiders teeming over the ridge, devouring the reptile patrol with the speed and force of a hurricane wind. A few spiders lost their legs, but within minutes all the reptiles were either paralyzed or dead.

The spider army marched past them, on to war.

"Let's get home," Sam said.

As the spiders continued their advance, they made a narrow opening for the van. The boys negotiated the path, careful not to hit any allies. As the van drove onto the road and back towards home, the mighty arachnid army disappeared in the rear-view mirror.

PART III

"You can only pull weeds so many times, before you decide to kill the garden, and start over."

– Loxtan Vhar

CHAPTER 27

OVER the next two days the war intensified.

The two armies clashed, giving rise to beastly screams that could be heard in every corner of the county. Sam and his group of survivors climbed to the ninth floor of the hotel, where they benefited from a higher view and a false sense of security. Through the binoculars they watched for miles. Although they couldn't see much of the actual fighting itself, except for a skirmish here and there, they smelled the heavy stench of war in the air. It came with a palpable feeling of pain and despair. Even before Bohai's updates from the deep woods, they knew it was bad.

"Dexter's compound may not have survived," Sam said. "And Walter. No idea if his team is still alive."

"Walter was pretty confident," Shane reminded him. "He had something up his sleeve. Underground bunker, maybe. He's the kind of guy who plays with a five-ace deck."

"What does that mean?"

"It means I'm sure his team is fine."

They had finished repairing the wall, complete with

broken glass shards embedded in the concrete, and an alarm bell was installed in the main tower. Guns were placed in key locations, and they added a new guard station on the ninth floor. Undermanned, they couldn't watch everything at all times, but someone looked out from the top floor at least once every two hours. They would have some warning if the lizard army broke through and marched on their camp.

The drone found its way back to the GPS base. The boys examined the video footage, but there wasn't much more to see. It showed massive armies of reptiles descending on Dexter's compound, and then the spiders pushing them back. On the return flight, the drone showed only empty woods.

Bohai had disappeared again for a full day. When he returned, he called a meeting with the group. His expression was hard to read, but Sam saw shadows of uncertainty on Bohai's face. Perhaps it was just because he was still wincing from the pain in his wounds He had returned alone; Zeus had not come back with him this time.

"The war is going bad for us," he informed them. "The lizards outnumber everything else."

"We knew that," Sam said.

"If the lizards are actually mutated people, there would be like millions of them," said Jason. "Right?"

Bohai nodded and continued: "But they are disorganized. They don't have a leader. They throw themselves at anything that moves, and there is no strategy to their fighting, and no art of war. The spiders have that advantage over them. The spiders are well organized."

"Awesome," Shane said and gave a mocking thumbs-up. This time he wasn't sure what he meant by that. *Our fate is in the hands of eight-legged creatures. Who have no hands.*

"And I just realized something else," Bohai said. "The lizards are mutations from humans, but the spiders are not. The reptiles are transformations, mutated from humans or human hosts. The spiders were always spiders; they simply got bigger as an effect of the same virus or biological weapon that mutated the humans. That's a big difference."

"So, that's why the reptiles have no leader," Sam deduced.

"And the spiders do. They have generals and war plans. They are smart and organized. But the numbers still work against them."

"And the bats?"

Bohai shook his head. "That I don't know. They seem to be further south. Not sure if they are mutations or not."

"Then, if it's going so bad," said Jason, "the lizards will eventually reach us. And take us down. Eat us alive."

Sam thought of Ken, devoured by the enemy. *What a terrible way to go.* This was the fate that awaited them, too.

"It's time to live up to our end of the bargain," Bohai said. "We have to help fight."

"I'm ready," Jason declared resolutely. He held up his

rifle. "They come up that road, I'll send them to hell."

"We have to do more than that." Bohai felt a twinge of pain in his chest and sat back. His side hurt, too, so he shifted position. "We have to go on the offensive, and backup our friends."

"How do we do that?"

"I need some of you to come with me. The spiders found something they want me to show you."

"Found what?"

"I'm not sure."

At noon, Stu took the wheel and drove the van with Sam and Bohai, out to see whatever the spiders wanted to show them. Meanwhile Jason, his arm still in a sling, stayed behind with Shane and the others to guard the fort.

Shane helped Camila clean up the kitchen. With her long black hair tied back, he thought she looked especially happy today.

"You like to cook," he observed.

"Always. I love it."

"You had a husband? Kids? Before all this?"

"Not yet." She continued scrubbing the counter. "I had a boyfriend. But he disappeared a few days before it all happened. Someday I want kids. Or, maybe not, because of all this..."

"We'll be safe again, someday. Trust me," he promised.

"We can adopt Lily and Mark, when Lucy drinks herself into the grave." She motioned to Lucy passed out on the couch.

"Sorry. I can't manage other people's lives. I can barely manage my own."

"I can. I'm hiding all the booze." She sent an angry look toward the passed-out rock star.

In the afternoon, Shane and Mark went out back to catch some fish. The young boy was an enigma. Years of dealing with a rock star mother and her abusive boyfriends had left him strong, but cold.

"Am I doing it right?" Mark asked. He cast his line out again, and it plopped on the water.

"You're doing fine. Is this really your first time fishing?"

Mark nodded.

"Sam and I used to fish all the time." There was a quiet pause. "Look, if you need anything you can ask me or Sam. Or any of us."

"I know." The boy shrugged.

"I can teach you to do stuff."

"I know."

Shane decided to let the matter drop. Maybe the kid didn't need a father or a big brother. So far he seemed to be holding up better than any of them.

They fished most of the afternoon. Mark had very little luck. He caught only one small fish, and Shane explained to him why they release the small ones. After a long uneventful hour, Shane caught a trout big enough to eat. He was disappointed at how hard it was to catch the fish with so many in the stream. Though he had a hunch it was the quality of their bait, a part of him believed even the fish were living in fear these days.

"Tomorrow morning we'll dig up some worms."

"Really? Cool," Mark said.

Shane managed to catch one more trout, and had just netted it, when the alarm bell rang. Jason was shouting something from his tower perch and making lots of commotion.

The birds squawked and scattered.

"What now," he groaned, dropping his fishing gear.

The bell continued to ring.

"Get your gun," he told Mark. "Follow close behind me."

They hunkered down behind bushes and cheated their way along the side wall toward the front. They managed to sneak back to the front gate without being seen, or seeing anything themselves. Shane's bow was drawn, and Mark held his pistol in both hands. They could see Jason up in the watchtower aiming his rifle at something on the road, and they heard the loud roar of something that sounded like tractors or heavy machinery.

Shane chanced a quick peek around the corner.

Holy hell, what has Dexter done now?

Four military tanks thundered up the road toward the gate. They sounded like engines of death, grinding out their metallic march. The clamor had startled everything, clearing the woods of all the birds, bees and butterflies; ribbons of color took to the air. The first tank thundered forward until it reached the front gate, a few yards from the newly repaired gap, and the others followed.

Oh hell, was all Shane could think. *We won't be able to fix the wall this time.*

The leading tank rolled to a stop, and the other three metal monsters lurched and halted on the road behind it. In the back of the line, the top hatch of the fourth tank popped open. Shane half-expected to see Mitch stick his head out and grin. Instead, a soldier jumped up from the hatchway and sat on its edge. His quick military movements were as sharp as his buzz cut. He dropped to the ground and walked up to the front gate. For a long ten seconds he scrutinized the lodge, its towers, wall and grounds. Then he put his hand on the pistol at his belt and spoke with a deep voice:

"Please lower your weapon, sir."

CHAPTER 28

THE van slogged as far as it could on a rough trail that was certainly not meant for a large van like theirs. It was more likely meant for a bicycle or motorbike, and now was consumed by brush and undergrowth. After a few miles, they couldn't travel any further on four wheels. The three of them spilled out of the van and continued the rest of the way on foot.

They followed a single spider. It was able to move faster through the trees than the men could on the ground. This fact forced it to continually stop to let them catch up, and Sam could sense its impatience. However, the terrain was rough, and hard to cross on foot. Tree roots and vines covered the path, signs of a long period of disuse. The further they went, the more obvious it was that they were the first to disturb this path in many years.

As the dense canopy of trees blocked out more and more of the sun, a syrupy darkness collapsed around them. The air felt sticky, humid, and the underbrush tripped them on more than one occasion.

A branch smacked Sam in the face. Annoyed, he

brushed it aside. "How much further? Are we still even in the same country?"

"I don't think we've reached Canada just yet," Stu said, "but it does feel like we're as deep in the woods as we can get. You sure this is the right way?"

"I'm sure," Bohai promised. "It's not much further."

"You know, I've met some real hermits in my day," Stu confessed, "but none of them lives this far deep."

"We're almost there, I think. I hope."

Their guide had scurried off and disappeared. They forged ahead, pushing aside tangled branches and bushes with great effort. It was starting to look impossible to pass, when they saw an opening at the end of the path. Light filtered in from what looked like a clearing, and hope of a conclusion spurred them on.

At last, they reached the opening, and stumbled out onto a wide glade. It revealed something none of them had ever seen before: what the spiders had found and wanted them to see.

It was a paved tarmac with five AIFV tanks parked on it, alongside five Gage Stingray tanks, two AH-64 Apache helicopters, and a military barracks. The base looked to be well maintained. Someone had been here recently looking after this place.

"Holy granola," Stu said.

"Tanks? Choppers?" Sam asked. "They want us to join the war with these?"

"This is how we can help," Bohai said.

"I don't know how to fly a helicopter, do you?"

"No, but we can drive the tanks."

"I don't know how to drive a tank either," Sam fretted. "I'm pretty sure it's not like driving a car."

"Why not? It can't be that hard."

Then a voice from the barracks said, "It's not."

A stout man in military fatigues, buzz-cut hair, stood in the building's doorway. He looked to be in his mid thirties. He studied them for a moment, then stepped forward, his boots thudding on the tarmac.

"Private George Sinclair, at your service."

Stu was the first to shake his hand. "I'm Stu Reese, this is Sam and Bohai. Have you been living here? Have any idea what's going on out there?"

"We lost contact with our command post two weeks and five days ago. Two by two the rest of my division went to see what was wrong. No one came back. Rex and I waited a week, then we went out to investigate ourselves. You wouldn't believe what we saw."

"Oh, I think we might."

They exchanged accounts of their experiences over the past week. George was one of a fourteen soldiers guarding this hidden base out in the middle of nowhere. No one knew why the base was here, including him. In small groups, they started going out to see why there was no communication from the outside world. The patrols never came back. George and Rex were the last to go out. In the middle of a lizard attack, they got separated, and George found his way back to the base.

"If he made it out alive, he'll come back here," George said. "I've been here alone for a few days. Thought I might be the last human on Earth. You're the first I've seen since I lost Rex." There was an innocent twang to his voice that was almost a caricature of an army man, the way TV likes to depict them, a cross between Gomer Pyle and Radar O'Reilly. It was comforting in its own way. But unlike those TV characters, George looked big and capable.

"How do you know you can trust us?" Sam asked. To the others, it was an odd question, but Sam wanted to know. He didn't think he himself would jump up to help just anybody – not after meeting Dexter.

"Son, I was a few days from shooting myself in the head, before you came along. I don't want to be the last man on Earth."

Sam understood. He understood completely. With a wan smile, he nodded and signaled for George to continue.

"So, if you don't mind. I'm tickled pink to see three other human beings on my base. You may have just saved my life."

"And you can show us how to drive those tanks?" Stu asked.

"Truth be told, it actually is a bit like driving a car," George smiled. "And I'm happy as a June bug to show you."

"We'd be taking these into war," Sam reminded him.

"War against the reptiles."

"I do understand that, son. Sorry I can't fly the Apaches. I'm not a pilot. Those would be real handy, but we got no pilots left. They'll have to stay grounded, least for now."

"The tanks will help a mighty lot," Stu said. "We have a fort of our own twenty-five or thirty miles from here. Others in our group are waiting., so we need to get some of these big machines back over there."

"Well, we can take four, I guess. There's four of us, each driving one."

"What about the van?" Sam asked.

"We can come back and get it later," Stu said. "But the path is a bit narrow for these beasts."

"We go out the other side." George pointed past the barracks. "There's a dirt road. That leads to a narrow path, but the Stingrays can get through anything."

George took them to the small barracks and handed out bullet-proof flak jackets. They also took a couple boxes of military rations for the Lodge.

It was George's opinion they should take four of the newer Stingray tanks. Lacking any experience of their own, they deferred to his better judgment; it was his party. Time was short, so they got a quick thirty-minute lesson from George, then hopped in.

Sam squeezed into driver's seat of the tank and leaned back. It was a tight fit. These things were not easy to get in and out of, despite what the movies portrayed. George had taught them that the pedals were gas and brakes, and the second throttle and gears were activated by hand. The square steering wheel moved like any car, or so George assured them. Sam was not so sure. His confidence was paper-thin.

The machine started and its vibrations resonated throughout his slim body. He worked the controls; the tank lurched forward, and Sam struggled with the wheel, fought to control it. Though he nearly crashed into the empty tank next to him, he avoided the collision and managed to straighten the wheel. He pulled out behind Stu's tank, and followed it.

Stu drove in the lead, followed by Sam and Bohai. George wanted to cover the rear, so he could watch the others and help if they got off course or experienced any problems with their vehicles.

As instructed, Stu passed through the open exit and followed the one and only road off the small military base. Sam kept his tank a safe distance behind Stu, in case of a quick stop. They drove slowly at first, crushing shrubs and destroying the path to the main road. Once they gained the paved road, a road that Stu was already familiar with, Stu sped up and cruised at 50 mph. Sam didn't like this, but he aimed to keep up.

I don't care what George says, this definitely isn't like driving a car, he thought.

Nothing blocked their way except for a single abandoned car, which Stu easily pushed aside with his armored vehicle. It dented one corner of the car and nudged it off the road. There were no enemy reptiles along this route yet; this part of the land was still in friendly hands.

Nothing about the drive was comfortable for Sam. The one saving grace was going to be the look on Jason and Shane's faces when four tanks pulled up. Some things in life are still priceless.

The tanks rolled up to the Peak Castle Lodge, and Sam saw Jason in the tower, ready with his rifle drawn. Shane was peering around the side corner at ground level. Sam couldn't get his lid open; he couldn't see any lever to release it. Through the viewer, he saw George approach Shane and ask him to disarm.

The hatch on the first tank slid open, and Stu popped his head out. "Look what we brung ya!"

Shane relaxed and stood back, taking a moment to absorb the impact of what he was seeing, and definitely relieved by it. Everyone lowered their weapons and let out a huge sigh of relief. Mark was in heaven; he walked around each tank, kicking the treads and soaking them in. With difficulty he tried to climb onto one.

George walked back and pounded his fist on Sam's tank. "It's the lever up behind your head."

Sam found the release lever and yanked it hard. The hatch made an emphatic *clunk* sound and opened. He was glad to be out of that tin can. It was hot in there, and he was starting to feel claustrophobic, like riding in an armored coffin. A second later, Bohai emerged from his hatch, too, and dismounted with some effort, holding his bandaged sides and wincing from the pain. He and Sam found their footing on the dirt road and ambled forward.

Sam felt dizzy.

Walking on foot is good, Sam thought. *This is natural, this is good.* He was glad to be rid of the vibrations and loud hum of the tank.

They brought George in through the side door, and introduced him to everyone. Lucy seemed the most interested. She felt his muscular arms, twice, and commented about "needing real men" a few times. This time she wasn't even drunk – just annoying.

Shane, Sam and Mark rode three of the bicycles out to retrieve the van. It was good for Mark to get out and feel useful. The kid was unbelievable in his lack of fear. He just needed something to do.

They reached the van without incident, loaded the bikes in back, and returned to the lodge before sundown.

The group gathered around the main table for dinner, and set about making a plan for the next stage of war. To Sam it seemed almost ludicrous: one cop, one soldier, and a bunch of kids planning for war.

Thank Heaven for Stu and George! Otherwise it would just be us kids.

"So, we've got four tanks," Stu said, "And can get more. But what exactly do we do with them?"

"Drive them into the heart of the enemy," Jason said

coolly. He smiled at the thought. "Go south and east, and keep shooting."

Stu raised an eyebrow. "I think we need a better plan than that."

"Yes sir, Stu is right," George said. "We need a plan. You can't just drive armored vehicles and shoot right and left. We need to decide on a formation and an objective."

"Take back Pittsburgh," said Shane. "And drive the enemy south. Kill as many as we can along the way."

Bohai shook his head. "We can't route them like a human army. They think like animals. They might not be so easily frightened into retreating like a normal squad of men. They'll keep coming at us, regardless of their casualties. And they have the numbers to outlast us."

Sam cleared his throat and spoke for the first time, his voice unsteady. "More than three hundred million people in America, all mutated into reptiles. That's a lot of enemies to fight."

"How many spiders, though?" Jason asked. "There have to be like millions, right? Or billions?"

"Not all of them were affected by the biological agent," Bohai explained. "Not all got bigger, certainly not three hundred million. More like twenty or thirty million. And a small percentage of them are in our area. We're badly outnumbered. And we don't know anything about the bats yet."

"Should we coordinate with General Tarantula, or whatever his name is?" Sam asked. "Not to sound ridiculous, but they're already fighting this war. And they found these tanks for us. Ask him what he wants us to do."

"I can try. I can go ask them tonight," Bohai said. "Come with me again, Sam?"

"Sure. I can do that," Sam agreed, although he'd really rather not.

"General who?" George asked.

"Uh, that's a long story."

"And it's gonna be a might hard to swallow," said Stu. "So buckle up."

They filled him in over dinner, and exchanged information about what both sides knew so far. They also told him about Dexter and his attack on their lodge. Jason and Shane told him what they knew about Walter and the secret lab. Like Stu, George was skeptical about some of it, but the broken world around him was starting to soften his hard head and his strong belief system. He hadn't seen the spiders yet, but he *had* seen the reptiles. That had shattered his entire outlook on life.

CHAPTER 29

AFTER dinner, Bohai took Sam on another trek into the deep woods to consult with the arachnid war counsel. Despite the full moon, it was dark inside the forest. The boys carried lamps and stepped carefully over the thick undergrowth at their feet. Where they were headed, no real paths existed.

When they arrived, a half mile into the forest depths, the spiders started to surround them and maneuver them into a clearing. Within the foliage, there was a hissing and a deep guttural growl. It sounded like a lizard.

Indeed the arachnids had a lizard with them, a prisoner they had captured and kept alive for some reason, and now two spiders dragged it to the clearing edge.

"What the hell is going on?" Sam asked.

The captive lizard, tied up tightly in silk web, hissed with rage. Two spiders held onto it and started to sever the web bonds. At the right moment, they thrust it into the clearing, and cut the last of its bindings.

It was loose!

A large tarantula nudged it forward toward Sam.

Another set of legs snatched the boys' guns from their holsters, and then the spiders backed away.

Sam and Bohai were unarmed, facing a huge lizard.

"What's happening?" Sam repeated.

"I don't know. I think they want you to kill it."

"They took our guns."

"You have other weapons, Sam. You know what I mean. You have to spark!"

They wanted Sam to use his powers. Was this a test, or something else? It wasn't clear, but what was clear was the set of fangs approaching them fast.

At first, the lizard was as confused as the boys, but it only took a few seconds for its instincts to kick in. The reptile lunged at the two humans, and Bohai fell backward on the ground. In the same instant, it swung its tail around and knocked Sam off his feet. Now it rush forward for the kill; its jaws opened wide. It leaped into the air and came down on top of Bohai.

Sam created an arc of blue electricity and sent the creature rolling off Bohai before its teeth could find the boy's neck. Sam raised himself up to his hands and knees and then regained his feet. He stood with his hands close together and generated a sphere of static power. He hurled it at the creature like a baseball.

The creature swung around as if to bat the sphere with its tail, and the ball exploded on impact. The creature's tail blew off. That didn't stop it. With blood dripping behind, the reptile spun around and headed for Bohai again. Sam produced another charged ball and threw it fast. The creature opened its jaws to swallow the blue projectile, and it landed spot on, directly in its mouth. Sparks bloomed, and the ball blew the creature's head clean off. Its lifeless body collapsed to the ground and spilled blood and guts onto the grass at their feet.

Breathless, struggling for air, Sam went down on one knee and rested a moment before reaching out to Bohai and helping him to his feet.

"What the hell was that!" he cried. He hated being forced to fight, and even more, he hated being forced to *power-up*.

Bohai stood up straight and backed away from the charred guts near his shoes. "That was pretty awesome, that's what that was! Amazing! I didn't know you could do that. Throw bombs like that."

"What?" Sam was still off balance, both mentally and physically. He had gleaned no pleasure or satisfaction from the ordeal.

"Impressive, man." Bohai slapped Sam on the back.

"That was terrifying."

"They want you to stop being afraid," Bohai said. "They need you to come out and fight with them. Like this. Not with arrows or guns, but with your gift, your powers. Your spark!"

"So they throw this beast at us?"

"They need you to stop hiding it."

"Screw them!"

Sam was angry, but he knew they were right. He knew he could do more for the cause if he stopped hiding his special abilities. This wasn't high school anymore. He knew it even before Bohai said it.

Bohai laid a hand on his friend's shoulder. "School's out, man. It's time to grow up, and wise up."

"I'm only one person. I can't fight a million of these lizard things."

"They say you're only using ten percent of your power. Is that true?"

Sam's breathing slowed and his heart stopped thundering, at least a little bit. He willfully began the process of calming down, coming down.

"I don't know. Just let me rest a minute."

He sometimes had trouble coming down from the high of powering-up. It was like a drug that sent adrenaline coursing through him, and then left him with a strange feeling when he was done. Sometimes he crashed. Maybe that's why he didn't use his power often: he felt guilty. It felt too good to use it, and remarkably bad when it was over.

Is this what junkies feel like? He wondered.

Bohai consulted more with the spiders, then the eight-legged creatures scattered. While the smaller two-foot spiders moved soundlessly, the tarantulas could be heard crunching through the foliage, like elephants.

"Let's go," he said. "You all right, Sam?"

"You know this isn't how I planned my life. I had a plan, and it didn't include... this."

"Life doesn't care about your plan, Sam. It doesn't care about your blueprint for four years of college and a wife with two and a half kids. All that is gone. Life just rolls on, with or without. Are you getting on board, or getting run over? It's up to you, man."

Sam looked down at the headless reptile body. Images of Ken filled his head, and at that moment he had no regrets. He would kill a thousand more of these things, and have no regrets. They weren't people, they were devils, abominations to be cleaned away.

"I'm with you," Sam said. He was agitated, but he wasn't angry anymore. "Whatever I can do."

The two boys walked back to the lodge in silence, but Bohai's words stayed with Sam all night.

School's out.

CHAPTER 30

INSIDE the lab, Walter and Max faced the cage and examined the subject inside. Max held the dart gun up to the bars and pulled the trigger. The dart pierced deep into the animal's scaly skin, causing the creature to scream and flailed against the bars. Entering its system through the carotid artery, the serum began to course through its cold veins, immediately affecting its vital organs. Frustrated and enraged, the animal snapped at the two men on the other side of the bars.

They watched to see its reaction to the serum. They were hoping it would undergo a major change. Reversing the mutation had proved impossible, so their new goal was to alter the mutation to make the creatures more docile. Since they couldn't change the deadly creatures themselves, their best hope was to remove the mutant's sense of rage, the instinct to attack.

Two previous subjects had failed. The serum had no effect on the first, and merely a minor effect on the second. Both subjects were later killed, and autopsies were performed. The experiences had earned the team very little insight or progress, and brought only scant new knowledge to the scientific effort. The mutation was far beyond their scope. And with more hordes clustering outside every day, time was running out.

Over the next hour, they studied the mutated reptile. It snarled and bit at the air every few minutes, then slammed its body against the bars again and again in a desperate attempt to attack the two scientists. Gradually its movements slowed, and its temper faded to a sleepy growl. The eyes glazed over. It lay down on the floor like a docile dog.

Max stuck a prod in the cage and tapped the lizard. It lifted its head, but didn't snap at the prod. Cautiously, the man reached in and touched its tail. When there was no reaction, he moved to the front and patted it on the head. The creature flicked its tongue, but did not try to bite the hand.

"A successful degree of change," Max said, and wrote notes on a clipboard. "This one looks promising."

"Monitor the subject overnight. We need to see if the effect remains, or if it is merely short-term."

"Exactly. I will check its reactions and its pulse every sixty minutes."

Walter felt good about this phase of the experiment. However, he was still bothered by the source of the original mutation. It wasn't from Earth, of that he was sure. It was a biological weapon from outside their world. *So, where did it come from? And where are those who sent it here?* The sophistication of the weapon impressed the entire research ream. But he wondered: *who would want to do this to our world?*

Who and why?

"I'm going to sleep. Wake me if anything happens."

In the morning, Walter was summoned to the lab. The reptile lay motionless on the floor of the cage. It was dead.

Max looked up when Walter came in. "We can try a smaller dose."

"What time did it die?"

"Four hours and twenty minutes after administration."

"I want an autopsy." Walter ordered. "Then get another creature. We'll try it again at half the dose."

"There's an upside." Max took his glasses off. "It kills them. We have a way to effectively kill the mutated beings."

"Yes, but not instantly. It takes time, too much time. Four hours and twenty minutes."

"Four hours isn't bad. We could wipe out whole swarms in less than a day."

"The real problem," Walter said, "is delivery. We can't shoot darts into a million creatures, directly into the neck of each one. We will need a better delivery system."

"Spray. I want to spray the next subject," Max put his glasses back on and wrote again on his chart. "Half dose, sprayed over the creature's head from a height of two meters. A fine mist."

"That is acceptable, but this serum is deadly to humans, too." Walter rubbed his eyes. "We'll need to be

277

well protected if we spray this out in the open air. And I want to know the effect on plant life. Put some plants in the cage with the next creature. I want a full report of the effect on the creature, the plants, and on us."

"Exactly," said Max. "We don't want to start the ecological end of the planet ourselves."

Walter stared wearily at the cage. "At this point only humanity is at risk. The planet will survive. Let's not make it worse."

For the next experiment they wore hazmat suits and sprayed a reduced dose of their new concoction into the cage. Two potted plants were added to the cage, three more in the room. The subject lizard snapped at the air and at the cloud being sprayed above its head. It smashed one of the potted plants with its tail. The toxicity levels in the lab rose to dangerous levels within two minutes.

Walter and Max watched intently for any reaction in their subject, or any change to the plants.

The first reaction came within thirty minutes: the plants started to wilt. One of them even turned brown. However, the creature barely reacted. It took an hour for a definitive reaction from the animal: it finally calmed down and looked to be sleepy. A test with the prod brought a halfhearted snap from its fangs. While it wasn't as docile as the last subject, it undoubtedly had lost most of its aggression. The experiment appeared to be a success. However, within two hours, all the plants were dead, and the toxicity levels in the room were still too high for human survival.

Walter and Max left the lab and unsuited.

"Failure," Max said impatiently. "At that dose, it didn't kill the subject, and its reactions did not even reach the desired level of docility."

"It would likely kill all humans in the same area." Walter sighed. "And all the plants. We can't spray this chemical agent out there. Delivery has to be via injection. Impractical."

"So we have nothing to offer. No way to kill or even disarm them." Max was tired. He lay on the sofa and closed his eyes.

"Don't give up, my friend. Back to the board."

At his own compound, Dexter was having an even worse day. Several of the lizards had slipped past his wall and managed to destroy some of his equipment. The Grinners even lost one of their generators. For now, the spiders were keeping the lizards at bay – a phenomenon he didn't yet understand – but he was grateful for the help. Unfortunately the battle front was moving back in his direction. The lizards were pushing forward hour by hour, and soon his compound would be at the front line again. He estimated less than a day.

"Should we evacuate?" One of his men asked.

"To where?" Dexter snapped. "Scurry into the mountains like rats? No. Not me. Never like that."

"So what should we do?"

"Shore up the wall for now. Make sure everyone has enough ammunition."

Mitch came into the room and sent the other man out. "Several of the men are leaving. They don't want to stay here any longer."

"Cowards," Dexter hissed.

"There's no point in staying, boss. Seriously... What's the point?"

"I don't need advice from you. I just got my lab set up, and I'm ready. If you hadn't failed to get me the last few components..."

"Pittsburgh is a lost cause, boss. Swarmed. It belongs to the creatures now. There was nothing we could do." He fidgeted with a cigarette, then put it back in his pocket. "We did the best we could. Really."

"I want you to take a couple of men and go north to Buffalo. There's a place there where you can get what I need." Dexter hadn't slept in days. He was growing impatient with these rubes. "Can you handle that?"

"I... I guess so." Mitch was uncertain if he wanted to go to Buffalo.

Some of the men were heading that way, anyway, but they weren't planning to come back. He figured he could ride with the others, and if the roads were clear, he'd bring back supplies. If not, it would be *adios Senior Dexter*. This one he'd play by ear.

"You're sure about this weapon you're building, you're sure it'll work?"

"For the last time," Dexter looked up. "I am sure.

Stop asking me stupid questions."

"Okay, boss. I'll get on it right away."

Dexter didn't reply, so Mitch left the lab and packed a light bag. He found eight bikers leaving the compound, heading northeast. He got on his Harley and rode out with them, comforted to see the compound get smaller in the rear-view mirror. Soon it would be overrun. If Dexter could get his weapon together, there was hope for all of them. However, if Mitch couldn't get back by tomorrow, then there would be no point in returning. The compound would be a graveyard.

CHAPTER 31

"SMALL craft have landed near every major city on the continent," Bohai explained at breakfast. He had news from his flock of spies. "Actually they landed weeks ago. I think these are drones, and I think they carried the bio-weapon that caused all of this mess to start with: the creature mutations. One probe is right outside Pittsburgh, and it's still operating. Or at least it appears to be working. They say lights continue flashing on its sides day and night."

"So you think destroying it will make a difference?" Shane asked.

"I don't know about that, but we could study it. Learn more about the enemy – the real enemy."

"You still think it's alien?"

"That's what we need to find out."

"Then let's go get it," Stu said, inspired to be doing something positive. "We have firepower now."

"If it's near the city, it's deep behind enemy lines," Sam reminded them. "It won't be easy getting there."

"We'll have to punch one helluva hole in their line," George said, "but we can do it."

What Bohai said next was entirely unexpected. "We have to go get to Walter."

There was an exchange of confused looks. Had they heard that right?

"Walter? Why?" Jason asked bitterly.

"He might be able to help. He'd be the best qualified to look at this craft, whatever it is: a weapon or a ship. But he's surrounded by a swarm. We need to punch a hole through it and get to him."

"If he is surrounded, how is he still alive?" Shane asked. "Are you sure he's still there?"

"Electric fences. For now, they're keeping the lizards away, but he's right at the front line of fighting."

"So why do we need to go save that bastard?" Jason asked again. It was a good question. "He didn't help us. Not at all."

"He has a lab. He certainly has more knowledge about biology and genetic mutations than we do, and he's better qualified to dissect the probe, if we find it. More importantly, the spiders want us to get his help."

"And Dexter? Is he still around?"

"His compound hasn't been reached yet. He's still in there."

"I'm not saving his poor ass," Jason spat.

"Oddly, he might be the second evil genius we need on our side," Sam remarked. "But those two hate each other, so let's just get to Walter for a start."

Stu laid out the map, and showed George where they needed to go to reach Walter's house. They plotted the best route, avoiding the Grinner compound and hitting the flattest roads and fields as possible.

And then Sam made an announcement: "Shane can take my tank. I don't need one."

"You're stayin' behind?" Jason was surprised.

"No, he's not staying behind," Bohai said. "But he doesn't need a tank."

"Oh, I see," Shane said, instantly pissed off. "So you're just going to take the van... maybe a few extra arrows. Walk out on the field and talk them to death?"

"I've been practicing," Sam said. "You know what I mean. The spark."

"He's almost ready," Bohai asserted, trying to be helpful, trying to be convincing.

"No." Shane shook his head. "No way. A few sparks won't stop them. You'll be killed."

"I won't be killed. I can do it," Sam insisted. He sounded certain this time. "I'll be okay. I can shield myself. And I'll be behind the line of tanks."

That part did appease his brother, if only the tiniest bit. "I don't like it. Listen: you stay behind the tanks. You promise? I mean... *way* behind the tank line."

"Yes. I will."

"This sounds risky to me," Stu said. "I'm not sure I understand your voodoo gift, but it still sounds like a bad idea."

Shane pointed his finger at Stu. "Thank you! I mean... right?"

"And I'm taking the jeep," Sam said. "Not the van."

"Oh, this keeps getting better and better." The older brother held up his hands in a plea. "Not a good idea, Sammy, but you never listen to me."

"I always listen to you, Shane," Sam said softly. "But we have four tanks and lots of spiders. The General has promised to protect me."

"Who?" George asked. "A General is here?"

"It's an inside joke," Bohai said. "He's not a real General, as such. He's a really big... hairy, um... We discussed this earlier, remember?"

"He's a tarantula," Sam said. "And he's protected us pretty well so far. Right? Now he promised to keep me safe." That wasn't entirely true; he had promised to be there and fight beside them. Sam just needed to convince his brother to sign off on this.

"Those tanks will surprise the hell out of the lizards," Bohai said, and he made a good point. "We've got lots of backup."

"Lots of spiders." Sam added.

"Awesome," Shane said. He gave them his signature sarcastic thumbs-up.

They prepared to take the road right before noon, and Mark gave Sam his favorite Magic game card for good luck. It was an important gesture to him.

"Leviathan 10/10," the boy told him. "It's always been good to me."

"Thanks," Sam said, and squeezed the kid's shoulder. He was actually a little touched by this.

"I'll take good care of it."

"It'll take care of you," Mark corrected him, then slipped the card into Sam's back pocket.

Sitting atop his Stingray, chewing on an unlit cigar in the corner of his mouth, George gave some last-minute advice: "The heavy rounds you carry are limited. Your 7mm cannon has 2400 rounds, but the big 14mm gun has only 8, plus 24 in the hull for reload. Fire that one with care. Any questions? ...No? Let's roll, soldiers." He twirled his finger in a motion to move out.

The four tanks thundered to life and lurched forward, driven by George, Stu, Shane and Bohai. Sam and Camila lagged behind in the jeep. With difficulty, they had managed to convince Mark to remain behind with Jason, Tina, and his sister and mother. Jason also argued that his arm was better, but they decided he should stay at the lodge to recover and to guard the tower. However, they couldn't stop Camila. She was dead set on coming, and she had been practicing with a rifle and pistol for two days. She climbed into the passenger seat while Sam started the jeep.

Bulbous clouds swept in from the west, choking off most of the sun, and set the tone for the ominous day to come. The tanks rolled out onto the road in single file with a mighty rumble; the jeep followed. Mark and Lily waved emphatically from the watchtower. Lily kept waving until they were completely out of sight.

Sam glanced at Camila in the passenger seat, pistol at her belt, her rifle gripped with both hands above her lap.

"Don't be nervous," he told her. "Take deep breaths, and aim for one target at a time. If you're calm, you'll hit more."

"From what I saw on the video you brought back, we can probably just point straight ahead and shoot. The targets will be close together, shoulder to shoulder."

He tilted his head. "Good point. But still, keep a cool head."

"And you? Not nervous?"

"Oh, I'm scared to death. I'm just trying not to throw up before we get there."

That made her laugh. "I get that. Look, I'll try to have your back. While you do your thing, I'll make sure nothing gets at you."

"Word to the mother ship!" he joked. "That's all I need to know."

The jeep bumped along behind the tanks, now crossing an open field in two by two formation. Even with four-wheel drive, the jeep had a hard time keeping up with the Stingrays. Walter's house was now in view, only a quarter mile away. A battle between the spiders and lizards raged all around it. Walter's house was literally the front line of a war zone. It seemed odd; Sam even wondered if Walter had something the lizards wanted, or if he was tormenting them.

As they approached Walter's electric fences, the spiders moved back. George fired a round from his tank.

As expected, the first volley startled the lizards. It most likely scared the hell out of Walter, too. A dozen lizards blew into pieces that were showered across the field. Stu fired the second round, and another half dozen lizards blew up. Others scampered out of the way. The tanks rolled forward.

George's tank was first to reach the electric fence, which the tank crushed without effort. Since there were no sparks, it was assumed Walter had seen them and cut the power. George and Stu advanced toward the house, crushing more lizards under their wheels.

The spectacle had an immediate effect on the horde of creatures. They scattered and retreated. The black mass drew back a few hundred yards. Shane and Bohai drove their tanks up alongside the house with the others. The jeep drove right to the front door.

Men rushed from the house and began fixing the broken fence. They righted and stabilized it within two minutes. Their efficiency was an amazing feat to watch. Apparently, this wasn't their first time.

The fence sizzled, now live again, and the men stepped back from it. Meanwhile, the Peak group exited their tanks and headed for Walter's front porch. Camila and Sam were already inside the house.

Walter was furious, now giving it to Sam with both barrels.

"What the hell! You can't just take down my fence like that. There are people in this house, and important work."

Stu raised a hand in peace, and said, "We brought tanks. We're here to help."

"So? Who asked you to?" Walter fumed. "We don't need your help. How do you expect to get those machines off my property without destroying my fence again? The gate is too narrow."

"Calm down," Sam said.

Then Walter saw Shane. "You! Is Dexter behind this?"

"Okay, Walt," said Shane in a cool tone, "I'm gonna tell you only one time, we are not with that douche-bag Dexter. I'll punch you in the mouth if you say it again. And – we're here to help you. You're welcome!"

"We don't need your help!" Walter wailed, red in the face.

"Honey, sit down," his wife said in a cool, composed tone. "Let's all sit down and talk about this. They're already here. Let's hear what they have to say." She was always able to disarm the quick-tempered man she had married. "I'm Margaret," She told them. "Sit, all of you. I'll make some lemonade, and we'll talk."

Shane recognized Jake and saluted him with two fingers. Jake returned a silent half-nod. One of the other men now came in the front door. "The fence is back up, Dr. Feynman." That appeased him a little.

"We'll talk, and then you go," Walter said, now sitting down at the kitchen table. His tone evened out a little bit. "What do you want with me? Why are you even here?"

"We know what started this," Sam said. That got Walter's attention, along with Max and everyone else.

Sam now wished it were true. It was a fib borne from a truth. They *suspected* they knew what started this.

"What do you know?" Walter took off his glasses.

"A bunch of small spacecraft landed near all the major cities a few weeks ago. We think these spacecraft, or probes, distributed the bio-weapon that caused this mess. We also know where one is, and we're going out to find it. The answers may be in there, in the craft."

"You know all this? How?"

Sam blushed and cleared his throat. *We talk to birds and spiders, you see.* "Well, that's hard to explain. But friends of ours saw it, and told us where to find it. We have a reconnaissance team."

Walter was skeptical. "So what do you want with me?"

"Come with us. You're the most qualified to study this object. I mean, it may be something from outer space. Don't you want to be the first man on Earth to examine it?"

Sam was wise to appeal to the scientist's ego. Walter wanted to be the first to discover everything. His ego had driven him all his life; it's partly what had started his feud with Dexter.

Walter chewed on the end of his glasses. "Even if that's true, are you sure you can find it? What makes you think you can get near it? It's probably protected by an army, or a force field."

"Our... sources... have been right up next to it," Bohai said, "and crawled all over it. There's nothing stopping us from studying it. Maybe even take it apart."

"This is a great opportunity," Dr. Max Witherspoon whispered in his colleague's ear. "We can bring it back here."

"How big is it?"

"Pretty big, from what I've heard," Bohai said. "A few meters wide. We might not be able to move it. You'll need to come with us."

Walter studied the faces of the intruders in his kitchen, as he pondered the idea of being the first scientist to study a probe from space. Perhaps something in this bio-weapon could be reversed, and he could be the one to stop the mutations. That would be better than winning the Nobel Prize.

He put his glasses back on. "If we follow protocol, let me do the examining, then I'll go."

"I should go, too," Max said.

"No, you stay here and keep working on our project."

"It will be dangerous," Sam warned. "We have to blast through their lines and keep them away from the object while we study it. If we fail, we'll be..."

"We'll be lizard chow," Shane finished the sentence. He enjoyed being blunt. "The odds of survival are two million to one."

"Is that true?" Margaret asked, furrowing her brow.

"No, no," Sam said quickly, flashing an admonishing glare at his brother. "He doesn't have those kind of math skills, he's not Mr. Spock. My brother just likes to be dramatic. The truth is, it may be dangerous, but we have a good chance of success. And most of all – we have to try."

"We'll look after your husband, ma'am," Stu said with bogus confidence and no idea if he could keep the promise. He smiled at her warmly.

Walter had made up his mind. "Okay."

"We need to go quickly," urged George. "We had a nice surprise effect getting here, but it will wear off soon. The enemy is sure to regroup."

"Let me get some things."

Walter collected a few special tools and instruments in a bag. He kissed his wife on the cheek, then squeezed her arm. Always more emotional, she hugged him tightly for a long minute.

"I'm ready," he said.

"Good Luck, Walt, and be careful," Max said to his colleague.

Walter nodded and shook hands with Max and two other men in the room. No one had been introduced. "The fence," he said to Jake, who had been silent up till that point.

"I've got it," Jake said.

"Turn the fence off and move it until we get out, then get it back up. Activate it immediately when it's up again. And best of luck!"

Jake signaled "okay" with his thumb and forefinger together. They had moved the fence a few times before; he had the routine down pat.

"We'll give you as much time as we can," George told him. "We'll keep the critters busy as long as we can."

Walter got in the passenger seat of the jeep, and Camila drove. Sam wanted to be hands-free in the back. His spark might be needed on this leg of the journey.

Walter's men parted the fence, and the tanks lumbered forward, two in the front, then the jeep, followed by two tanks in the back. At the lead, George and Stu shot round after round into the black horde. Dead reptile bodies flew in all directions. The rapid fire of volleys sent the lizards running again. They backed away, and gave the procession room to move forward. The spiders had scurried to the west hills to stay clear of the tank blasts. They were keeping thousands of lizards from joining the rest of their scaly army. Everyone was doing their part.

Behind them, Walter's men realigned and activated the fence again.

To the front, thousands of vicious creatures slowly retreated, but could be seen mustering in a valley no more than a mile ahead. Getting past that would be a bloody task, and the group still had fifty miles to pass in order to reach the alien probe.

"You okay with driving?" Sam asked Camila.

She nodded, but didn't look at him. She kept her eyes fixed on the road.

"Doctor, take this," he handed Walter a pistol. "You might need it."

Walter put his bag of tools on the floor, and gripped the pistol with both hands. He looked back at Sam. "I've never fired one of these. I've never *held* one before."

"Plenty of practice coming up ahead," Sam motioned to the front. "You'll get the hang of it, I'm sure. Just don't shoot your own foot. And don't shoot *me!*"

The two rear tanks trundled up alongside the jeep on each side, and started firing. The loud blasts unsettled Walter, and even Sam, for that matter. Today was gearing up to be a rough day, and this was just the beginning.

CHAPTER 32

THE tanks continued to fire as they moved forward, and the jeep bumped along with them, struggling to keep up. A rolling metal chain of destruction over open fields and rocky terrain, the armored vehicles pushed the enemy back. At several points their blasts blew holes in the terrain ahead of them and formed trenches which the vehicles then would have to drive over. This was no problem for the tanks, but the jeep was certainly being pushed to its limit. On several occasions its wheels got bogged down or stuck in the furrows and ditches. Adding to choppy terrain were all the dead bodies of dismembered lizards, which forced the jeep to slow down even more. Avoiding holes, dirt mounds, body parts, and other obstacles was making Camila's job difficult. They were forced to grind on in low gear.

More clouds converged overhead, crowding and darkening the sky with the threat of rain. If that happened, it would turn this dirt into mud, and the jeep would be in real trouble. As long as the ground stayed dry, they could still forge ahead, albeit slowly.

At first there was little resistance from the lizards. The

spiders kept most of them out of their way, and the rest were easily blown to smithereens. The war party thundered ahead all afternoon, slowly making progress and getting closer and closer to the city. The tank patrol put more than forty-five miles behind them before they hit their first real snag. A few miles from their objective, a river needed to be crossed by a steel tied-arch bridge spanning four hundred feet. This was blocked by a tightly packed horde of creatures. Any shelling from the big guns might bring down the whole structure and remove their chance of crossing the river. They faced the possibility they might need to get out and clear the bridge with guns, hand to hand and face to face with the reptiles. Given its length, clearing it on foot would be a serious challenge.

George stopped his tank just short of the bridge entrance, and popped up out of his hatch. "Any ideas?"

The others emerged from their own armored vehicles, guns in hand. They looked visibly shaken by the drive so far.

"We can get out, push them back with gunfire," Shane said. "We'll move forward in a line, and shoot until the bridge is free."

"You're crazy," Camila said. "That won't work."

Stu agreed. "Look on the other side. Plenty of reinforcements to keep at us. It would take us a week to kill all these things with just pistols and rifles."

"Use the tanks, the smaller 7mm guns?" Shane offered.

"That bridge is already about to collapse," George observed, pointed to the cracked supports. "It's old and the weight of all those things on it... even the tanks might be too much. One or two blasts, and it's coming down."

"He's right," said Walter. His face was pale, and he looked ill from motion sickness. This trip was taking its toll on him. He was a scientist, not a soldier. "The construction looks old. It's unsteady. I do not think it can withstand any violent disturbance."

Bohai came up behind Sam and put his hand on his shoulder. "Sam can do this."

"Me? Do what?"

"You can clear the bridge, Sam."

"Me? I can't."

"You can." Bohai sounded sure.

School's out, man.

"What's he talking about?" Walter asked. George was a little puzzled, too.

"Just watch," Bohai said. "It's easier than explaining."

"Sam, no," Shane pleaded. "You don't have to."

Sam hesitated, then stepped toward the bridge, and Bohai walked beside him. "I'll go with you, man. I'll stay right behind you." Bohai got his pistol out and held it ready. "Be strong. Don't be afraid."

"If I get eaten, my brother will kill you," Sam warned. "I'm just saying..."

"You got this, man."

They stepped onto the bridge, and Shane came up a

yard behind with his rifle loaded and ready. The others watched with astonishment, not at all sure what was happening.

As the two boys closed in on the reptiles, the first line backed away. It was as if the creatures sensed something was wrong. When Sam sparked up his hands, they flinched. Primal fear glowed in their red parietal eyes.

Sam created two spheres, one in each hand. He thrust them forward and blew four lizards into the water. The others stepped backward, as Sam continued to walk forward. He closed his eyes and created a shield about six feet high and ten feet across, and held it in front of him as he walked. He could hear Bohai's steps behind him.

A group of confused lizards found courage at that moment and stopped backing away. When Sam was toe to toe with the front line, he push forward and burned several of them with his electric shield. It created a searing charge of blue sparks when each creature touched it. One brave reptile attacked; it rushed forward and leaped into the air toward Sam. It hit the shield and was instantly fried. Its body rolled off the bridge and into the river.

Sam concentrated and expanded the shield. In a thrust, he pushed it forward and toasted another two dozen lizards. Some of the dragons behind them started to retreat, climbing over each other to back away. A few dove into the river. Stu and George aimed their rifles at the water and started to pick them off, making sure the beasts would abort any plans to swim to their side.

Sam pushed forward again. A headache swelled in his right temple. His ears began to ring.

Bohai and Shane ran back to the others, shouted, "Come on! Quick!"

They got back into their tanks, and started the engines. Bohai's armored machine lurched forward onto the bridge. The others disappeared back into their own tanks and followed him in single file, leaving several yards between each other. Camila started the jeep and entered the bridge last.

A dozen giant spiders appeared from nowhere, scrambling out from the deep grass, and formed a barrier to protect the jeep. Their objective was to keep this side of the bridge safe until the vehicles crossed. Sam pushed forward again and again, and more reptiles fell into the river. Those who survived the dive swam to the nearest shore. Another squad of spiders immediately killed them at the top of the river bank.

At last, the bridge was theirs. Sam stepped onto the other side, and sank to his knees. He was spent. The lizards saw this and tried to move forward again in a fresh assault on the boy, but the tanks began to fire again.

Bohai was now across the bridge and shot several rounds into the enemy horde. George followed suit, and they managed to hold them back until the jeep could reach Sam. Bohai jumped from his tank and helped Sam into the jeep. He nearly had to carry him. Shane also dismounted and ran to his brother.

"Talk to me Sammy, you okay?"

"Keep going," Sam said. His voice was weak. "Don't stop."

Bohai touched Sam's cheek and forehead, both burning with fever. "You are incredible, man."

Stu and George continued shelling the front line, and pushed it back another twenty yards. Bohai and Shane climbed back in their tanks, and the group started forward once more. They blasted the disorganized lizards mercilessly, and punched another hole in their lines. Full speed ahead, the jeep and four tanks barreled on.

Walter sat in the back with Sam and checked his vital signs. Sam assured him that he was fine, but Walter insisted. "I am a doctor, son. Be quiet and let me check you."

"I just need a couple hours to rest."

"That was incredible, what you did," Walter remarked. "I would love to know how you achieved that electric field. Later, we should talk about this."

"That should be fun." Sam closed his eyes and rested.

An hour later, they reached their mission's target. The alien object they sought lay in front of them: a round probe sat on loose soil a hundred yards away. Sam opened his eyes and took a moment to realize they had arrived. It was here.

The object wasn't what he had expected. He had assumed it would be a small probe, some device looking like a miniature satellite, or an alien probe droid. Instead, this was much bigger, more than twenty feet in diameter, and looked like a big gray onion. It actually bore a close resemblance to a flying saucer from any of a hundred old sci-fi movies he loved to watch. A glass dome covered the top half. It was tinted glass, partly masking what lay underneath, but a slow spinning mechanism could be seen below the curves of the dome; they could barely make it out. Black numbers appeared distinctly on the dark gray metal surface of its outer hull: 40050.

The entire machine rested at a slight angle on uneven ground in a gully, which hid it from view for miles in any direction. It was unclear whether the gully was a natural formation or had been made by the landing of the craft itself. The object sat motionless and appeared to be lifeless, except for a small blue light blinking at its crest, and the spinning orb inside.

"Aliens use the same numbers as us?" Stu asked.

"Anything is possible," Walter whispered, mainly to himself. He stood still for a moment, then walked toward the craft.

There were no lizards in the area. After the tanks and spiders had punched their way through a sizable part of the army, the horde now started to scatter. The spiders helped push them further south. Yet none of them appeared anywhere near this object.

When Walter reached it, he extended a hand and touched its metallic side. He laid his right palm down against the surface, and felt it tremble ever so slightly – the pulse of an engine or battery inside.

"Well, it didn't melt his hand off," Shane said. They all

looked at him. "That's good news, right?"

Sam stepped up next to Walter and examined the object, whatever this was. He also touched it, and felt the low power it generated. The light at the top still blinked; it showed no concern for the intruders touching its surface.

When the tanks had all been shut down, the area became quiet, and they heard the object's low hum. The wind picked up, and the skies still threatened to rain. The clouds turned black but held firm for now. It was an eerie scene, in the middle of a field situated less than a mile inside the Pittsburgh city limits, on the city side of the river. In the distance ahead they could see the tall skyscrapers of the downtown area, the iconic US Steel Building and PPG Place. Behind them lay the destruction they themselves had brought to the land. Mounds of blasted dirt and lizard body parts stretched out for many miles in their wake.

And here before them was a metallic object from space. It squatted on this Earth and mocked them with a single light that said: *you don't matter, your time is over.* It didn't care they were there at its side. The object was confident they could do it no harm. *Weak Earthlings, you cannot hurt me.*

They were out to prove it wrong.

Walter ran his hand along the entire metal surface, searching for any cracks or breaks, any sign of a door that might open. He circled the object, examining its round body. The only apertures were two round vents the size of tennis balls, open at either side. Then he checked underneath, running his hands along its surface. He couldn't find any other rifts or fissures.

"Unless something is on top," Walter said, "I can't find any way to open it. I'm too short to reach up there." The object stood twelve feet high.

"Boost me up," Sam told Shane. His brother helped him up and let him stand on his shoulders while Sam checked the top of it. He ran his hand along the dome and flicked the light with this thumb and forefinger. It did not react. He jumped back down.

"I don't see anything. Looks pretty solid."

"Maybe we can shoot something into those holes," George said. He pointed at the vents. "Maybe even use the big guns."

Walter shook his head. "Let's call that plan B. I'd like to get into this thing without destroying it. This may be the key to everything." He reached into his instrument bag and pulled out a hand-held scanner. It buzzed to life. Slowly he scanned the surface of the object and recorded the results.

"I've never seen anything like that before," George said in a low voice to the others. "Did this guy just beam down from the Enterprise? Or from CIA? Roswell or something?"

Walter overheard, turned to him and said, "Something like that. Can you give me a hand here? Hold this scanner right up to the opening here."

While George held the scanner, Walter listened at the

second aperture for any signs of change.

"So what does it tell you?" Sam asked. He and Camila were both touching the side of the object again, dazzled by its sleek alien configuration. Sam loved its cool smooth surface. He did not want to stop touching it.

"Micro-organism living on its hull," Walter replied.

Sam and Camila yanked their hands back. Camila instinctively wiped her hand on her jeans. She stepped away from the object.

"Is it dangerous?" She asked.

"Maybe," Walter said. He was never one to sugar coat anything. He didn't see the need. "Most of these organism are on everything here on Earth. Simple bacteria, nothing to be too concerned about. But there are unusual fungi fighting for the same space." He continued to read the results on his scanner. "Very strange. I've never seen these before."

The scientist wiped the hull with a cotton swab and sealed it in a small tube. He tucked the tube in a pouch within his bag. Then he began examining the craft with a series of more bizarre instruments.

"You think this is what distributed the bio-weapon?" George asked.

"This and others like this," Walter answered. "I do think so, yes."

"So let's turn it off." Sam said

"I'm not sure exactly how to do that. Do you have any ideas?"

"Yeah. I got one," George said, his frustration

showing through. He stepped up and put his pistol directly into the closest vent hole. He fired. Nothing happened. The bullet disappeared with no effect.

"I am sure there is a mechanism to retain projectiles inside there," Walter explained. "This thing has traveled across galaxies, I do not think they overlooked the possibility of a gun-type weapon upon landing here." He paused and turned back to George. "Please refrain from doing that again."

George shrugged and holstered his gun.

Sam already had another idea. "Could you step back, please, doctor. Give me some room."

Walter took two steps back but never looked up from his scanners. He intently studied the readings, scarcely paying any attention to the others.

Sam held out his right hand, palm up, as if to offer up something like a gift. He sent a lightning bolt from his palm, up into the air and back down into the top of the saucer. The lightning struck the metal object and sizzled around its hull. Sparks covered it from all sides, ran down top to bottom like water drops, then dispersed. The object stopped humming, and the blue light went out.

"Damn," George said. He still didn't understand what was going on with this kid, but let it go for now. It would be better to ask questions later. There's a time and place for everything. Walter did not share the same view.

"Good work, man," Bohai said. "You killed it."

Shane also slapped him on the back, proud of his little brother.

"I don't know what you did," said Walter, a bit disapproving. "You may have just made it angry. And this will certainly get someone's attention."

"Good," said Sam. "Let them come out and fight. We turned off one bio-weapon; we can turn off more. We're taking our planet back."

Bohai smiled, threw his hands in the air, and shouted: "Finally!"

CHAPTER 33

THE motorcycle sputtered and complained as Mitch turned the corner for the last road back to the compound. The bike was on its last leg, literally. Almost every part rattled and needed to be replaced. He was also low on gas, and prayed he could make it the last two miles to the compound. He was surprised to see the road deserted. All around were signs of a battle, dead reptile parts and amputated spider legs, but now nothing stirred. The road sat still in the aftermath of an event that Mitch was glad to have sidestepped.

Helluva party I missed here, he surmised.

Only one man guarded the gate to the compound, instead of the usual five or six. Inside, fewer than a dozen Grinners had stayed behind. Most had split after the war broke out, and now just a skeleton crew remained, and many of them were now packing. Large groups had headed north for Canada, where it was rumored to be safer. Mitch had found little action in Buffalo where only a few lizards had stood in his way – easy enough to dispatch.

After getting the last few chemicals Dexter needed,

Mitch came back alone. No one else wanted anything more to do with the mad scientist. They didn't believe his "weapon" would work against the growing army of creatures. Mitch believed, though. He had to believe – hope was the only thing keeping him going. He wasn't cut out for this post-apocalyptic world, not like the other guys were. Mitch hadn't been a survivalist before this happened. He was all bark and no bite.

On news of Mitch's return, Dexter ran out and met him in front of the lab building. "You got it? All of it?"

"Everything on your list, boss."

"Good. Good." Dexter pawed through the two boxes of chemicals, making sure nothing was missing. He lifted a box. "Bring the other one inside. Come on."

The lab was now up and running. Glass tubes bubbled with fluids, and the whole place smelled of sulfur and something worse. It was foul. The lab looked to Mitch like something from a monster movie. He carefully placed the box on a table.

"So now you can end all this, right?"

"What?" Dexter was preoccupied with unpacking the final ingredients.

"You can kill those things out there and end this thing now, right?"

The scientist turned away from his work and looked at Mitch as if just realizing he had been standing there. He noticed something yellow sticking out of the man's shirt pocket.

"What's that?"

Mitch looked down and pulled a dandelion out his pocket. "Oh, I forgot that was there. It's just a flower." He and his sister used to pick dandelions for their Mom, but he wasn't about to share that *mémoire* with this madman.

"It's a weed, isn't it?" Dexter spat the words irritably.

"Yes, I guess so, technically."

"You put a weed in your pocket?"

Where is this conversation heading? Mitch wondered.

"Um... yeah. Is that a problem?"

"Up to you, but I don't know why you're keeping weeds and calling them flowers."

"Um... yeah, well, I always liked the yellow flower on the head. And when it turns white and its seeds blow off... it's nice," said Mitch. Actually it was his mother who loved them so much.

Why does this crazy scientist care so much? Is he coming unhinged?

Mitch stuffed the yellow flower back in his pocket. "Weeds to one man, are flowers to another, am I right?"

"Not really. Taraxacum officinale is a weed by any name, and regardless of who is holding it or naming it."

"Um.. okay."

Dexter turned back to his work, and seemed to have forgotten Mitch again. He spoke mostly to himself, "Weeds are meant to be pulled. It's what I was taught since I was a child. It's what I was taught."

"Okay... whatever. Need anything else?"

The scientist continued his work, and only grunted an

inaudible reply. He turned on a machine that looked like an incubator. His work was his single concern now. Pleasantries with others, while never his forte, were now completely forgotten.

"Okay, boss, shout if you need anything."

When Dexter didn't answer, Mitch turned and walked out. The odd fellow just needed some time alone to work, he figured. Let him work his magic and kill off all these creatures terrorizing the world.

"It will all be over soon, thank the five heavens!" Mitch said aloud to no one.

Unfortunately, all the good men had left, including his friends. The people who now remained in the compound were the dregs of society. Mitch didn't feel like talking to any of them, so he wandered off and ate dinner alone. After dinner, he tinkered with his bike. He had a feeling he might need to get back on it soon. After Dexter got his mysterious weapon to work, Mitch wanted to get as far away from him as possible, put some distance between himself and the madman... and the Grinners! He was tired of pretending to be on the psycho scientist's side, pretending to be a Grinner. He was tired of a lot of things. The only question remaining was: would he kill Dexter or not? Would he leave the madman to his own devices?

I'm not a killer.

"Maybe I'm not a killer, but he is," he told himself. "That psycho is a mess."

Night washed over the compound. A few raindrops

fell from the starless sky, a mild spritz. Mitch could not see the moon, but he stared at the sky for a long time. Half an hour later, he retreated to a building and found a hard bunk to lie on. Like so many nights since the end of the world, he rested, but could not sleep. In his past life he would have watched re-runs of old cop shows to fall asleep. Now he sorely missed having a TV.

CHAPTER 34

THE group set up camp in the gully just a few yards from the alien object. Stu and George built a fire, and dinner consisted of apples and military rations – not the most appetizing, but nervous stomachs would have kept them from enjoying any meal, even steak. The spiders kept the reptiles away, and they would continue this for as long as possible. Outnumbered, at some point, the lines would break; but for now this gave Sam's group a little time to rest. Their camp used the sunken side of the gully to remain hidden from view. The seven of them sat around the fire and planned the next day's strategy.

"We need to do more to draw them out," Shane said.

"Who are the '*them*' that you keep talking about? *Them.*" Walter asked.

"The aliens or the foreign government, whoever started all this," Bohai said. He held up his arms. "Whoever sent this weapon."

"If we draw them out, we can fight them," Sam said. There was determination in his voice. He was not the same boy he was two weeks ago. "We can't fight reptiles forever. We need to hit the source of the problem. There has to be a reason they didn't just attack us themselves. Maybe their weapons are weak."

"Listen, what do you think their end game was?" Shane asked rhetorically. "Jason and I talked about this. I'll tell you my idea: to turn all the inhabitants of this planet, humans and animals, into these mutations we've been fighting. They use these mutations to kill off the rest of the planet's inhabitants, all the people, at least. Then the mutations turn on each other. In the end, the cities are empty, but the buildings are still there. They rid the planet of everyone, but keep the infrastructure in place. Then, when the time is right, the aliens come down and kill off the rest of the mutations that are still left alive. Boom! They own the planet, infrastructure and all. They don't have to build from scratch."

Shane sat back with his hands folded behind his head, quite pleased with himself. He was proud of his hypothesis. "After they kill off the mutants, it's all theirs, baby. The whole world is theirs."

"They probably have a death ray," Bohai said with a bit of awe in his voice.

"Right. They land and take over the planet without destroying any building, pipelines, or what-have-you... they have it all for themselves. A few upgrades for their technology, and it's a free set of cities ready to host millions of people. Or blue aliens, bugs... whoever!"

"Sounds plausible," Walter agreed. "Not the death ray part, but the rest. And Sam is right – they might not have conventional weapons. Maybe that's why they use biological agents. It's a solid premise, given the situation. Biological purging."

"They could do this to every planet they find," Sam said. "Assuming there are other planets to take, I mean. This is a good plan. Take over planet after planet without firing a shot."

"Peaceful invasion," Walter muttered. He was lost in thought, seemingly unaware anyone was listening to him. "And keep the insects alive so that the plants and greenery don't die off. Keep the ecosystem alive... oxygen and clean air. Nuclear weapons would destroy the atmosphere for them, so those are of no use. But this way, the ecosystem is kept clean." He took off his glasses. "It's brilliant."

"But they hit a few snags here on Earth." Bohai said. "For one, they didn't expect the spiders to get bigger. They also didn't expect them to organize and fight back."

"Or maybe this is an expected side effect," Walter mused, again talking mostly to himself. "And they are prepared for it. Think about it: the spiders are just killing off the reptiles. That's something that needs to be done anyway, at some point. Maybe they know about this possible effect, but it doesn't matter to them."

"Right," Shane said. "They don't care about a war on Earth between two species of animals. No buildings are being damaged. The plants and skyscrapers are safe and not being torn down. Well, except for a few trees that got blown up. Eventually, one side will win, and it's a good wager to bet on their mutations. Later, these aliens come down and take the planet. Either way, they win."

"It's really a beautiful plan. A beautiful design," Walter repeated. He put his glasses back on. "It's ingenious."

"Glad you're so impressed," Sam said, flagged and irritated. "But we need to screw with their plan. We need to fight them. We start by doing something to get their attention."

"You mean besides killing one of their probes?" George asked. "That's probably gonna piss someone off. What else can we do to mess with their plans?"

"Infrastructure," Sam said. "We start to destroy the buildings, the sewer systems, the power plants. We mess with their golden plan."

"That should catch them by surprise," said Walter soberly. He furrowed his brow and looked at each of them eye-to-eye. "It might bring down some big visitors. Are we ready for that?"

"Yes," Sam said, increasingly scared and angry at the same time. "We're ready."

"I'm sure as hell not fighting lizards the rest of my life," Shane said. "Let's take down some buildings."

"Scorched earth strategy," George agreed, nodding his head. "Don't leave anything for them to use."

"We start there," said Shane, pointing at the US Steel Tower, 64 stories tall and one of the nation's tallest buildings. It stood in the background like a mighty dagger, slicing upward from the skyline. "That should get someone's attention."

Together, the humans contemplated the city stretched

out before them. Dozens of skyscrapers punctuated the sky. They loomed like towers in ancient time, or like teeth that speared up from the ground and split the view. To Sam it looked beautiful, as the late evening sun formed spokes piercing through the rain clouds before disappearing over the horizon. It started to sprinkle, just a little, as total darkness closed in. Fortunately the tiny bit of rain only spat for twenty minutes, then moved on.

They slept on the ground with only grass as a pillow, and Sam imagined the planets and stars hidden above the clouds. He wondered which of the stars their alien invaders came from. How many other planets had they conquered on their way to Earth? Was it always this easy for them?

"Seven of us," Shane said.

"So?" Sam sat up on his elbows.

"Remember that show: *Blake's 7?* They had seven crew members. That was a cool show. It's just like us."

Sam sat back and closed his eyes. "Sure, if that helps you. Go to sleep, man."

Camila snuggled in between the two of them, and fell asleep. Somehow Sam and Shane managed to drift off just as easily – a side effect of total and utter fatigue.

In the morning, they ate a quick breakfast and put out the fire. The alien object had not moved or reacted in any way to their intrusion. Shane tapped its hull with his knuckles. A metallic echo replied.

"Still no one home," he said. "Let's head out."

The tanks rumbled to life and lurched forward onto the wide empty street that would lead them to Forbes Avenue, and then downtown. The jeep followed third in succession, with Stu taking up the rear. They took Forbes Avenue to the Hill District and looked down onto the city's downtown skyline, a quarter mile ahead and below them. So far nothing had stood in their way to reach this point. A few straggling reptiles slithered off the road to avoid the loud tanks invading their space, but the route to this point had been easy. Straight ahead stood BNY Mellon Center and to the right towered the US Steel complex.

Sam looked down and saw a writhing mass of lizards in the streets. Thousands of the reptilian monsters crowded the downtown area, nesting in alleys and in the buildings that massed together shoulder to shoulder. It was a sickening sight to behold – even more so, given the origin of these creatures.

George's voice squawked through the walkie talkies, "Are we ready for this? Everyone sure?"

Sam hesitated only a moment, thinking this was a point of no return.

We really doing this? There is no un-doing something like this.

Then he picked up his talkie and said, "Light her up, guys." There would be no ceremony for this moment of destruction.

We're doing this.

George put a cigar in the corner of his mouth, loaded

his 14mm cannon, and aimed it at the tallest building. He fired. A round met the sixtieth floor and exploded. Bohai and the others followed each with a round of their own. The sound of impact was deafening. When the shells entered the building, the ground shook. Chunks of two floors spat out the other side. The shock of the explosions sent large pieces of concrete, steel and glass plummeting to the street, and the top floors imploded and collapsed. The lizards clambered over each other to get out of the way. One of them was beheaded by a sheet of glass.

"Here we go," George grunted, the half-chewed cigar still in his mouth.

George shelled the fifty-eighth floor twice more, and the top of the building severed from its whole. The top seven floors came crashing to the ground – the 64-story building had been cut down to 57. It now looked like a giant monument to the spiked head of Bart Simpson. Thousands of lizards screeched and raced away from the streets surrounding the building. Many of them were crushed under steel debris that now piled high on the pavement, rods of rebar sticking up haphazardly. Two lizards were impaled.

Sam let out a whistle. "That should wake someone up."

The tanks fired again, and again. Five more floors blew away. Steel girders poked up from the forty-ninth floor – everything above it now gone. A zigzag of jagged metal clawed toward the sky, where solid floors used to exist. Pieces of stone and steel continued to fall to the ground far below, seemingly in slow motion. Lizards screamed and fought with each other, then turned toward the tanks and attacked *en masse* in large numbers.

Stu began shelling the streets to keep the horde at bay.

George turned his cannon to the second tallest building. The shiny glass tower of the financial building took a blast to the fortieth story, then another. Immense glass windows cracked and imploded. A two-story chunk of its corner fell to the ground and crushed many of the creatures below, pushed others to scatter. It looked like Godzilla had taken a bite out of the building's side.

The lizards rushed them again. This time the numbers were beyond anything they'd ever faced. Sam guessed fifty thousand, maybe more. The swarm of demons now descended on Sam's group in blind fury. No amount of shelling would stop them.

The tanks aimed for the streets and blared out shot after shot. The monsters didn't care; they kept coming. A group of them reached Shane's tank and turned it on its side. They bit and clawed at the hatch, trying to get the prize out of the jar.

This is going to end badly, Sam thought. *Do something.*

Sam was paralyzed with panic. It wasn't until anger and frustration overcame his fear that he moved. He grabbed the railing of the jeep. In minutes they would all be under a pile of creatures. If that happened, he doubted any of them would survive.

Do something!

Sam jumped down from the jeep and walked forward to meet the assault head-on. Scared, he stumbled and fell on the ground. His arms thrust forward and scuffed the concrete. He did not get up; instead he raised himself to one knee and bent his head to concentrate. The boy was seconds from being clawed to death, when he opened his arms and let fly a wave of lightning bolts bigger than anything he had ever before generated.

Like a tidal wave, the power arc swelled and surged forward in the direction of the swarm. It struck the first pack of creatures and sent them flying backward, spinning and rolling. At least two hundred of the beasts were tossed back; they cascaded over each other in a roll of carnage. The ripple of energy continued for more than a mile. It covered three quarters of the downtown city, and touched most of creatures in the surrounding area. Their bodies sizzled and twitched; the smell of burning flesh flooded the nostrils. Blue electricity shimmered across the air and reached its climax, then fizzled out. This was no flash like a camera bulb, this was an explosion of fireworks.

The whole event happened within a mere few seconds. And then it was over.

While it had only killed the first several hundred lizards in the front lines, it has singed many others and scared them into retreat. Even the light static shock, received at the rear lines, was enough to make the creatures back away.

George fired his tank again, and the lizards turned tail

and ran – those still alive, anyway. The power arc and the shelling were too much. The demons made a mass retreat to the other side of town, back to the third river. Many crossed the bridge to the stadium and did not look back.

When Sam stood back up, he was dizzy. He gazed out at the path of destruction he had caused. The city lay silent, except for the hissing of a few rogue lizards now crawling up from hidden cavities and trying to decide whether to flee or fight. They had escaped the power arc, and now scurried away under buildings and behind cars. Their ultimate decision was to flee. The breeze carried the sickening stench of death. One dead lizard was curled up and burned from head to tail; it looked like a fossil. The city tableau resembled a horrifying Monet painting, if Monet painted in only red and black.

Sam fell over, and Walter ran to catch him. The scientist and Camila helped Sam to the jeep.

"I'm okay," Sam said, but his voice cracked. "Get Shane out of there."

George and Stu dragged Shane's body out of his toppled tank. It wasn't immediately apparent if he was still alive, but he regained consciousness and started coughing.

Bohai ran to Sam, grabbed his face with both hands and kissed him on the cheek. "You rock, man!" He laughed and ruffled his hair. "Incredible. The Amazing Sam."

Everyone gathered around the jeep.

"I'm fine, I'm fine," Sam assured them. He still

needed a minute to catch his breath. He was getting better at this, sparking and recovering. The tips of his fingers trembled, his heart raced, as the high came crashing down.

Sam looked at what he had done and briefly wondered if he might have saved Ken this way. That was an absurd notion, of course; Ken would have been fried alive. Still, this was a guilt Sam would wear forever, like an old jean jacket, torn and ragged. Something he would never be rid of.

Shane stopped coughing and stood on shaky legs. His body was badly bruised, but he had suffered no broken bones.

"Are you all right, Shane?" Camila asked.

"Just some scrapes. I'm okay." Shane grabbed his brother by the shoulder. "Look at me, Sammy. You sure you're all right."

"Fine. Really."

"How many fingers am I holding up?" Shane gave him the finger.

"Two," Sam lied, and forced a laugh. "I'm fine."

"Um, guys..." Stu pointed up to the sky that was now shifting. "We may not be so fine."

A new spaceship appeared, larger than the probes, moving fast and blotting out one of the clouds. It dove from the sky and headed straight for them.

CHAPTER 35

THE ship plunged from the clouds and rapidly descended in a spiral. Much bigger than the probe object they had deactivated, this was at least fifty feet long and thirty feet wide. It had ten-foot wings on either side, and spikes running along the top. Although they knew nothing about it, Sam's guess was a small warship. It looked menacing. Its blue and gray metal flashed in the light.

Two more ships swooped out of the sky, a few miles apart on either side, east and west. They had the same appearance and configuration as the first, and the scene of three of them together, landing in unison, looked impressive... and scary.

"No offense, Sam, but I'm gonna say you did it." Shane said. He always joked when he was nervous, and right now, he was panic-stricken.

"Something's hitting the fan, that's for sure," George asserted through his cigar. "Should we start the tanks?"

"I don't think so," Walter said. "I doubt the tanks will have any effect against those."

"Can we try?"

"No. I doubt they intend to kill us," Walter said confidently. "They could have done that already, I would assume."

Stu exhaled. "Really hope you're right. You know what they say about assumptions."

Sam drank a bottle of water, and regained his focus. He watched the closest ship land on Bigelow Boulevard, just a hundred yards away. Lights flickered on all sides and down the length of the wings.

A hatch opened and a ladder descended from the body under one wing. They waited anxiously to see who or what might climb down the steps. Sam half expected to see a talking lizard pop out and extend his claw to shake hands.

King of the reptiles.

Instead, a simple man climbed down the ladder – a human man. He wore a gray military uniform of unique design, decidedly not from any Earth nation. It bore an emblem on its left shoulder that resembled the probe they found earlier. Looking well into his forties, black hair barely starting to go gray at the edges around the ears, he stood up straight and tall. The man walked out alone, and surveyed the destruction around him, the damaged buildings and the hundreds of dead creatures. He soaked in the scene for a good minute.

Then a soldier wearing an intricate helmet came out of the ship and stood next to the ladder. His uniform was simpler but also bore the probe emblem on its left shoulder. The soldier carried no weapon, as far as they could tell. He stood his ground by the ship and did not move.

At last, the first man began to walk up the street toward the group of seven. He did not hurry, each step was careful and calculated. No one else came out of the spacecraft, and his soldier did not join him. He approached by himself. It took him ten long minutes to reach them, and when he did, he simply smiled and opened his palm.

"I come in peace," he said.

They did not know how to respond to that. Sam, Shane and Bohai exchanged looks of both confusion and slight amusement.

"That was a joke," the man said. Seeing the joke had not landed, he continued, "This situation is out of control. I will need to kill at least one of you today. I thought I might lighten the mood first with a joke. But... I guess you're not in the mood."

No one said a word. It took a few seconds for his words to sink in. "I believe this was a common phrase in your entertainment media." He paused, then asked, "Did I say it wrong? Should I place the inflection on *come* instead of *peace*?"

"You said it perfectly," Walter told him. "We did not expect your first words to be a joke... or to be in English"

"Well, it is a serious day, isn't it," the man said.

"We did not expect you to be human, either."

"What did you think? Green skin and antennae?"

"To be honest... yes," Shane said.

"At the least," Bohai agreed. "And with claws."

"Sorry to disappoint you. I am humanoid, as are all the inhabitants of this galaxy, and most other galaxies, too. There are few worlds without humanoids; and you'll probably never meet them. And I speak many languages. *Perituraque defectum*. Is that right?"

"Not exactly," said Walter. "So you originally came from Earth?"

That irritated the man, and he could not hide his displeasure. "Why are you people so egotistical. You think life started here or ended here, and that your planet is the center of the universe. No, I did not come from Earth, and we are not the same race, by the way."

"You look the same to me," Stu said.

"But I am not the same," the man snapped. "I am a Sayan, part of the Saraid Empire. In this galaxy, we occupy Neptune's largest moon, Triton. We live beneath the surface. You are Earthenians, part of the Earthenian Empire. This was their home world, the seat of their government over a millennium ago. They left it behind for better worlds, set up a new home world on Earthus and haven't been back since. They moved on when they saw the planet-killer asteroid on course for Earth."

"You mean, there were humans here before the ice age," Walter sputtered.

"They left for greener shores, and have no idea the few humans who remained actually survived the asteroid hit. The world here had to start over."

"Start over," Walter muttered. His mind raced, and he

had a million questions.

"That's why you're so far behind in technology. This is your second age for Earth 1."

"Earth 1?"

"The name of your planet. There are many Earths in the Earthenian Empire, along with Earthus, and Earthkhen and Eartious. But yours is the most primitive. My home world is Neptune Caliphen, but in this galaxy we live on Neptune 2, what you call Triton, Neptune's moon."

"Triton," Walter said, lost in thought. He was starting to sound like a child repeating an adult's words.

"Before our invasion, we waited to be sure that Earthus did not know of this planet's continued survival. We wish to avoid another war with the Earthenians. Living on Neptune 2, Triton, is not easy; we cannot live above-ground. We have always been jealous of Earth 1. It is time we take it for our own. Our people are peaceful, we deserve to enjoy the sun, deserve it more than you."

"How presumptuous of you," Walter said.

The alien man snorted. "You who are barbarians fighting always, even within your own world, every day. We deserve this sun-filled paradise more than you. Our time has come."

"But you really caused the mutations?" Sam asked.

"Ah, our man Sam. You disabled our probe, good for you!" The alien clapped his hands together twice in mock applause. "But you didn't knock out the communications system. We heard everything you said last night. And you are right about everything. Almost everything. We want the infrastructure to remain whole and intact for our settlements here. Which is why this..." he waved his hand at the destruction of the city, "...has to stop. You have to stop destroying our new world."

"It's not yours," Shane said. "And we'll destroy whatever the hell we want."

"We won't let you have it," Bohai growled. "If we can't have it, you can't either. We can take it all down."

"No. No, you won't," the Sayan said. "We'll kill one of you, and then another, until you stop. Accept your fate. Earthus doesn't even know you still exist. Earth 1 is lost. Surely you realize that."

"No," Sam said. "We won't let you take it."

The Sayan turned to Sam and smiled, "Our wayward son. The one who is different from the rest. Let me show you something."

The alien held out his hand and sparked a small plasma ball. It hovered a few seconds, then rose in the air until it disappeared in the clouds. He held his smile, quite pleased with his small display.

"What the hell?" Shane cried.

"Recognize that trick?" The alien asked.

"No," Sam said, defiant. "I don't."

"You're not an Earthenian, Sam. You're one of us."

Sam shook his head. "No. I don't think so."

This was a trick. It had to be!

"A few of our people were put here on Earth, years

ago, to keep an eye on the planet and to test the waters for invasion. Your father was one of them. He was one of our greatest scientists, a loyal agent. However, he fell in love and married an Earthling, and they had two sons, two half-breeds. Sam, you inherited some of your father's Sayan abilities, it seems."

"This is bull crap," Shane hissed. "I don't believe a word of it!"

"Maybe so. But it is the truth," the man stated without a hint of humor or guile. "The truth is rarely what you want it to be, son, but it is what it is. Didn't you ever wonder why there were no relatives on your father's side of the family? He has family, but they do not reside on Earth. They are on Neptune 2."

"No," Sam mumbled, even though he felt it might be true. This suddenly made a lot of sense. His dad had been highly secretive about his work, his past, his family. And their last name was Summer, after Dad's favorite season. A fake last name for Earth.

"Dad wasn't an alien!" Shane bellowed, but even he held no conviction for the words. It made sense to him, too, that Dad wasn't from Earth. The boy remembered his father's odd observations about the simplest aspects of the world.

The alien man ignored the outburst, and continued: "We developed skills after centuries of living on Neptune's moon. Our DNA changed and adapted. The powers were a means to survive our harsh world. You got some of that, Sam, and Shane... maybe even a little, too. You just don't know it yet. You'll inherit the Earth with us, both of you. You're part of us, and we will take good care of you both."

"I don't want that. What about my friends?"

"Oh, come now, son. They're already dead. Do not fret about them."

Sam's anger welled up in his chest, and he shot a thin bolt of lightning toward the man. His power had been drained from the day's events, so it wasn't much of an assault. The man deflected the tiny burst easily without lifting a hand, and the lightning fizzled. The sparks faded to nothing.

"You can't hurt me, Sam. I am too strong. Our abilities are all that separate us physically from the Earthenians. As for other differences, there are some..." The Sayan man sighed. "Their Earth religions promote weapons, while ours forbids them. They have crusades, and we have peace."

"I am an Earth boy," Sam said. "I'm not one of you. I won't follow you. I'm here with my people, my friends."

"It doesn't matter, Sam. Stay or go. I do not care; it makes no difference to our invasion. This isn't about you. You are merely a bee sting." He thought a moment, then added, "An interesting bee sting, I'll admit that. Do you know what we call you Earthlings on my world?"

They shrugged. Of course, no one knew.

"Weeds. We call you the weeds of Earth, or Earthweeds. It's a nickname the kids gave you. I think there's even a school rhyme about it. *Earthweeds in our garden*... something like that. *Pluck them, pull them*.... I forget."

He smiled to himself, lost for a moment in a childhood memory. Then he shook himself free and returned to the present. His smile remained but was no longer warm.

"And today, we..." the alien held out his hands toward the ships behind him, "We are the gardeners. And the gardeners are pulling weeds today."

"Well, these weeds are fighting back," Bohai said defiantly.

"We'll keep taking down buildings, we'll be thorns in your side, forever," Sam said. His anger and confusion were preventing him from being more clever. He felt like a child fighting for control of a sandbox with just a plastic shovel and a Dixie cup.

"We'll be your worst nightmare," said Shane. "We'll take down every pipeline and brick on this planet—"

"No. No, you won't," the alien man interrupted calmly. He didn't seem worried at all. "You'll stop this mess now. Surrender, and cease your efforts. Or I will start to kill your friends one by one."

A chill thought reached Sam just then: were soldiers already at the Peak? Would they kill Tina or Lucy, or even the kids? How far would they go?

"We'll..." he started to say something, but didn't know how to finish the thought.

"It's over, Sam," the man from Neptune said in a clear, matter-of-fact tone. "You must surrender, or I will start to kill your friends today."

Tension leaked out of the air, and was replaced by utter despair. In that moment when one realizes his chances are gone, that he's not holding any more Aces or Kings, when it's time to fold and go home. That moment when he realizes his bankroll, his savings, his life are over, that same feeling of anguish... it now enveloped the group as a whole.

You are just weeds, and the gardener has arrived.

CHAPTER 36

ᴀᴛ that moment, an unexpected voice spoke from behind the group, an oddly familiar voice. It startled Sam, and at first he thought the voice was in his head, in his thoughts.

"No. He won't," the voice said. "He won't kill anyone."

They turned and saw the specter of a man walking toward them, and it took a second to realize it was Dexter. His henchman, Mitch, stood next to a pickup truck several hundred yards away. In all the commotion, no one had noticed their approach. Mitch stayed at the truck, standing with his shotgun in hand, and staring in awe at the tall buildings in ruins, while Dexter took deliberate steps toward Sam and the alien.

"He won't do that at all," Dexter said. He reached the group and glanced coolly at Walter, then glared at the Sayan. "Kiern! The Devil of Saraid."

The alien's eyes widened. "You know my name?"

"I do," Dexter said with his trademark know-it-all self-assurance, although slightly out of breath from his journey. He and Mitch had rushed to get here.

"Commander Kiern You served with my brother. I never met you, but I'm sure you're as big a prick as he is."

"You're Sayan?" Kiern was genuinely surprised. "How?"

"I was exiled here years ago," Dexter told him. "I was injected with Methyl to reduce my sparking abilities, and forced to live among the backwards rabble of this planet."

"You're a criminal?"

"We outlawed capital punishment a century ago," Dexter explained to Sam and his group. "Criminals are sent to primitive planets to live out the rest of their lives. Earth was my prison."

"Wait! We're a prison planet?" Shane croaked. "I live on a prison planet?"

Dexter held up his hand to shut the boy up. "In every sense, yes. And it's been hell for me."

"What was your crime?" Sam asked, his voice cracking a little. He was slowly regaining some strength.

"Intelligence. I was too smart," Dexter said bitterly.

"Seriously, what did you do?"

"Treason. In simplified terms you can understand, I opposed our government's increase in national authoritarianism."

"You?" Bohai asked. "Of all people, I don't see you as a revolutionary."

"I publicly opposed the actions of my government. It's more complicated than that, but such protests had recently been outlawed by my brother, Loxtan, head of the Security Council."

"You're Loxtan Vhar's brother?" Kiern could not hide his amazement. His interest had been piqued by this newcomer, but now he felt a little intimidated. This Sayan living on Earth, this criminal, was somebody. He was the President's brother! Kiern had only heard rumors of the brother being cast off-world.

"I am Dextan Vhar. I go by Dexter on Earth. My brother is a heartless war monger. And he's a jackass."

"You are President Vhar's brother?" Kiern was still thrown off balance by this information. In all his imagination he had not expected this twist of fate, and was having trouble coming to grips with it.

"President? That bastard is President now?" Dexter laughed. "You really are all lost. Idiots. And I thought Earth was stupid."

"Hey," Shane objected, but the protest was half-hearted.

"He's not going to kill any of you," Dexter informed them brusquely and with some impatience. "He can't. Sayans are forbidden from killing other beings by their own hand. It is part of our religion. That is why they have created bio-weapons to do their dirty work."

"But in the end these creatures wouldn't all be dead," said Walter. "Some would remain alive after the fighting. How would they remove the last of them without guns, without killing them?"

"The new gene sequence of the mutations requires X02," Dexter explained. "It's an invisible odorless chemical compound released into the air. It does not affect humans, but the mutations need it to live. When the time is right, the Sayans stop pumping the X02 into the air on Earth. The mutations die off. That is the purpose of those devices – what you call probes, like the one you disabled. Right now they are pumping X02 into the oxygen to keep the mutations alive."

"Brilliant," Walter whispered to himself.

"Weird science," said Shane.

"So you see," Dexter continued, "he won't kill any of you. If you keep destroying the buildings and infrastructure, he can't stop you. He can only throw more and more mutations your way. But you've proven quite adept at handling those, so far."

Bohai whistled through his teeth. "That's a strange form of invasion, man. And the spiders? An accident?"

Kiern remained silent, still stunned by the news that the brother to Neptune 2's President was living here on Earth 1.

"Every planet has its aberrations," Dexter said. "I'm sure they did not expect certain species of arachnids to increase in size, but again, they have the mutations to do their fighting for them."

Finally Kiern spoke again. "Does your brother know you're here, Dextan?"

"No idea, and he can go to hell."

"I should inform him right away," Kiern said.

"I've created a surprise for you, Kiern. I started working on it the minute I saw your invasion, the moment I saw the green fog come down."

"What do you mean?"

"I've created a concoction, a mixture of elements for release into the air. It's the perfect weapon."

"What are you talking about?"

"My own toxic formula to screw with you," Dexter spat the words and relished every syllable. "I released it in the air this morning. It's brilliant, really. I was actually able to compose it from the primitive chemicals here on Earth. I am a genius."

"What did you do?" Kiern's face fell dark.

"I developed a compound that removes the X02 from the air, it nullifies it. I released it this morning," Dexter grinned. He enjoyed gloating. "By tomorrow or the next day, all your mutations within a hundred miles will be dead. Over the next few months, I can cover the planet."

"You are a traitor," Kiern said.

Dexter put his hands out and smiled again, "As advertised."

"Help us now," Kiern pleaded. "I can bring you back home, reunite you with your brother, your family. I'll get you reinstated, I promise."

"I thought you said I am a traitor."

"Help us now, help your own people. We need this planet! Our people are dying on that cruel moon. I'll get your record wiped clean."

"You will?"

"I promise. Your life back, your home back."

I miss my home. I miss it so much!

337

"What do you want from me?" Dexter asked.

"First, stop spraying the air with your twisted concoction. Let the X02 do its job."

"And second?"

"Kill these people," Kiern said, his voice regaining strength and confidence. "Kill all the remaining Earthians on this planet. You can do it, you're not a true Sayan anymore. Do it and I will bring you back."

Dexter inventoried the seven people staring back at him. He certainly had no love for Walter, or Shane for that matter. He pulled out a pistol from his vest. It was a semi-automatic Walther P99. "How can I trust you, Commander Kiern?"

"We are Sayan. We do not lie."

Dexter raised his gun and aimed it at Walter.

"Don't do this," Walter pleaded.

"I need to kill all of them?"

"Absolutely. Kill all the Earthians," Kiern ordered. "Even your companion back there." He pointed to Mitch.

"What about the half-breeds, Sam and his brother?"

"Them, too."

"Really? One of them has the spark."

"Get rid of them all," Kiern demanded. He could smell victory around the corner.

Dexter smiled and pointed his gun at Sam, Shane, and then Walter again. His grin took on an odd appearance, and at that moment he looked like a madman at a shooting gallery.

"Don't," Sam said in a whisper.

The others stood helpless and silent. No one had a clue what to say. They stood like deer caught in the headlights.

All of a sudden, Dexter shifted his aim to Kiern and fired the gun. Three shots in rapid succession to the man's stomach, and the alien commander fell to his knees.

Kiern looked up at Dexter and hissed, "You will die alone on this forsaken planet."

"I never doubted that. I've been dying here every day," Dexter said poetically. He put his last bullet in the commander's head.

Kiern fell over dead. His body slumped onto the street, blood oozing onto the pavement. Seeing this, the lone alien soldier turned and quickly climbed the ladder back into the belly of his ship.

"Sayans die the same way Earthlings do," Dexter muttered, looking down at the dead body. He looked up at Walter and added, "Just so you know. We're all human."

He turned to the others, and they flinched. He realized he still had the gun in his hand, and put it back in his vest. "Calm down. I'm not going to shoot you."

"Thanks, man," Shane said. "Seriously."

"Thanks," Bohai echoed. "And not just for helping us, but for not shooting us. That's solid, man."

Dexter ignored them and walked directly up to Walter. "I want my box back."

"The box?" Walter sounded confused. "Why? Those formulas are worthless to you, aren't they? You never really had any interest in the projects we worked on. Now that I know who you are... I don't know why you would want them."

"I don't care about your primitive work, idiot." Dexter had not lost any of his charm. He took a deep breath. "I need the box itself. It's a communication device. I need it to contact someone. It's not your concern."

"Why would you hide something like that in a box of chemical formulas?"

"It's not in the box, it *is* the box. Hidden in plain sight. I never thought it would be out of my reach."

Walter remembered kicking Dexter off the team and sending him away. The man's behavior made sense now, and Walter regretted some of his own actions, some of his sharp words. Their past had been fragmented by multiple petty slights.

"It's fine," said Walter. "I'll take you to it."

"Wait, who are you gonna call?" George asked. "Are we sure he's not using it to call down reinforcements?"

Dexter sighed impatiently. "In case you haven't noticed, reinforcements are already here." He gestured toward the three spacecraft. "It's nothing to do with you. It's something for me."

"It's okay. I believe him," Walter said. He believed the man's hatred for his own people, for the invasion. Walter had learned to recognize stale hatred over the years.

"I do, too," Sam agreed, not sure why, but fairly

certain that Dexter would not betray them. The Sayan was a traitor, but not to them.

Dexter regarded Sam a moment, said, "You're not a Sayan, son. Don't ever let them convince you of that. You're whatever you want to be. You're an Earthling, if that's who you are." He tapped Sam's chest. "Listen to no one."

"Thanks," Sam said. He didn't know what else to say. It was an odd piece of advice.

Listen to no one.

Through weary bloodshot eyes, Sam and the others looked out over the land. The three alien ships remained, but all the reptiles in sight were now dead. Apparently those in hiding would be dead by tomorrow, without the X02 in the air. That is, if Dexter spoke the truth.

The city wasn't in ruins, but it had seen better days. Its downtown corner was a flaming, broken mess. Rubble and debris covered half the downtown streets. A fire burned on the top floors of the US Steel Tower, eating the desks and other wood pieces like a ravenous devil. Fractions of the top floor's contents – bricks, furniture, pipes – sporadically continued to plummet to the ground below. A shelf unit severed the torso of a dead lizard, and a burning wall soon covered it up. Patterned steel bars poked upward from concrete slabs, one with the head of a hapless lizard impaled on its end, like a macabre scene from the gates of Transylvania.

Overhead, the sky darkened with more storm clouds, thunder rolled faintly, but still no rain fell. The scene was haunting and surreal, an image not soon forgotten by those unfortunate enough to witness it.

The stink of dead bodies intensified. Rain would be welcomed to wash the blood off the streets.

"What about them?" Sam asked, pointing to the other ships.

"They will not do anything today," Dexter said. "Not yet. They have no guns with which to fight you. I told you: guns are illegal in our religion. The mutants are their only weapons."

"No death rays or laser beams?" Shane sighed. "I'm almost disappointed."

"They still control most of the planet," Dexter reminded them. "We shall have to do something about that soon enough. But not today. I want my communication box first."

Walter consented to let Dexter come to the lab and take his box. With a fresh perspective on his old colleague, he shed some of his bad feelings toward the man. Wonder and a little admiration took the place of bitter rivalry, for today, anyway. His former adversary and friend was an alien; it's hard to top that.

Sam and Shane, the sons of a Neptune agent, carried a great deal on their shoulders, as they began the journey back home. A lot of new information had been thrust upon them in a very short time. That's a strain only the strongest minds can bear. In the coming days, both of them would have to struggle not to break under the weight.

Walter, Dexter and Sam's group of Peak Lodge survivors drove away and left the broken city behind. The jeep and pickup followed the tanks, while the alien ships remained silent and still, poised like sentinels watching the Earth – watching the Earthlings.

It feels so creepy to be among them, to be watched by them, Sam thought.

That view was shared by everyone.

CHAPTER 37

THE combined parties drove back to Walter's house. There was an uneasy tension between Mitch and the others, especially with Camila, who glared at the man constantly. She wanted to stab him, but managed to suppress the urge for the time being. They took separate vehicles and didn't interact with each other.

Again the tanks took up the front and rear for protection, with the jeep and pickup in the middle. The return trip to Walter's house was quiet and without incident. Nothing appeared on the empty roads for miles – not until they passed a fourth ship. It was parked in a field, just sitting there with landing gear fixing it to the ground, lights spinning along the hull and wings. Further on, they spotted a fifth ship perched on a hill, distant.

These ships dotting the land, like crows on a power line, watching our every move. Calculating.

The presence of the ships unsettled Sam and his friends, but they passed on without engaging them.

At Walter's house, Dexter had a few more words for Sam and Shane. While he never knew their father, he felt he knew something about the two sons. Like them, he was an outcast. He could empathize with Sam in particular.

"Don't think too much about this," he told them. "Maybe you're Sayan, maybe you're Earthian. Or something in between. It doesn't matter a whole lot, does it?"

"Can I ask you something?" Sam asked. "Do you think the Sayans killed my parents? It was a car accident, but... do you think it wasn't really an accident?" He sounded like he had already made up his mind.

Dexter furrowed his brow and thought for a moment. He wasn't thinking about the answer, but how to phrase it. "It is possible, if he had been voicing opposition to an invasion. Possible."

"So you think so?"

"I don't know, young man. I lack the information needed to form a conclusion."

"Thanks... for your honesty."

"I did not know your father, but it seems he found a bit of solace on this planet that I could never find. Good for him."

He squeezed Sam's shoulder, pointed his finger in a form of wave toward Shane, then walked away.

They split into two parties at Walter's house. Walter, Dexter and Mitch stayed at Walter's place, while the tanks and jeep headed back for the Peak Castle Lodge. They hoped Jason, Tina and the others were still safe, and wondered if the war had reached their walls.

Sam's party entered the lodge near nightfall, and were relieved to see a calm quality shrouding the hotel and grounds. The fort stood strong and untouched. The Peak had seen no fighting today.

As ever, Jason sat in the watchtower with his gun and scope. His hair was short now. Later they would find out Lucy had cut it.

Sam hugged Tina and Mark, then touched Lily's cheek. He was glad to see them all. All of them slapped hands with Jason, and then found Lucy cooking and sober in the kitchen; Tina had kept the wine bottles well hidden.

Quietly Sam slipped the Magic game card out of his back pocket and handed it back to Mark. It was creased and damaged now, but Mark just smiled and took it back. They exchanged a moment that needed no words, warrior to warrior.

The group enjoyed a reunion dinner around tables pushed together in the hotel reception hall, and exchanged stories about the last few days. There had been no decisive victory this day, but the dinner felt like a victory celebration. Information can do much to ease one's mind, and now they had more information about the state of affairs on their planet, the cause and reason for the changes that had brought them together.

Later during Shane's turn in the watchtower, Sam accompanied him to talk in private. They had a lot to talk about.

"So," said Sam. "We're half aliens."

"Dad was an alien, but we are simple Earth boys," Shane said firmly. "Same as everyone else."

"Except I'm not the same. I'm different."

"You're one of us, Sammy. You're different, but the same. Maybe a little bit special. And definitely a little weird."

"Thanks. You're just as weird, you just haven't found your *chi* yet."

The older brother laughed. "Yeah, maybe. Time will tell. Someday I'll wake up with psychic powers, like an X-Man."

Sam rubbed one of the bruises on his left arm. "Do you think Mom knew? She had to have known, right?"

"I doubt it. She never let on. And there was no reason for Dad to tell her. I doubt he ever intended to go back to his home... planet. That sounds funny to say: home planet."

"To me, they seemed in love. Maybe she wouldn't have cared where he was from."

"We always hid your lightning, Sammy. Dad didn't even know about your abilities, or else he might have clued us in."

"I think you're right." Sam smiled and sighed. "They were good parents. Dad was a good father. A lousy double agent, but a good father."

"He couldn't come up with a better last name than Summer?"

"I guess not," Sam laughed.

Bohai and Jason climbed the steps and joined them.

347

"So, I heard," Jason said. "You guys are like Martians and whatnot. That is so righteous. Can you plow Martian girls, now? I mean, it all works the same, right?"

"Screw you," Sam laughed again. "I'd rather be an alien than a weed. You're all weeds, you know. Didn't you hear?"

"Yeah, yeah, we're all weeds in some cosmic Garden of Eden." Jason flipped a middle finger at the sky.

"What's with the hair?" Sam asked, running his hand over the top of Jason's head. "Your trademark seventies flashback look is gone. You look all modern and stuff. Normal-like."

"Long hair makes it real hard to aim and shoot," Jason explained, pushing Sam's hand away. "Survival and fashion don't mix. I needed a change."

"It's an improvement, trust me."

Now Shane took his turn and ran his hand over Jason's short hair. "Too bad, I was hoping you'd start an 80's hair metal band."

Jason pulled away, laughing, "Okay, okay, are you finished? Stop touchin' me."

"Almost," Shane said. "I just want to rub it one more time for good luck." He reached across and rubbed the top of Jason's head again and received a light punch in the arm for his efforts.

There was a pause, before Sam got serious. "Look, guys, does it bother you at all? I'm from the enemy. My brother and I are part of them. We are *Neptunes. Neptonians*, or something like that."

"I think he said *Sayans*," Bohai corrected him. "...and the hell with that. You're with us, aren't you? You're no more an enemy today than you were yesterday. And besides, we've all got a dodgy past. I'm a freak who talks to animals, and Jason here... well, Jason is just a freak."

They laughed together, but Sam would not drop the subject.

"Everyone looks at me differently now."

"They've always looked at you different, dude, your whole life." Bohai forced him to recall those painful growing years. "Same as with me."

"But this is worse. Before, I was just the sparkler boy. Now I'm the alien sparkler boy. "

"That will change," Bohai assured him. "We're with you, all of us. This place is important, this fortress of ours. If we stick together, we can keep it and make it work."

"Okay, this is getting way too *After School Special* for me," Shane said. "Do we need to hug it out? Or can I get back to my job?"

"No hugs!" Jason pleaded. "Please, no more touching!"

They quieted down as Camila came up the stairs. They stopped talking, the way students stop joking when the teacher enters the room.

"Don't let me interrupt," she said.

"We'll leave you two alone," Sam whispered to his brother. He winked and kissed the air. "Come on, weed-boys. Let's find some food. I need a snack."

Shane flicked Sam's ear and told him to get lost. The three boys disappeared down the stairs, arguing about what they missed most at night: the internet or TV. It was a tie, until Bohai pointed out he missed internet-TV.

Camila handed Shane a bottle of Cherry Cola. He took it and held it up to read the label.

"Wow, what's this?"

"We don't have many," she said, "but we're celebrating our first victory. So go ahead."

"I'm not sure it was a victory, but I'll take it anyway." He pretended to examine the bottle as a wine connoisseur would. "Nice vintage. Split it with me?"

"Yep. That's the idea."

He took a swig from the bottle and handed it back to her. They talked for hours, alone just the two of them. He felt comfortable with her.

After his shift, she spent the night in his room. Even though they had only kissed and fallen asleep together, at dawn his only thought was: *What if we have half-breed alien babies?*

Somewhere in between late night and early morning, Sam woke up frightened by a nightmare. His body felt cold, even though his chest and arms glistened with sweat. It took a long minute for him gain his bearings and to realize he wasn't in a classroom, but in a hotel at end of the world.

He had dreamed he was back in high school, had green skin and could morph into a cold black creature not unlike the lizards they had been fighting. In the dream, he ate Billy Morsky alive.

Sam groaned, covered his head with a sheet and went back to sleep. Being a non-Earthling was going to take time to digest.

CHAPTER 38

THE next day the air felt thin to Dexter. He could hardly breath, as he unfolded the cloth surrounding his precious box. Its design was so ancient, the dinosaurs would have been impressed by its antiquity. And it had been resting here on Earth, right under Walter's nose. That zealous scientist had never known he was keeping a mechanism of alien origin, protecting it, touching it, and even disregarding it. The answers to so many questions lay within his grasp all these years. Like a man dying of thirst and charged with guarding a small obelisk that turns out to be a thermos full of water.

That thought made Dexter smile with a genuine shred of humor. For the first time in a decade, he almost laughed.

Have I ever laughed? He wondered, then dismissed the notion. Of course he had, but not on Earth. Nothing good had ever come to him on Earth. He missed his home.

He thought about the half-breed Sayan boys, especially the one with the spark. A small part of him wanted to save them from the inevitable future of this planet. But a larger part of him simply didn't care anymore. There was a time when he cared about everything, perhaps too much. Those days were long gone now, left behind like so many broken childhood toys.

Dexter sat down before his communication box that — at long last — lay on his desk, his treasure regained once more. He had retrieved it from Walter without incident, as the animosity between the two scientists had already begun to fade into mere dislike. The two could not be considered friends again, but certainly were no longer enemies. He suspected Walter only wanted the secrets of Neptune from him. The man was a scientist first, above all else, greedy for knowledge; but Dexter was not going to be so accommodating. He did not intend to spill any secrets just yet.

How many years ago had this all started? How had he come to this place? Dexter could scarcely remember. Or he could remember, but didn't want to.

"Loxtan, my brother," he said aloud as if exhaling a poison. In his mind, his older brother was the source of all evil in Dexter's small world.

The mistakes made in his life, he could hardly count now. He pushed aside the pool of self-pity starting to well up, and steeled himself for the future. There still was a future for him, he partly believed that. He *had* to believe that. And now, at least, he had a way to send a message to the only person who mattered anymore. Until now, the timing had not been right, and the means out of reach.

Gently he placed one hand on the box, like a pirate fondling a gold bar. It felt smooth and warm to the touch.

The glyph on its top surface, a character of his moon's written language, lit up and glowed orange.

Carefully he crafted his message in the local dialect of his home moon. He had to get the words right, no miscommunication. In a moment the machine would encode the words that Dexter had yearned to speak for so many years.

"No more waiting. It's time now," he said to himself. He had waited too long already.

Dexter activated the device with a swipe of his hand. The top glyph now turned blue, a cool color, soothing to the Sayan's weary eyes. Symbols on the side lit up one after the other in yellow, then orange, then blue. The box hummed imperceptibly. It was ready to send and receive.

After a deep breath, he leaned in closer to the box.

And he spoke.

To Be Continued in
SONS OF NEPTUNE, BOOK 2 :
REVENGE OF THE SPIDERS

For more information about the "Sons of Neptune" book series, and other books by **Rod Little**, visit the author's website:

www.rodlittleauthor.com

About the Author

Rod Little has written for two dozen science fiction, fantasy, and horror magazines over the past two decades. He has also written novellas for the Wayward Pines series and The 100 series, and five novels, including his own series: *Sons of Neptune*.

Born in East Peoria, Illinois, Rod later moved to Pittsburgh, Pennsylvania, and worked as a translator. In 1994 he opened a sci-fi gaming store called Starbase One on Pittsburgh's famed Forbes Avenue, which he kept open for eleven years of fantastic fun. In 2006 he moved to Thailand to begin writing again.

Rod travels often around Asia, but prefers the rare indulgence of intergalactic travel. He is partial to the Carina Nebula, where he still has friends of an alien nature.

"Reading sci-fi should open your eyes and make you think, but it should also be fun."

26764873R00211

Printed in Poland
by Amazon Fulfillment
Poland Sp. z o.o., Wrocław